nulla somniant. non edimus et non acecui
conficimus et non morimus. Sanguem
bibimus et solem vitemus et totus est.

(We) never dream. We don't eat
and we don't ~~acquire oldness~~
age and we don't die. We ~~blood~~
drink blood and we avoid the
sun and ~~all is~~ nothing more.

Published by Crimson Tree

Cover design by Barbette Jensen
with contributing art by Eric J.Foxhill

neverdream.com

ISBN 1-59109-936-6

never dream

Scott Charles Adams

ACKNOWLEDGMENTS

Special thanks to the following:

'Light' Mike Mastroianni, for his Latin expertise; Barbette and Eric for a very cool book cover; Art for beer, pool lessons, and support; Michael for beer, cigars, and support; Mom, Dad, and Syd for support and faith; Darlene and Keith for text, laughs, and *incredible* support; and anyone who read the book before publication (too many to list) (or remember). Without their positive feedback, I'd only be a very good typist.

This book is dedicated to Nikolette

I love you

Arthur

France, 1298

Rain fell from a gray October sky as a horse swiftly carried his armored rider along a dirt road. Dusk was approaching, although one could barely tell. The bleak chill of November had come a few days early this year.

The rider turned the horse from the road, cutting across an open field of high grass and heading directly towards a monastery. The animal gave gruff, nervous noises of protest, but obeyed dutifully as the knight urged him faster across the uneven and uncertain terrain.

Arthur tried not to think about Anne.

The knight took the bell rope in his mailed hand and pulled repeatedly, the dull tolling summoning silent men in plain, brown robes from within. "Where is she?" Arthur demanded as he dismounted, but their only answer was to take him inside as others led his horse away.

Soon he was within the monastery, facing a monk who wasn't afraid to meet his eyes. "Where is Charlotte?" the knight repeated.

"You are Arthur Talon?" the small, round-faced man asked in response.

"I am Sir Arthur Talon. Where is my wife?"

"She is here." The monk took the knight's arm, but quickly

withdrew his hand when he felt the freezing steel. "We should get you in front of a fire—warm you up a bit."

"I would see her now," Arthur said. He towered over this little holy man, but his tone was more desperate than threatening.

"Very well," came the man's response.

Arthur was brought to a cell and allowed to enter. A small oil lamp lit the room, giving the frail woman on the cot a deathly cast. The knight was immediately on his knees beside her. "Charlotte," he whispered gently, stroking her blonde hair with a steel-covered hand.

"Your servants thought there was something unnatural about her illness ... something unholy," the monk said. "Given the way of her sister's passing, it was thought best that ..."

"How long since she's eaten?" Arthur asked.

"Three days," the monk replied. "How long since *you've* eaten? Or slept?"

"I do not know," the knight confessed, his eyes never leaving Charlotte.

"I will bring you something," the monk said, moving towards the door.

"I'm not ..." Arthur began.

"You will eat," the monk said steadfastly. "Your wife has no strength of her own, and may need to borrow yours."

"Arthur."

His head bolted upright at the sound. The combination of warm food and days of determined riding had sent him into sleep still kneeling by Charlotte's bed, his wet head on her chest. "Yes, Charlotte," he said quietly. "I'm here."

"Arthur, she's coming."

"Who's coming, Dearest?"

"Anne. Anne is coming."

Arthur grimaced at the mention of the name. There were times when he thought the last six years had eased the pain of his first wife's passing. They hadn't. Even now, with Charlotte dying right before his eyes of the same illness that had taken Anne, his thoughts weren't *Dear God, I'm losing Charlotte*, but *Dear God, I'm losing Anne again.*

Guilty tears streamed down his cheeks.

"Anne is with God now, Darling," Arthur said, reassuring his dying wife in a quivering voice. "She flies with the angels on soft, downy wings."

A panicked look crossed Charlotte's face. "She is here ... now ... in this room," she stammered in terror. "She wants to kill me so she can have you. She told me. She's telling me, right now. Oh God, Arthur, I'm so afraid."

"Don't be afraid," another woman's voice said from behind Arthur.

The knight leapt to his feet and turned, his eyes telling him what his ears already knew. His misty vision gave her white-robed form an angelic sheen, and for a few seconds Arthur could feel his heart stop beating ... just stop. He barely managed to breathe the word, "Anne."

"I've missed you, Arthur," she said, taking two steps towards him. "Have you missed me?"

For long moments, the violent tremble of his mouth made response impossible. "Yes," he finally said in an unsteady voice. "Yes, I have missed you. Please don't take Charlotte away. She's all I have left of you."

"I haven't come for Charlotte," she said, moving closer to Arthur. Her scent—familiar and yet near-forgotten—over-whelmed him, and he had to close his eyes. "I've come for *you*," she finished.

"Don't let her kill me, Arthur," Charlotte wept from the bed. "Please don't let her kill me."

"Oh, Charlotte," Anne said as she circled around to the other side of the bed. "Charlotte ... my dear whore-sister. I'm not going to kill you—Arthur is."

"What?" Arthur asked, suddenly confused. "I'm ... what?"

"You're going to kill her, Arthur," Anne said as she swept the hair away from her sister's face. "She should never have married you ... especially not a mere four months after you put me into the ground. Besides, you have to sever your ties to this world. Only Charlotte's death can free you."

The wall met the knight's back, and Arthur realized he'd been moving away from them. "I'm not ... you ... you're not an angel," he managed. "You're the Devil, sent to tempt me into damning my soul."

Anne slowly stood from the bed. "I'm neither, Arthur," she said. "And I'm not here for your soul. After you've been reborn, neither God nor the Devil will have any claim to that. You'll be immortal, as I am. You and I can have forever together. Look at her, Arthur."

Arthur looked down at Charlotte. Pleading eyes stared up at him from a face that was damp with fear. "She's suffering," Anne said. "She's suffering because her husband will never love her like he loved her sister. She's close to death already, so close. How much longer does she have? Twenty years? Thirty? You can spare her so many painful days ... you can spare her infirmity and dementia and the other ravages of time. You can send her to Heaven while she is still beautiful."

Slowly, Arthur's hand went to the hilt of his sword, and he drew it from its sheath as Charlotte's eyes widened. She was right, of course—about everything. He'd never loved Charlotte like he'd loved Anne. The words hadn't been spoken between them, but both knew them to be true. Without ever wanting to, he'd inflicted a great deal of pain on this poor creature who stared up at him from a monk's cot. Arthur had it within his means to ease her pain.

And he would do just that, right after he slew this Godless Beast wearing Anne's shape.

"Back to Hell with you, Devil!" Arthur screamed as he lunged for Anne, the blade slicing through air where her neck had been. His eyes frantically searched the tiny room, but it was gone. The Devil had failed, and fled.

The sword clanged loudly to the floor as he rushed to Charlotte, sitting beside her on the bed. "It's over, Darling," he said as she broke down into tears. "The Devil is gone. It's over."

"I was sure you'd choose her," Charlotte said, her trembling hands caressing his face. "I was so sure of it. Arthur, I love you so much."

"I'm sorry," Arthur said, leaning towards her to kiss her forehead, her cheeks, her lips. "I'm sorry for the last six years. It's taken me this long to see ... my grief blinded me ... I don't love you with *some* of my heart, Charlotte. I love you with *all* of it. You need never doubt that again."

Arthur wasn't sure what happened after that. One moment, his lips were on Charlotte's ... the next, his body had slammed against the wall and slumped to the floor. Then there was the scream, and wet warmth on his face. When his eyes could focus again, his own sword stood perpendicular to the bed, driven through Charlotte's heart.

"Charlotte!" Arthur screamed as he struggled to reach his feet. Anne was suddenly on top of him, pinning his arms at his sides with inhuman strength, her wet lips at his ear.

"Charlotte is with God now, Darling," she hissed angrily. "She flies with the angels on soft, downy wings. In time, you'll see it was for the best."

Arthur yelped at the sharp pain in his neck.

Spain, 1986

The decor in Tito's was that of a cave. The walls were made to look like natural stone, the lighting was mostly recessed, and fish swam beneath the transparent stairs. This was one of Arthur's favorite clubs in the city, even though it didn't have the privacy of the Rojo y Negro because so many of the patrons here were English-speaking American students from the nearby University of Salamanca. But he supposed all vampires preferred their hunting grounds to their meeting places.

Arthur brought his glass to his mouth, allowing the gin and tonic to wet his lips only. He knew the consequences if he actually consumed some of the drink—it would come back up *immediately*. The only way he could drink alcohol was to feed from someone who'd been drinking, and if the alcohol content of their blood was too high, that too would come up. Most unpleasant, and considering it was blood he was vomiting, very messy.

Jennings was a different story. Jennings could eat or drink anything he wanted and bring it back up at an appropriate time and place. Conditioning, he claimed, but Arthur's own belief was that he was just Gifted that way. At times like right now, Arthur envied Jennings that Gift. It was a minor Gift as Gifts went, but it enabled Jennings to blend with the mortals in a way

Arthur never could. The lack of a more powerful Gift also compelled Jennings to be twice as crafty to survive, and Jennings was crafty. He had the ability to read people—so well, in fact, that Arthur wondered if this might be another Gift, but Jennings claimed he'd been able to do it even when he was alive. 'Keen observation,' he'd said. Jennings had been Made in Victorian England—maybe he was Sherlock Holmes.

"Hello, Arthur," Jennings said as he sat down beside him at the bar, reminding Arthur of his only weakness: the damned conspicuous Cockney accent that made his greeting sound like *'ello, Ahthah.*

"Evening," Arthur replied. "What news?"

"He's here." *'e's 'ere.* "He was spotted at the airport in Madrid. Won't be more than a few hours reaching Salamanca."

"Damned upstart," Arthur mumbled to himself. "It appears Lyle is going to have to be taught a lesson."

Arthur stopped talking as the woman behind the bar approached. "*Cervesa*," Jennings said, his accent evident even in Spanish. He didn't have to specify—she knew what Jennings drank. "I think he's going to need more than a lesson," Jennings said quietly.

"Don't talk like that," Arthur reprimanded in the Whisper. It was an ancient vampire trick: part lowering one's voice to a level mortals couldn't make out, part speaking without moving one's lips. It was like Telepathy, but it wasn't the actual mind-to-mind communication that Raymond—another member of Arthur's cabal—was capable of. "Vampires don't kill other vampires," Arthur continued in the Whisper.

"Lyle does," Jennings answered in a normal voice.

The woman returned with Jennings' beer as Arthur replied, returning to his own mortal voice. "We couldn't take action against him unless we could prove that."

"I don't need proof," Jennings said. "I know he does."

"*I* need proof," Arthur said finally, ending the discussion.

"Have you turned up anything on the Book?"

"Nothing, but I think we may have fallen into some luck. There's a group of students ... company."

Arthur turned on his stool, half-expecting to see Lyle. What he found instead was a young girl—maybe twenty, if that—approaching them from across the dance floor. Her long dark hair was swept to one side, nearly covering one of her deep, brown eyes. She wore a black leather miniskirt, a white blouse, and black stockings on long, flawless legs. Arthur was tempted to feed on her right here in the bar, but knew that white blouse would show the blood if things became ... untidy.

"She looks good enough to eat," Jennings said. The message was clear. This was Arthur's hunting ground, and Jennings could not have her without his permission. Arthur was generous, but not that generous. Maybe if Jennings had delivered the Book things would be different, but a Mark like this came only once a decade. Arthur's silence was Jennings' refusal.

"Buy you a drink?" she said in English—whiskey-voiced, American English. It was no wonder American vampires were dullards: how could one remain lean and hungry in a place where the food walked right up to you? But the fact that she had used English rather than Spanish when she'd approached made him a little wary.

"I have one, thank you," Arthur replied. "Won't you join us?"

Jennings stood, offering her his stool. Arthur noticed that she stood slightly taller than the other vampire, so she would be several inches taller than himself. In his own time, Arthur had been a large man. But that was seven hundred years ago, and five foot seven was no longer considered tall.

"I've seen you in here before," she said.

Arthur *really* liked her husky voice. "You are a student at the university," he stated.

"How did you know?"

"Because every American in Salamanca is a student at the university. What's your name?"

"Terry," she answered.

"I am Arthur, and this is my associate, Mr. Jennings."

"Nice to meet you," Terry said, turning her attention to Jennings. "Are you a teacher?"

"No. Why would you think that?" Jennings replied, his tone somewhat guarded. *He doesn't trust her either*, Arthur thought to himself.

"Oh, an Englishman," she said, almost under her breath. "I've seen you at the university, after hours. I thought perhaps you taught there."

"What are you studying?" Arthur asked, remembering too late that in the 1980s they said, 'What's your major?'

"Language and Anthropology."

"And what do you want to be, when you grow up?" Jennings asked.

Arthur regarded this curiously. Jennings would not have spoken to Arthur's Mark—except in response to a direct question—unless he had a specific agenda in mind. He watched Terry's reaction carefully, just as he knew Jennings was.

She seemed to hesitate a moment, as though considering a direct answer. Her eyes and her response did not match. "I don't know yet," she said. "Maybe a teacher. I'm considering graduate school."

"Hmm," Jennings said, nodding and obviously satisfied with the response. He'd apparently gotten something from it that Arthur had missed.

"What do you do?" Terry asked, turning her attention back to Arthur.

"A little of this, a little of that," Arthur replied. "I do some dealing in antiques. Objects of age hold a great fascination for me."

"And for me," she said, locking her eyes with Arthur's in a manner that suggested some hidden knowledge.

"Arthur, we still have that meeting with Mr. Wayne tonight," Jennings interrupted. "If you like, I'll tell him you were detained—I'm sure it's nothing I can't handle myself."

"No, I'd better come along," he replied, getting up from his stool. "I'm sorry I didn't get a chance to talk to you more, Terry. Business, you know."

"I'm sure I'll see you in here again," she said.

"I'm sure you will," Arthur responded.

Jennings leaned on a wall in an alley, trying to keep the beer he was vomiting from getting on his shoes.

"All right, what did you see that I didn't?" Arthur asked, no longer amused.

"You really didn't see that?" Jennings asked, a rainbow of crimson saliva hanging from his smiling lips.

"See *what*? Yes, she knew something—or thought she knew something. But what?"

Jennings retched the last of his beer, coughed, spit, and wiped his mouth with a handkerchief. "She knows we're vampires, man," he said with a smile.

"What?" Arthur asked, stunned. "How could she know that? What on earth would make you think she knew *that*?"

"You *really* didn't see it?" Jennings asked again, still smiling as he smoothed down his dark hair. "Should I tick off the clues?"

"By all means."

"One: has a woman that attractive ever simply walked up to you, without you using the Voice on her?"

The Voice—that was what Jennings had called Arthur's Gift of Influence ever since he'd read *Dune*. "No, but ..."

"Two: did you see her reaction when I asked her what she wanted to be when she grew up? I could see the words 'A vampire' on her lips, even though she lost her nerve at the last moment. Three:" in an arrogant, self-important tone, he mimicked Arthur's words of just a moment ago, "'Objects of age hold a great fascination for me.'" Then, in a flaky, feminine voice, "'And for me.' Four: did you see her wheels turning when I mentioned that we had a meeting with Mr. Wayne?"

"What the hell was *that* all about?"

"Mr. Wayne? Bruce Wayne? Bloody *Batman*, for crissake. *She knew exactly* what I was talking about."

"I still don't," Arthur confessed. "If you thought she suspected we were vampires, why would you make a reference to Batman for her? Do you *want* her to know?"

"She knew when she approached us. I was just letting her know that we know she knows. Ya know?"

Arthur and Jennings began walking towards the university. "I have difficulty understanding why any mortal would walk up to a couple of vampires and practically invite them to feed. Do you think she's working for Lyle?"

"It's certainly possible, but I really don't think so. Her demeanor was all wrong. Lyle prefers his women nice and stupid."

"Why, then?" Arthur said, somewhat unnerved. "What other motives could she have?"

"Haven't you read *Interview with a Vampire* yet? Anne Rice has made us very vogue. Apparently, having all of your blood drained is better than orgasm." He seemed to reflect for a moment, and added, "Bloody Hell, she probably thought we were Louis and Lestat. Too bad you weren't with Raymond, then she really would have got her money's worth."

"I think I preferred it when we were scary monsters," Arthur said.

Jennings stopped smiling. "I know *I* did."

Arthur leaned against a building across from the bus stop, waiting for Lyle.

Salamanca hadn't changed much over the centuries, although Arthur had been familiar with it only for the last two. That was when he'd moved the Book here from its last hiding place, a monastery in Italy. War was what frightened him, the possibility that the humans would begin squabbling and that the school—or the entire city, with the new generation of weapons—would be taken out by a stray bomb. He had many times considered moving the Book again, this time to America. But America had a tendency to change so quickly that within a single decade the skyline of any given city could become barely recognizable. Arthur felt comfortable with the familiar, and Europe remained familiar. Some little bits and pieces, here and there, were the same as they had been back when he was a human. The Roman Bridge in Salamanca had been a thousand years old when Arthur was born. And the church that the Salamancans referred to as 'The New Church' was begun twenty years after Columbus had come to this city to speak before the University, and completed forty years before the colonists on the new continent gained their independence from the British. Of course, even the Plaza de Mayor had seen some changes. Although he couldn't remember exactly all of the shops in the plaza when he'd first come here, he was relatively certain there'd been no Burger King.

Maybe this time, he wouldn't hide the Book. Maybe this time, he would hold on to it. He'd considered that before moving it the last time, but hadn't wanted to be a target for vampires older and more powerful than himself trying to obtain the Book's secrets. Arthur was no longer sure there were even any of those vampires left. There had to be some somewhere, but he had no idea where they'd gone. Carelessness, complacency, and the *Ennui* could be held accountable for the Final Deaths of a few—but all?

Arthur checked his Rolex—Lyle's bus was running late. There might have been an accident, he mused. Lyle would die in any accident involving fire, as would any vampire—burned up like dry paper, leaving no physical evidence for modern scientists to ponder. He had no desire to kill Lyle himself, but he certainly wouldn't begrudge an accident. Arthur's un-life would be much simpler if Lyle was killed by something arbitrary and mundane. But Arthur hadn't survived for seven hundred years by relying on luck. Lyle would simply have to be dealt with, like countless other foolish young upstarts before him. Not destroyed, like Jennings wanted. Just ... dealt with. He'd seen others like Lyle learn respect, and finally realize that just because they no longer had to obey the rules they'd obeyed as mortals didn't mean they had *no* rules. Hell, forty years ago Jennings had been one of those vampires.

Lyle's problem was that he was still living in the world of mortals. Of course, the same could still be said of Jennings. He didn't respect any of Arthur's vampiric codes, but he did respect Arthur, and adhered to the old codes because of that respect. It was his hope that Jennings would someday follow the codes because he saw their importance, that he would someday teach this respect to any kin he decided to create, and the long-dead Society of Vampires would return through his own teachings.

He heard the bus coming from a long way off. What was

more, he could sense Lyle and three fledglings on that bus. Jennings' sources were accurate as always. Arthur could draw in his Presence when he wished, so that Lyle would not be able to sense him—instead he pushed it so that Lyle would know he was waiting. Even the fledglings would be able to sense something, but Lyle would have to explain to them what it was their new perceptions were telling them.

The vehicle squealed to a noisy halt across the street from him, and Arthur waited while the passengers disembarked. Arthur could sense no fear from Lyle, which he would have respected if the source of his bravery hadn't been ignorance. When the bus pulled away, not four but five of them stood staring at Arthur. Lyle's companions were all beautiful women, dressed in the tight-fitting leather of rock groupies or something. Three of them were the fledgling vampires he'd sensed—but the fourth was a mortal. Arthur wondered if Lyle was perhaps less stupid than either he or Jennings thought.

Lyle wore a contemporary suit, very expensive looking and probably tailor-made. He wasn't a bad looking man. Considering he lacked the power of Influence, he would have to be good-looking to seduce his four companions with only mortal charm at his disposal. The defiance in their stares made him want to gut one as an example.

"Come on," he heard Lyle tell his girls, even though they were forty or fifty feet away. "Let's talk to Arty."

'Arty?' A demonstration was clearly in order.

"Not them," Arthur whispered as he stood away from the wall. "Just you. Have your pets take your things to the Salamanca Hotel ... you have a room already waiting."

"We have arrangements, thank you," Lyle shouted back like a mortal.

"Your arrangements have been canceled," Arthur continued as walked towards them. "You will stay at the hotel as my guests for the day. At dusk, you will put yourselves on another bus, and head back to London."

"You know what I'm here for," Lyle said.

"Please, not in front of the children. You four run along now." The mortal and two of the fledglings obeyed, but one remained by Lyle's side. "Your Jedi mind-tricks won't work on her, she's deaf," Lyle said arrogantly as Arthur reached them.

"Deaf?" Arthur asked, an amused lilt in his voice. "That's very close to being clever, Lyle. Very, very close." Arthur focused his full attention on the fledgling. "You look tired, my love ... very, very tired. Why don't you go back to the hotel and sleep for a week? But don't forget to kiss me good-bye."

She walked up to him, staring at him with the same desperate longing he'd created in mortals a thousand times, took his face in her hands with violent passion, and kissed him long and hard. Arthur had Pushed her harder than he'd intended, and had to physically take her by the arms and force her away.

"That's enough for now," Arthur said as he straightened his short, blonde hair, his collar, his tie. "Go on to the hotel. Lyle and I have to talk."

She kissed him one more time before she left, and continued to cast glances back at him until she was out of sight. Lyle was shaking with anger. "Now it is *you* who have broken *my* rules."

Arthur stepped back and spread his arms invitingly. "If I've broken your rules, Lyle, perhaps you should discipline me." Lyle silently declined the offer. "I thought not," Arthur said, lowering his arms and closing the distance between them. "I could have asked her to stick her own hand in a blender. It would be months before she could carry your luggage again."

"Listen here, old man ..."

"No, *you* listen. You drink blood and you don't age and you think that makes you something. But if you play games with me, you're going to learn some harsh realities. I can push you just as easily as I pushed her—I can wipe out you and your little cabal just by asking you to kill yourselves."

"The Book is the only thing that separates you and me," Lyle said. "That's why you're afraid to let me see it; you're afraid I'll learn your secrets."

"Seven hundred years separate us," Arthur said. "The truth is, I don't use the powers in the Book. The cost is too high. You don't even have the wisdom to govern the powers you have, let alone handle something like that. Have you taught your children about the Mark?"

"We don't use the Mark in London. The strongest hunt where they please, the weak fend for themselves."

"You aren't the strongest in Salamanca. Hunt anyplace that's Marked in this city, and you'll be dealt with accordingly. Believe me, *I* can enforce *my* rules. It would be a shame for you to lose one of those beautiful fledglings just because you failed to teach her proper etiquette."

"Whatever," Lyle said.

"You need to learn more than respect ... you need to learn manners. Now, limp to your hotel."

"You bastard," Lyle mumbled to himself as he walked away, dragging one leg behind him.

Arthur had to feed. As an older vampire, he didn't have to feed as often as most, but it was time. Between that girl in Tito's and the kiss from Lyle's fledgling, he was in the mood to feed.

He walked in the direction of the Roman Bridge, specifically towards the nearby Gypsy camp on the edge of the city. Gypsies made excellent food for many reasons. They considered it a sign of good fortune if you fed on them without killing them, because they knew it meant they were Marked by a merciful vampire and therefore under his protection. They didn't report strange occurrences to the authorities, and finally, their blood had a unique taste Arthur enjoyed. The Gypsies were another reason Arthur preferred Europe to America.

He walked unseen into the camp, passing trailers and campers, walking towards the music he heard. Not flutes and fiddles, as he would have found in past centuries, but a modern rock band being played on a portable stereo. He found its source—a large fire in the center of the camp where dark-eyed, dark-haired youths danced spiritedly around their fire—and watched from beyond the edge of the fire's light. One young girl caught his attention, a slightly built thing with a slender neck, long legs, and the body of a dancer. Her half-shirt showed her brown stomach and the curve of her breasts when she moved just right.

Arthur didn't know her name. He'd fed on her before, and

she knew who he was. He pushed his Presence, showing her he was here without commanding her to come. She would come on her own. That was when the feeding was the best, when they came on their own.

She stopped dancing and looked around. Oh yes, she knew he was there all right. She smiled a little and began to dance again, and Arthur knew she was dancing for him. The girl caressed herself, her naked stomach, her blue-jeaned thighs, until Arthur thought he might leap from his hiding place and take her right in front of the others. When the drunk men and boys around the fire noticed the change in her dancing, mouths fell open and hormones young and old raged. An old woman smiled at their good fortune, nudging the man beside her and speaking of the *Guardián*.

The song ended, and a deejay began chattering in Spanish. Out of breath and sweating, both from the dance and her excitement, she left the fire and walked into the darkness. Arthur silently moved to intercept her. She was lying on her back in high grass when he reached the girl; naked, eyes closed, arms stretched above her head. Gently, he put his hands on her, stroking her throat, her breasts, her stomach. When he reached the soft hair between her legs, she bit her lip and made a quiet moaning sound, and he left one hand there while the other stroked her brown legs. His fangs extended as he lifted her foot, and she let out a slight moan of pain as he bit her ankle and fed.

Then he was on top of her, and she threw her head to one side, offering him her throat. He bit her again as she writhed beneath him, and again the iron taste of blood ran into his mouth. She'd been drinking tonight, and the alcohol burned his stomach and instantly intoxicated him. It wasn't so much that he would suffer any ill effects, but it was enough.

Then came the Shame. Seven hundred years hadn't changed that. The greater the pleasure, the greater the self-loathing afterwards. It usually began just as the ecstasy of feeding abated, and lasted right up until the Hunger for blood drove him to feed again. He could have fed every night, but for the Shame. It was the Shame that made him ignore the Hunger until his reason was nearly blind. It was the Shame that could keep his feedings more than a week apart as long as he didn't tax his unnatural abilities too much. He'd spent the last seven centuries spacing his feedings to keep a delicate balance between the Shame and the Hunger, like a modern diabetic monitored his sugar. It was something else he envied Jennings—Jennings, like many of their kind, didn't feel the Shame. Arthur wondered if pedophiles felt something like this after one of their diseased encounters—if the hours of self-deception, of convincing yourself an eight-year-old boy had the faculties to want sex with an adult man, rapidly dissolved brief moments after orgasm.

Arthur kissed her lips a single time, her response barely noticeable. He'd taken a lot of blood. "I'm sorry," he whispered, before standing and leaving her naked in the grass. The Gypsies would take care of her.

Arthur walked into Tito's earlier than he had the night before—just after dusk. There were a few faces he was accustomed to seeing, students mostly, but it would be a while before the place began to get crowded. Even if Jennings were only a mortal, he would have no trouble finding him in here this evening.

No sign of Terry, he thought to himself. He found himself wanting to see her again, which he didn't like one bit. Why did he find her interesting? Was it just her beauty? Her voice? No, there was something more, something that made him think of her even at inappropriate times—like now. It was the fact that she was attracted to the idea that he was a vampire. The Gypsy girl did what she did because her people told her it would bring them protection from others like him—she even allowed herself to enjoy the feedings, and that made them extraordinary while they lasted. But she had no understanding of what she was doing. She had no comprehension of the un-life she was sustaining with her superstitious ritual. Perhaps Terry would understand. Perhaps with Terry, there would be no Shame. That was stupid. It was the voice of the Hunger speaking

There was too much unknown about her. She could be working for Lyle, or another vampire who wanted the Book. Arthur couldn't shake the idea that she wanted something, be it the Book or not. Perhaps Jennings was right, and she just wanted to be a vampire. This Anne Rice had apparently made his affliction so attractive that mortals *wanted* to drink his blood. He wondered if he would see a 'fledgling-boom' over the next few years, and he wondered what the long-term effects of that would be. He didn't like the idea of Making Terry merely because it was fashionable.

He was reminded of a conversation he'd had with Jennings just after he'd read *Interview with a Vampire*. 'Read it,' Jennings had urged. 'Although some minor details are inaccurate, it will remind you of what you enjoy about being a vampire.' Arthur thought that perhaps one day soon he would do just that. In all honesty, he was beginning to forget.

Jennings came down the stairs to the bar two at a time, with a newspaper under his arm and a distressed look on his face. "No luck last night?" Arthur asked rhetorically.

"Did you talk to Lyle?" Jennings demanded, his anger not directed at Arthur.

"Yes. Why, what's happened?"

Jennings slapped the newspaper onto the bar, and Arthur picked it up and saw the cover. He recognized the word 'MUERTE' in bold black, but the rest would take concentration and patience to decipher. "What does it say?" Arthur asked.

"Apparently our boy's had a little public feeding," Jennings said quietly. "He left the body about a block away. Good luck feeding in here tonight."

Arthur scowled at the newspaper, and he scowled at himself for allowing Lyle to walk away last night. *"Telephono, por favor,"* he asked of the woman behind the bar.

"Forget it," Jennings said, holding up his hand in a gesture that told her that it wasn't necessary. "He checked out of the Hotel Salamanca before dawn this morning."

"He really knows how to push his luck, doesn't he?" Arthur said.

"He knows you won't kill him for it," Jennings replied. "You know, Lyle would make a fine example for the next *schmuck* who came along. He wouldn't be missed."

"Not yet," Arthur said, regaining his composure. "Let me talk to Drew. Maybe he'll be able to control him. Did you get anywhere with the Book?"

"I wasn't able to finish telling you last night. There is a group of students cataloging every Book in the library. Once they stumble across it, it'll be a simple matter to find it and spirit it away."

"Maybe one of them has found it already," Arthur suggested. "Maybe that's how Lyle got word of it."

"Unlikely. They're cataloging every book on a computer database, one at a time. It's not cataloged yet, and I doubt any of them would intentionally exclude it."

"How long before they've gone through the entire library?" Arthur asked.

"That's a tough call," Jennings answered. "The project is supposed to go on for months."

"We don't have months," Arthur said. "I can't afford to have you sitting back waiting for the mortals to do the work for you. I need you in there, checking through every book ..."

"I am, I am," Jennings interrupted. "But that alone is one Hell of a bloody project, without having to browse their database on a nightly basis *and* keep track of Lyle. I wasn't saying they were going to do the work for us, I was only saying that they could make this job a lot easier. Have you seen Terry yet tonight?"

"Terry?" Arthur asked.

"Yeah, sure. We got time to play bloody games. The girl from last night? *Bat*girl?"

"Ah, her," Arthur said. "No, I haven't seen her. Why?"

"Because now might not be a bad time to bring her into this," Jennings said.

"I'm still not convinced she can be trusted," Arthur insisted.

"That's not the point, is it? Either she's working for Lyle—or someone else—or she'd be willing to help us. She's a mortal, she can make contacts during the day that I can't."

"I should let you handle her," Arthur said.

"I'll trade you: you play night-librarian at the university, and I'll deal with Terry. Of course, that'd be a terrible waste of your Gift," he said, referring to Arthur's Influence.

"I don't want to use that on her," Arthur protested. "She's not food."

"She could be an enemy."

"She could be an ally."

"My point exactly. But you need to talk to her to find that out. The Voice could make it real easy, but use craft if you have to. You do remember how to be crafty, don't you?"

"I didn't reach this age by being stupid."

"Of *course* you didn't. That's why I'm in your cabal. That, and the fact that you're a sharp dresser. I have to get to the library. If I find Lyle there, what are your specific orders?"

"Inform him that he's on my Mark," Arthur said. "Defend yourself using whatever means necessary. Punish him if you have to. But don't destroy him if you can avoid it."

"I'm telling you—and remember these words—now is the time to take him out," Jennings said, his eyes meeting Arthur's squarely. "Drew should have done it forty years ago. Lyle's going to do something so destructive one day you'll wish you had. What are you going to do if he gets the Book?"

"If he gets the Book, I'll destroy him," Arthur said. "But if he had the Book, he wouldn't be in Salamanca."

"Unless Terry or someone else has already stolen it for him, and he got it last night—or plans to get it tonight."

Arthur considered that: the power of the Book in Lyle's hands. The Book had the secrets to unlocking the potential held by all vampires, and Lyle would surely twist the world into a dark place if he had it. Arthur shivered.

"Exactly," Jennings said. "I'd better go. He may be there already."

"Go ahead, I'll handle things out here."

Jennings shook his head, still regretting the fact that he didn't have permission to kill Lyle if he came across him, and climbed the stairs that lead out of Tito's. Arthur took the newspaper from the bar and struggled to understand the Spanish print.

The body had been found at eleven last night, so it had probably been done right after Arthur left Lyle. The victim was a young Spaniard, eighteen years old, probably chosen at random and probably chosen by Lyle's girls while he attended to other business. What other business? Finding another place for them to stay? Meeting with someone to buy the Book? With five of them—well, four now that one would sleep for six more days—it would be difficult to track Lyle's movements. The ironic part was if he would just use the secrets in the Book, he could simply locate him and destroy him like the rabid dog he was, right from this barstool.

No. Not yet, anyway. He knew the price of such power, and he wasn't prepared at this stage to pay that price. But Lyle could not obtain the Book—that had to be prevented at any cost.

Arthur suddenly had a very strange, very disturbing feeling. Lyle was using his vampiric Gifts, and pushing his Presence as a result due to his lack of experience. Through this fleeting connection, the elder vampire received a vague sense of Lyle's emotions. Although he couldn't tell what the younger vampire was thinking, the underlying heartlessness and selfishness of those thoughts—while not entirely new to Arthur—were nonetheless unsettling. Perhaps he was wrong about Lyle. Perhaps he wouldn't mature.

"Anything interesting in the news?" a husky voice at his shoulder asked.

Arthur was so lost in his thoughts that he'd actually been

startled, and he turned his head at the sound much faster than a mortal could have. To Terry, it would have seemed as though his head had begun turning at her approach, but he'd heard the voice and his eyes were suddenly just *there*, on her. *Careless*, he thought to himself. *Sloppy. Jennings would never have been caught like that.*

"What?" Arthur said, hoping she would elaborate on her thoughts.

"That murder," she said, peering at the paper over his shoulder. "I never thought of Salamanca as a dangerous city. But they say the Gypsies here ..."

Another flash of emotion from Lyle touched Arthur like a single strand of spider web. *Glee.* He couldn't see more. He wasn't sure he wanted to.

He distractedly defended the Gypsies to Terry as he listened to the whisperings in his head, trying to learn more. To his dismay, they quieted again. Lyle was some distance away, but not nearly far enough. He was still in Salamanca.

Arthur silently cursed the coincidence—that Lyle was doing this while he had Terry here. There was too much to learn about her for this conversation to be a distracted one. He spent several minutes focused on finding Lyle and doing his best to respond to Terry, accomplishing neither feat well. If only Jennings were here ... but their meeting this evening wasn't for another couple of hours, and it wasn't going to take place at Tito's.

"Do you believe in vampires?" Terry asked for the second time. Somehow, she'd managed to direct the conversation to space aliens and vampires. Next would probably be Bigfoot or the Loch Ness Monster.

While he carefully danced around Terry's question, Arthur wondered if perhaps he should bring more of his cabal to Salamanca. But who? Raymond was his first choice because of his telepathic talents, but those talents were required in London at the moment. With a couple of telephone calls, Jennings could have ten vampires here in three day's time. However, such an action would only serve to exalt Lyle's importance in everyone's eyes. No, it would be far better if Arthur and Jennings could handle this situation alone.

The force of Lyle's emotions suddenly stuck him like a gentle blow from a light hammer. The fledgling was feeding, and his passion made his Presence shine like a distant beacon. Finding him now would be simple.

"I have to go," Arthur said, getting up from the bar.

"Hey, I was hoping I wouldn't have to walk home alone tonight."

It took a second for Arthur to remember what she was referring to—last night's murder. "You'll be safe enough," Arthur said. "Can you meet me here tomorrow night?"

"Yes, I think so," she answered.

Another image from Lyle came to him, the face of his victim. Vague urgency became certain urgency when he recognized that face—the face of his Gypsy girl.

Arthur mumbled something to Terry and headed for the door. It required all of his self-control to move slowly, like the mortals did ... one foot in front of the other, gently pushing through sparse bodies while the nameless girl was murdered less than two miles away. The flavor of Lyle's emotion left no room for doubt—murder was his intention.

Once Arthur was clear of the bar and the crowd, he broke into a preternatural run.

Arthur knew it was too late long before he got there. The grieving wails had assailed his ears for the last half-mile. Something terrible had happened, it was just a matter of finding out what it was.

The beams of electric torches flashed through the trees, near the sight where Arthur had fed the night before. No, not *near* the sight, he realized as he grew closer. *On* the sight.

Arthur walked through the Gypsies, and most went silent at his presence. None had ever seen his face before, but they knew who he was. The Guardian. The supernatural creature who fed on them, in exchange for his protection; his protection which had turned out to mean nothing. His protection that put them in danger in the first place.

He walked into their center, finding the object of their grief. Her skin was pale, and the flesh of her throat was torn open as if by an animal. Lyle had done this.

Someone was shouting at him in broken Spanish. Arthur didn't attempt to translate, but he understood the gist of it. He was supposed to protect them, the man was saying—probably the girl's father. Where was he? Where had he been in their time of need?

Arthur went to one knee, reaching down to close her unseeing eyes. The man had quieted, and he noticed that an old woman was approaching him. He could see in her eyes a shared sense of responsibility. She'd probably been the one who'd told them they would be safe.

"You are still our *Guardián*, no?" she said in Spanish. "You will not let this go without punishment?"

Arthur couldn't think of the words, but he shook his head that No, he would not let this go without punishment.

"Because if you do, they will not have trust for you anymore," she said. Quietly, she added, "Or for me."

Arthur knew what he wanted to say, but didn't want to think of how to say it in Spanish or Romanish. There were too many thoughts racing through his mind—too many resolutions dissolving. Language was too much of a burden at this point.

No one moved or spoke as the *Guardián* left.

"I got your message—what is it?" Jennings asked as he seated himself across from Arthur at the Rojo y Negro. It was decorated in red and black, just as the name implied, with low tables and lower leather chairs. The place was relatively quiet, a club where a mortal couple would go after a night of drinking and dancing to wind-down and talk. The soft furniture absorbed the sound of voices, and most spoke in hushed tones here anyway. Although Tito's was good because only a vampire could make out what was being said in the din of the music, Arthur preferred to meet here, away from the distraction of easy prey.

"Destroy him," Arthur said, his voice little more than a whisper. "If you can find him, destroy him."

"What happened?" Jennings repeated.

"He killed a Mark—a Gypsy girl. My scent was so thick on her a mortal could have picked it up. He did it just to prove a point—an attempt to convince me that he was a force to be reckoned with. I'm convinced."

"Bloody Hell," Jennings said. Gingerly, he added, "You sound like you loved her."

"I didn't love her," Arthur pronounced steadfastly. "I didn't even know her name. But she certainly didn't deserve the death he gave her. It was brutal. She died in pain. I could still smell the fear on her dead body."

"Are you going to call Drew?"

"It's beyond that now. When I intended to call Drew, it was for the chance to get Lyle under control." Arthur nodded his head as he spoke, his eyes staring at the light reflected from the glossy black surface of the table between them. "There's no controlling him. You were right. I should have destroyed him last night. If Drew has a problem with it, then it's ... then it's Drew's problem. He never should have Made Lyle in the first place. If I were going to be a real bastard, I'd have Drew destroy him. If Drew gives me any trouble, I'll take his hands for Making that psychotic."

"I agree with you absolutely, and I'm behind you one hundred percent."

"Let Drew get angry," Arthur rambled. "That stupid son-of-a-bitch has a lot to answer for. It's a wonder I don't destroy them both. Vampires that stupid are a threat to us all. What kind of lovesick cow Makes a mortal like Lyle just because he's pretty? Yes, let Drew complain about this one. I'll take his arms *and* his legs, the stupid bastard. I should find the bloodsucker who Made Drew, and punish him as well."

Jennings just nodded, saying nothing.

"Six hundred years ago, this wouldn't have been a problem," Arthur continued. "Six hundred years ago, when we had a Society—when we had *laws*—no one would have ever done something like this. It was unheard of. You followed the laws, or the rest of the Society joined against you. Now, we've got fledglings Making fledglings and no one is accountable. Only one thing teaches these children respect. You've got to show them. You've got to show them what they're up against. Otherwise, they don't have a clue. Drew is to blame. Drew should have taught his child respect, before unleashing him on the world."

When Jennings spoke, it was with great hesitation. "My French is a little rusty, but I'm fairly sure I agree with you."

"Your what?" Arthur asked, suddenly realizing that he'd switched languages at some point. "Oh ... I'm sorry."

"No apology needed," Jennings said with a gentle smile. "What's a little French between friends?"

Arthur said nothing for a moment, and when he spoke, his voice was heavy with fatigue. "Did you have any luck at the university tonight?"

Jennings sighed, reluctant to say. "The Book isn't there," he finally said. "Someone's beaten us to it. It's not Lyle, or he wouldn't be playing these games."

"No, you're right," Arthur said. "He doesn't have the Book. Any suggestions on how we find him?"

"In this day and age, there are a thousand ways," Jennings said. "If he's used any credit cards, I can trace them. If he's called Drew, I can find out where he called from. If he's been seen on the streets, or in any bars, I can find him. He can't hide from me."

"Find him then," Arthur said coldly. "Let me worry about the Book for a while. Someone knows something, and I'll Push whomever necessary to find it."

"Start with Terry," Jennings said. "She knows what we are, and she's hiding something. You Push her, I guarantee you'll learn something."

Arthur nodded. He couldn't remember ever having been this tired. "If it comes to that, I will."

Sunday night found Arthur in Tito's again. It had been three nights since his Gypsy girl's murder.

In that time, Arthur had questioned every scholar at the university, and was now satisfied that not only did they have no knowledge of the Book's existence, but no knowledge of any book leaving the library where the old manuscripts were kept.

Jennings had as much luck with his search for Lyle. His reports to Arthur consisted of 'waiting to hear back from this one' or 'waiting to hear back from that one.' No more bodies had been reported found, although reports of missing persons flooded every media.

Arthur hadn't fed in four days, and the Hunger was getting stronger—not quite strong enough to compel him to feed, but stronger. He considered a feeding just to clear his head, but realized the moment the thought crossed his mind that this was the voice of the Hunger talking.

He went into the bathroom and rinsed his face with cold water. An animal stared back at him from the mirror. He pulled back his lips to see that his canines were extended—an involuntary reaction to the thought of feeding not unlike the erections he'd had in life.

Over his shoulder in the mirror, Arthur noticed a young man staring at Arthur's reflection, transfixed. Arthur had been so caught up in his own thoughts he hadn't noticed him, and the boy had probably seen the canines. The vampire turned on him. "What are you looking at?" he demanded, his Hunger dangerously close to the surface. The boy, apparently deciding there were things more important than hygiene, turned and ran from the bathroom.

He turned back to the mirror. The image there was more alien than it had been just a few seconds ago. Arthur only rarely got a good look at this side of himself. Bestial, irrational, inhuman. He was repulsed, but his gums throbbed—the Hunger liked what it saw, even if it was the only part of him that did. He thought of the Gypsy girl as he ran more cold water over his face; thought of her laying dead in the grass. She hadn't deserved what Lyle had done to her, but she hadn't deserved what Arthur had done either. The throbbing subsided, his canines retracting, leaving a dryness in his mouth that water would not assuage.

When Arthur came out of the bathroom, Terry was there. She hadn't noticed Arthur yet. Good. It was about time *he* surprised *her*. He was the vampire, after all.

"So glad you could make it," Arthur whispered into her ear. Big mistake, he realized soon after. The closeness of her, the scent of her, had reawakened the Hunger.

Four days. With everything that was going on, he never should have tried to push it to four days.

"You spoke to her?" Jennings asked. "What did she say?"

They were back at the Rojo y Negro for another report. The Shame now was worse than usual—Shame for the way he'd dealt with Terry, and Shame for the feeding shortly after. "I'm not entirely sure," Arthur said.

It was rather a small lie, as lies went. But it was a lie nonetheless. He remembered far too much about that conversation. He remembered that he was very, very close to snuffing out that delicate mortal life last night—and all because she'd called him 'Arty.' He also remembered the look in her eyes. She'd *known* how close he'd come. If there'd been a chance at trust between them, it was almost a surety that he'd eliminated that chance last night.

Fortunately, Jennings didn't need more details. He'd probably known three days ago that Arthur would fast after the Gypsy girl's death. He'd probably silently watched the denigration of Arthur's reason as the Hunger grew stronger and stronger. He understood, without being given the details, what had happened with Terry—and Arthur was immeasurably grateful for that.

"You've fed since then, right?" Jennings asked.

Arthur nodded that he had, and tried not to think about the obese young man he'd left unconscious in the bathroom at Tito's last night. There'd been nothing sensual or pleasurable about that feeding. The Hunger had been in full control by then. A woman never would have survived that feeding.

Terry never would have survived that feeding.

"I think I might have ... I might have given her a better idea of what we're *really* like than perhaps would have been appropriate."

"Did you tell her about us?" Jennings asked, hesitantly.

"Yes," the elder vampire replied. "Yes, I did. I told her about us, and I let her go. If she wants to help, she'll be at Tito's tomorrow night. I think I want *you* to talk to her this time."

Jennings nodded, his fingers idly drawing abstract figures on the glossy black table with the condensation from his drink. "Do you trust her?" he asked without looking away from his fingertips.

Arthur considered this. "I don't know."

His tone suggested Jennings let the subject drop, and Arthur was thankful the other was perceptive enough to recognize that. "There's something that's got me concerned, Arthur," Jennings said.

"The missing," Arthur said.

Jennings stopped his drawing with a quick strum of his fingers, and met Arthur's eyes. "The missing, yes. The missing have me *extremely* concerned. And Raymond reports that several acquaintances of Lyle's have left London. I think we have to assume that his group numbers at least twenty at this point. Probably closer to thirty."

"Perhaps. Perhaps more. But the only thing that concerns me about their number is the fact that they can search every nook and cranny while you and I are reduced to tracking their movements. What have you been able to find out?"

"I know that Lyle's called London several times, but I don't know who he's called or where he's called from. And if he's using credit cards, he's sleeping someplace different every day. Actually, that's beginning to seem likely, even if he's paying cash. It's what I'd do."

"Lyle is not you," Arthur said absently.

"No, but he definitely seems to be taking advice from someone with at least a modicum of wit, doesn't he? Have you spoken with Drew yet?"

"You don't think he's doing this with Drew's approval, do you?" Arthur asked.

"He may be," Jennings answered. "He calls London every other day, as if he's reporting his progress."

Arthur shook his head, dismissing the idea. "No," he said. "Drew doesn't have that much ambition. Or that much courage."

"How much courage would it take? Drew can get a lot of mileage out of 'I can't control the boy.' And think of what he stands to gain: the power of the Book."

"I don't think Lyle would turn that over to Drew," Arthur argued. "In fact, I think the first thing Lyle would do is destroy his Maker."

"I agree, but Drew may not realize that. You should call him."

Jennings was right. "I will," Arthur said. "I'll call him tonight. He deserves at least a phone call before I destroy his kin."

"Hello?" the male voice on the telephone answered in a uptight-British accent.

"Good morning. I need to talk to Drew."

"Who shall I say is calling?" Positively bitchy—probably Drew's latest boy.

"Tell him it's Arthur."

The bitchiness was suddenly gone. "One moment, I'll get him." Jennings nodded and smiled, hearing the change in his voice on another extension across the room. He was taping the conversation, and making mental notes as they went along.

"Hello, Arthur. So nice to hear from you."

"Hello, Drew. How's business?"

"The theater is doing very well. We're doing a splendid little show now, perhaps if you plan on being in town any time soon, you could see it."

"When I make it back to London, I'll be sure to. We need to talk."

"Really? What about?"

"It's Lyle. He's been behaving rather badly."

"Lyle?" Drew asked, almost desperately. "Have you seen him?"

Arthur and Jennings exchanged a look. "Yes, I have," Arthur said. "He's here, in Salamanca."

"What the hell is he doing in Salamanca?"

"He's causing a bit of trouble, I'm afraid—sticking his nose where it doesn't belong."

"That's Lyle," Drew said. "You know kids these days. You can't teach them respect."

"Spare the rod, spoil the child."

"Now, now, Arthur. I'm sure whatever he's done, it can't be so bad. He's young. Even *you* were young ... once."

"I was never this young. Steps will have to be taken."

Drew took a deep breath, composing himself. "Do whatever you feel is necessary. But if you could, as a favor to me, avoid doing anything that will scar him permanently—he is a very handsome young man after all."

"You don't understand. I was referring to steps a little more drastic."

"Oh, Arthur," he said reproachfully, but the concern in his voice was evident. "Are you certain you're not overreacting?"

"You know me, Drew. You know I don't overreact. And you know I don't come to such decisions lightly. The die is cast."

"Why did you call me then?" Drew snapped. "Why didn't you just do it?"

"Because there's something you can do to save him."

"And what would that be?"

"Get him out of Salamanca."

"I didn't even know he was *in* Salamanca. We had a fight and he left ..."

"How long ago?" Arthur interrupted.

"I don't know," Drew answered. "It's been a few months, I guess. But I have no way of contacting him—unless you would give him a message for me."

"When I find him," Arthur said, "I won't be passing along any messages."

"Please, just listen, okay?" Drew begged desperately. "He couldn't have done anything *that* bad. Whatever he did, I'll make the compensation personally if you just let him live."

"Lyle's a big boy—he can handle his own reparations. Besides, you have reparations of your own to concern yourself with. After all, *you* Made him."

"Arthur, if you harm a hair on his head ..."

"Excuse me?"

Drew took another breath. "Our friendship is at stake here."

Arthur kept his tone calm and even. "Yes, it is. But I place the responsibility for that on *your* head. He is your offspring, and you must bear full accountability for his actions—that is why we are supposed to create offspring with great care. Compensation will be expected from you even if you cannot convince him to leave Salamanca and the worst occurs. Am I being entirely clear on this point?"

"Yes," Drew answered, his contempt thinly veiled.

"Good. Always nice chatting with you, Drew."

Drew's response was the click of disconnection. Arthur returned his phone to the receiver, mumbling an obscenity in French before looking up to Jennings. "Any thoughts?"

"I know Drew's an actor, but if that was an act, it was a great performance."

"So you think he's telling the truth?" Arthur asked.

"I don't know," Jennings said. "He might well be. Or, he might be a better actor than I ever gave him credit for. He's had a century to master the craft. His feelings for Lyle are real, I can tell you that. He was genuinely concerned that Lyle might come to harm."

"Well, that's his own damn fault," Arthur spat.

"You're right—but don't believe that Drew is ever going to see it that way, because he won't."

"That's his problem. So what do we have?"

"We don't have anything we didn't have before the call," Jennings said.

"Dammit," Arthur swore. "We've got to end this soon."

Arthur and Jennings approached Tito's from across the street, and stopped a few buildings away. Arthur said nothing, and Jennings followed suit for several moments.

"I'm going inside," the younger vampire finally said. "If I'm not back out in five minutes, she's here already. Give me half an hour."

Arthur nodded, and watched Jennings until he'd disappeared into the noisy bar. Thirty minutes ... that wasn't such an unbearably long time, was it? He could wait and wonder for that long, wonder if the damage he'd done last night was irreparable.

He'd know in thirty minutes.

At minute thirty, Arthur decided that perhaps it would be best to give Jennings another ten minutes. After all, he was extremely good at what he did, and the extra time could only help. By minute thirty-two, that resolve had changed to five extra minutes—and by minute thirty-three, he'd come to the conclusion that three extra minutes were plenty.

The smell of bodies and blood were much less appealing to him than usual. Their allure would return to him soon—just like it always did—but for right now, the pounding music and the resulting dancing children were only a physical obstacle course to be woven through to reach his objective.

He was well into minute thirty-four by the time he found the two of them, hunkered into a booth as if hiding. He elected not to wait a few moments inside of vampiric hearing distance and eavesdrop before he approached. It was an advantage he didn't deserve.

"Good evening," he said, seating himself next to Jennings. "What are we talking about?"

He wanted to watch Terry for her reaction to his presence, but found he could barely look at her.

"We're talking about the fact that you have a magical way to tell if I can be trusted," Terry said, "and the fact that you won't use it for some dumb reason."

Insolence. It was insolence that had triggered his outburst

the night before. He couldn't remember much of what happened, but he knew that much. But Arthur found this insolence extremely comforting. He may have bent her last night, but he hadn't broken her. The vampire found he could meet her eyes again.

"You don't understand," he explained. "It's not a pleasant experience. I don't know for certain that we're all going to end up friends when this is over, but we may—and assuming complete control of someone isn't something one does to friends."

"No, *you* don't understand," Terry said. "You're right—I don't know if we're all going to end up friends when this thing is over, either. But I want to help, and I don't want you two watching me for a knife in the back the entire time. I *need* you to do this, Arthur. It's important to me."

Impossibly, he felt the stirrings of the Hunger again, just at the fringe of his consciousness. She was begging him to place her under the control of the Influence, and the Hunger saw that as clear indication that she wanted to feed him. Arthur's disgust with his reaction so soon after a feeding made it easier to dismiss—easier, but not quite *easy*.

"You don't know what you're asking," the vampire said steadily.

"Then show me."

Arthur looked to Jennings. The younger vampire gave a slight, almost imperceptible nod.

So be it, then.

"Are you working for Lyle?"

"No," Terry answered. As always with the Influence, her mouth had answered without her willing it. The expression on her face showed that the experience was as disconcerting as Arthur remembered it being.

"Have you ever met Lyle, or anyone you suspect might be Lyle?"

"No," she answered again.

"Have you met with anyone who has mentioned the Book to you, besides myself?"

"No."

"Did you have any knowledge of the Book, before I ..." Arthur's voice abruptly trailed off, and his eyes assumed a far-off look.

"What is it?" Jennings asked.

"One of Lyle's fledglings," Arthur said quietly.

"Where?" Jennings said. "In here?"

"No. Outside, I think. But close by."

"This may be our first real stroke of luck. Is she alone?"

"I believe so," Arthur answered.

Jennings was instantly on his feet and pulling Arthur out of the booth. "Let's go," he said urgently. "I can't spot her without you."

Arthur and Jennings slipped through the front door and stood together, looking up and down the street. A few people wandered about—a couple holding hands crossing the street, a student walking hurriedly towards some unknown destination, an old Gypsy begging for money.

"Where *is* she?" Jennings asked.

"I don't know," Arthur confessed, still staring at passersby.

"You know, that thing would be a lot more helpful if you could fine-tune it," Jennings said.

"This *is* 'fine-tuned,'" Arthur retorted.

The only ones on the street were common mortals. There weren't even any suspiciously attractive women about.

"Are you sure she's still around?" Jennings asked. "Maybe she's left, or she's out of range."

"It's not a wireless," Arthur snapped. "You don't just ... oh shit." Arthur turned around, facing the door to Tito's.

"She's inside," they both said together, bolting back into the bar.

She wouldn't have been that difficult to spot, even if Arthur hadn't recognized her from the bus-stop. Gone were the leather and chains—she now wore a short dress; high enough, low enough, and tight enough to leave very little to the imagination. And it was red, so it wouldn't show blood. 'Dressed to kill,' so to speak. She was on the dance floor with her next victim, a young Spaniard who inwardly stroked himself for what he believed to be his good fortune.

"How did she get in here?" Jennings asked.

"I don't know. A back entrance? It hardly matters, does it?"

"It might," was Jennings' uneasy reply.

They separated, Arthur walking right up to her on the dance floor. "Excuse me," he said in Spanish. "May I have this dance?"

"No," the young man replied, attempting to brush him off.

"Don't move, don't speak," Arthur said to them. "Forget anything that's happened in the last five minutes," he said to the boy. "Return to your seat and have a drink." The boy wandered off in a daze, and Arthur turned his attention to the girl. "Come with me."

She did as she was ordered, and Arthur led her back up to the booth. Jennings fell into line behind them as they walked, following them to their seat.

Terry saw them coming, and stood at their approach. "Where are you going?" Jennings asked—but Terry made no response. She simply left, without a word spoken.

"Let her go," Jennings said quietly.

Arthur gave Jennings a few moments to explain further, but he said nothing more than those three words. The elder vampire decided to simply obey for the moment. He directed the enthralled vampiress into the booth, and all three seated themselves—Jennings beside her, and Arthur across from the both.

"Where is Lyle?" Arthur asked forcefully.

"I don't know," she answered in a British accent.

"Where do you go during the day?"

"Always someplace different, and we don't stay together. Last night, I stayed with Benjamin."

"Who is he?"

"A fledgling we made four nights ago."

Arthur sighed—this was the question he wasn't certain he wanted the answer to. "How many fledglings have you made since you came to Salamanca?"

"Nine," she answered.

"How many fledglings have you, Lyle, and the others made since you came to Salamanca?"

"I don't know exactly."

"Take a guess."

"Perhaps fifty."

Arthur and Jennings exchanged a look. *Fifty.* Fifty could be a huge number. Fifty years wasn't a particularly long time, and fifty playing cards wasn't quite enough. But fifty vampires was an enormous amount. Salamanca wasn't large enough to support fifty vampires trained to kill their victims. Very few cities in the world could.

"If you don't know where he is or where he sleeps, how do you find him?" Jennings asked.

Her response was a dull, defiant stare, until Arthur said, "Answer his question."

"We meet someplace every night," she said.

"Where?" Arthur asked.

"It's different every night."

"Where will you meet tomorrow night?"

"I don't know."

"Where will you meet tonight?"

"At the Plaza de Mayor," she answered.

"When?"

"At five."

"That's cutting it a little close to dawn," Jennings said. "He probably has a place nearby—at least for tomorrow."

"Does Lyle have the Book?"

"No," she answered.

"He didn't find it when he ransacked the library last night?" Jennings asked.

Arthur stared at Jennings. "Terry told me, just now," the younger vampire explained.

Suddenly, he was furious. The collection of books at that library was worth a thousand of these fledglings, and Lyle had destroyed it without a thought, a doubt, or a hesitation. When this was over, Lyle would suffer a little bit extra for that.

But first, this fledging would suffer.

"You haven't answered Mr. Jennings' question," Arthur said to the girl evenly. "Do you feel that's wise?"

"We didn't find the Book when we ransacked the library," she said quickly. She was frightened, but not quite frightened enough. Still, there would be time for that in a moment.

"Does Lyle have any idea where the Book might be?"

"He thinks *you* have it," she said.

"How did he find out the Book was here?"

"A mortal stumbled across it and word got back to Drew."

"Who is this mortal?"

"We don't know."

"All right," Arthur said to himself as he decided the fate of the fledgling. "I want you to find an open field and go to sleep for three days."

The fledgling started to cry, knowing she wouldn't be able to deny the command. "But I'll die," she said.

"That's right," Arthur said. "Go now."

The girl moved to stand, still crying, but Jennings didn't get out of her way. "No ... wait," Jennings said to her in vain as she began to climb over him. To Arthur, he quickly said, "Stop her."

"Stop," Arthur said. She did as she was told, now crouched on the seat with one foot on the table. "What is it?" he asked

Jennings.

"You really think we're going to *chassé* over to the Plaza de Mayor at five and destroy fifty vampires?" Jennings asked.

"Why not?" Arthur retorted.

"It's a trap," Jennings said.

Arthur snorted at Jennings' overestimation of Lyle. "Is it a trap?" he asked the fledgling.

"No," she answered, still half-out of the booth.

"She doesn't know it's a trap, but it's a trap," Jennings argued. "You're going to have to trust me on this."

Arthur thought about this for a moment. "What do *you* want to do?"

"Give me control over her, and I'll show you."

He considered this for a moment, before saying to her, "You will obey everything Jennings says, as though it came out of my mouth."

"First of all, sit back down," Jennings instructed. "Disregard what Arthur told you about falling asleep in the field."

She looked to Arthur for permission on this order, and Arthur nodded as she slid back down into her seat.

"You will not mention you ever came in here, or spoke to us," Jennings continued. "You will go to your meeting, as planned. Every night at nine, you will come to this bar to tell us where the next meeting is, unless it would arouse suspicion with Lyle. What is your name?"

"Stephanie," she answered.

"Good. You will act exactly as you would have before you met us, and follow every order Lyle gives you unless it would directly involve harming any of us." Jennings turned to Arthur. "There," he said, "How's that?"

Arthur turned back to Stephanie. "You will obey every word Jennings just spoke, to the letter, as though commanded by me. Is that clear?"

"Yes," she answered.

"Good. Now, leave."

Jennings stocd, and Stephanie slid across the seat and stood beside him. She didn't move for a moment, seeming to struggle with her orders, before giving Jennings a quick kiss on the cheek and walking away.

"What was that?" Jennings asked, resuming his seat with his hand on the spot where she'd kissed him. "Did I ..."

"You saved her life," Arthur said. "At least for now. You or I had nothing to do with that—that was just her."

"Amazing," he said to himself. "It's a good thing *I* don't have the Voice, or I'd keep her as my slave forever."

"What do you plan on doing, exactly?" Arthur asked.

"I don't have anything exact planned, but at least now we have some options. We don't have to kill them all tonight if we don't like the look of the situation, because we know where they're going to be the next night, and the night after that. Also, if he's got this army searching for the Book, they're going to have an easier time finding it than we are. If we give them a few days, they may save us some trouble."

"If we give them a few days, their numbers could go from fifty to two hundred and fifty," Arthur said steadfastly. "Your idea with that fledging is very clever. God help us if we need to use it."

The Plaza de Mayor was a large, square courtyard, perhaps two hundred meters across, surrounded by four stories of ornate, tawny-orange stonework. The alcove that rode the plaza's outer edge provided four or five meters of shade in front of the many shops within the plaza. Above the alcove were hundreds of arched windows with closed wooden shutters—shutters that could conceal both mortal and immortal eyes.

"This place is a tactical nightmare," Jennings said to Arthur as they surveyed the plaza. It was only midnight, five hours before the scheduled meeting, but it was far from safe here.

"Any suggestions?" Arthur asked.

"What's up there?" Jennings said, referring to the wooden shutters. "Are those flats?"

"Yes," Arthur answered.

"Think we could get into one?"

"I could own one by tomorrow night."

A hard look was the only response Jennings needed to give.

"I know, I know, we need it in five hours," Arthur said.

"I could get us into one, but your way would be tidier," Jennings said.

Arthur nodded, even though the idea of using the Influence turned his stomach at the moment. "We'll do it my way," Arthur relented.

Arthur knocked on some doors, asked some questions, and found the flat of a man who had 'gone to the pueblo' for a few weeks. Jennings picked the lock without difficulty, and the two of them entered and examined the place without turning on the lights. Just as they'd been told, no one was home. Two-thirty found Jennings in a chair by the window, and Arthur laying down on a sofa.

"Do you have any idea what you're going to do yet?" Jennings asked.

"'Do?'"

"Yeah, tonight."

"No, I don't," Arthur answered. "I could just command all of them to go to sleep, and allow them to burn at sunrise. But one of his fledglings is a deaf girl. I need to push a little harder to Influence her, and if she's hiding someplace there isn't much I can do without Pushing everyone in the plaza—both mortal and vampire."

"You can do that?" Jennings asked.

"Maybe. The trouble is, every one of those vampires is going to have different Gifts, whether they've been trained in the use of those Gifts or not. Odds are, some of them are going to be immune to the Influence. Those will have to be dealt with hand-to-hand."

Jennings nodded. "So that's it then? You think you'll be able to deal with them all tonight, in one fell swoop?"

"Could be. We'll have to see what it looks like down there."

"Have I mentioned that I think this might be a trap?"

"Yes, you have," Arthur replied. "But Stephanie said it wasn't."

"That would be part of the trap, wouldn't it?" Jennings asked.

"What do you mean?"

"Let's forget that we're dealing with Lyle for a minute," Jennings began. "Let's say for the sake of argument that you're going up against me. First, I would want to somehow ensure that you wouldn't leave the city as soon as you found the Book. Easiest way to do that would be to piss you off, so you were gunning for me."

"The Gypsy girl," Arthur said.

"Exactly. Then, I would use the knowledge that you have the Voice. I would send out some little fledgling to get your attention, tell her to specifically violate your Mark whenever possible to increase your odds of finding her. I would tell her where I was going to be at a specific time every night, so that you would eventually find me. And finally, I would have preparations so that when you did come, I would be ready for you."

Arthur thought about this for a moment. "What kind of preparations?"

"Bloody Hell, *anything*. In this day and age, there are thousands of ways. And with the meeting being so close to sunrise, he doesn't even have to kill you, does he? He only has to incapacitate you for a short time. A bullet through your brain'd do it."

"*Might* do it," Arthur corrected.

"From what Raymond tells me about these people, they know what will and what will not kill a vampire. Lyle will think of something new, and Make a fledgling just to try it."

"Is there a point to this, or are you just trying to make me nervous?"

"You *should* be nervous," Jennings said gravely. "This is some serious shit we're getting into here."

"We're dealing with children," Arthur said. "They're dangerous to mortals, yes—but they are still children. Whatever Lyle thinks he may have learned from his sick experimentation may or may not work on me."

Jennings nodded his head slowly. "I hope you're as good as you think you are."

Arthur gave a slight laugh. "I'm even better."

Two more hours passed. The mortals in the plaza below had thinned considerably, but there were still quite a few ambling around—much more than Arthur was comfortable with.

"You ever been bored?" Jennings asked, staring at his hands.

"Sure. I'm pretty bored right now. I wish I'd brought a book."

"No, I mean bored with life—bored with immortality. After seven hundred years, one would think life could get a little dull."

Arthur considered this question carefully. "No, not really," he finally answered. "There's always been too much to do."

"Like what?"

"Like keeping the Book hidden. Like protecting the secret of our existence by enforcing the laws of the old Society. Think about it: you've been with me for about a hundred years, have we ever been idle for very long?"

"No," Jennings answered, unsatisfied.

"What is it?"

"I haven't been alive for that long. There are mortals alive now who are nearly as old as I am—and some of *them* get bored with life. I just can't fathom having been alive for seven hundred years."

"It's really no different than being alive for seventy, it's just ... more."

"'More?'" Jennings said, almost laughing. "That's it? Just, 'more?' That's very profound, Arthur."

"What is it you want me to say, exactly?"

"I don't know. It seems to me there would be something different about being seven hundred years old. I don't know, like maybe you'd have the secret of life or something."

"Stay busy," Arthur said. "That's the secret of life. Stay busy."

"In *The Vampire Lestat*, Lestat goes underground for a couple of decades."

"Underground? How do you mean, underground?"

"You know—he buries himself."

"Really?" Arthur said derisively. "And what did Lestat feed on while he was underground?"

"He didn't," Jennings replied. "He just slowly wasted away while he listened to the world above him. When he finally resurfaced, he was stronger—more powerful. Have you ever done that?"

"No, I've never done that."

"Could it be done?"

"Sure, if you were some kind of Zen master. I couldn't take it for three days. And I don't know if you'd come out of it stronger. We get our strength from blood. I suppose there may be some folds to the nature of Vampire I'm not familiar with—but I doubt it. Why? Does the thought of spending several decades under the earth sound appealing to you?"

"Maybe, sometimes. She made it sound like sleep. Remember sleep? Remember waking up feeling better than when you went to bed?"

"I remember sleep," Arthur said. "Mortals have to sleep because of the poisons that build up in their systems after being awake all day. Those poisons don't develop in us."

"How do you know?" Jennings asked. "You're always saying that all vampires are different. Maybe those poisons still affect some of us."

Arthur shrugged, unconvinced. "Anything's possible," he said.

"That's one thing I miss about being a mortal: sleep. That comatose-state that comes over us at dawn just isn't the same."

"Maybe you should go to Antarctica, and sleep through one of their six-month summers when the sun never sets."

Jennings smiled, still thoughtful. "I wonder if that'd work," he said, turning back towards the window.

Five o'clock drew close, bringing with it a faint, orange glow in the eastern sky that made both of them nervous. Each stood behind one of the slatted wooden doors, eyes carefully watching the plaza below.

It was a poor time for a meeting of vampires. Many of the mortals in the apartments around them had awakened, and some had already begun their daily routines. Arthur counted seven bodies in the plaza, his unnatural senses unclear on whether any of them were vampires. Drawing in his own Presence—which he'd been doing all night—had that effect on his perceptions.

The two of them watched and waited in silence as the minutes ticked by. Seven bodies became twelve, then nineteen, then twenty-six. They formed little groups of anywhere from two to seven, ambling about, talking casually.

"Looks like a goddamn cocktail party down there," Jennings whispered.

"Do you see him?" Arthur asked. They couldn't risk saying his name, but both knew who they were talking about.

"Not yet," Jennings answered. "He could be in the alcove below us, where we can't see." Jennings pointed with his chin. "Looks like our friend made it here."

Arthur followed Jennings eyes and found Stephanie, walking from group to group.

"Can you hear what she's saying?" Jennings asked.

"Hush," Arthur hissed back, watching as more came into the plaza. Their numbers pushed sixty by now, maybe more. Mortal whispering he could have heard—but the vampires below them were whispering at a level their own senses could just barely hear. Arthur's ears were sharper then theirs, there was simply too much distance between them.

"There he is," Jennings said, the volume of his own voice rising to that of a whispering mortal.

There he was all right, surrounded by the largest group of fledglings in the plaza. He spoke to each of them, one at a time, and each in turn reported back to their smaller group. Some of them were already beginning to leave.

"If you're going to do something, now is the time," Jennings said quietly.

"Is that your recommendation?"

"Our friend told us that they numbered fifty. There's better than seventy out there right now, and by tomorrow there'll be a hundred or more. If you think you can really do this, then Yes, that's my recommendation."

Arthur relaxed his hold on his Presence, searching the plaza for vampires. Lyle, and many of the others, seemed immediately to notice the change, and Arthur heard his name being whispered by several of them.

"That window, there—third story, second from the corner," Arthur said to Jennings. "There's your ambush. There are at least three vampires behind that closed window, and they're confident. They have something, but I'm not sure what. You handle them, and I'll take care of the rest."

"Do you mean destroy them, boss?" Jennings asked.

"Yes, destroy them. Now cover your ears, and scream at the top of your lungs."

Arthur threw open the window, Jennings shouting at the top of his lungs behind him. He focused all of his power, all of his

Presence, into a single word, and spoke that word with such strength that Spaniards half a kilometer away would be late for work that morning.

"SLEEP."

The vampires in the plaza staggered under Arthur's power. Some went to their knees, and fell forward to the stone; some went straight back like trees; some clutched at each other for support and found none. But they all went down, until the plaza was littered with their bodies.

Arthur noticed that the screaming behind him had stopped, and turned to see Jennings laying on the floor of the flat, his hands still at his ears. "Wake up, Jennings," he said, as he leapt over the banister at the window, to the plaza thirty feet below.

There were vampires everywhere. Arthur hadn't seen so many Creatures of the Night all in one place since the old days. He opened all of his senses to their highest degree, searching for any sign of movement, anywhere. Arthur was focusing on the window that hid the ambushers when he was engulfed in sound and thrown off his feet.

Arthur knew what hand grenades sounded like. Jennings kept him up to date on all forms of modern weaponry. But it was one thing to know a hand grenade, and quite another to *know* a hand grenade. This was Arthur's first proper introduction to Hand Grenade, and it didn't take him long to realize that he didn't much care for her.

Arthur was at a cocktail party, talking to Stiletto. Not a bad fellow, really. He'd met Stiletto on several occasions, and found him to be quite personable. Handgun came walking over, and the three had a nice little chat. He'd only met Handgun once or twice, and on both of those occasions the bullet had passed right through him and the wound had healed shortly afterwards. No, he had no quarrel with Handgun.

Arthur's thoughts refused to clear. The explosions had stopped—there had been seven or eight of them, timed sporadically. The crazy bastards had pulled the pins before they'd come into the plaza, knowing they'd go off if anything happened to them. That much, he was rational enough to see.

Across the room was Flame Thrower. He'd never met Flame Thrower, but knew from what he'd heard that he never wanted to. Flame Thrower had no manners and no discretion. He was sticking close to Nuclear Warhead, who was even more of a boor than Flame Thrower. The only one actually speaking to Warhead was an American General, who had his arm around him and joked loudly.

Arthur's trembling hands searched his body, finding a piece of shrapnel lodged in the side of his head. *That* was why he couldn't think straight.

Lyle came up to him, handing him a drink. "Good to see you, old boy," he said casually. He'd brought a friend over with him, and suddenly realized that he'd been remiss in his introductions. She was a beautiful woman—in fact, she looked just like Stephanie.

"Arthur," Lyle asked. "Have you met Miss Hand Grenade?"

"Met her?" Arthur responded. "She just fucked me in the plaza."

"Really?" Lyle responded, laughing amusedly. "Well, if you liked her, you'll love the woman you're about to meet. Dawn should be by any moment—in fact, I should probably be going. I haven't seen Dawn in years, and I wouldn't want to break my streak now. Toodles."

"Don't get too close to him," Arthur heard a voice saying. "Leave him right where he is. The sun will take care of him."

"Help me," Arthur breathed, reaching out with his mind. "Someone ... anyone ... please help me."

Arthur tasted blood.

It had been some time since his mind was clear, since his thoughts were his own. Exactly how long was difficult to say. A day? Two? It didn't feel like much longer than two days, but vampires were funny that way.

His jaws were clamped to an arm, as were his hands. He was holding on and drawing mind-clearing, healing blood from it. It was vampire blood, and that made it a little more potent. But he needed more.

As if in response to his unspoken request, Terry's shaking voice said, "I think there's more where that came from."

Questions bombarded him from within faster than he could ask them, or decide which order they should take. How did they get into the mountains? Why was there a huge dog sitting at Terry's heel? Where had this dead vampire come from? Where had 'more' come from? Where was Jennings? How long had he been out?

Blood. Blood first. The questions would wait.

"Bring me the next one," Arthur said.

Arthur pushed a narrow stick into the chest of the fourth vampire. He'd taken all the blood from it—and the others—that he could. It was impossible that they would escape the rising sun, perhaps less than an hour away. Still, no sense taking chances. Not anymore.

"So, that thing about a staking a vampire's heart is true," Terry said.

The mortal girl seemed very far away. He supposed he couldn't blame her. Whatever had happened must have been extremely traumatic for someone with her lack of experience with such things. She sat huddled on the ground, her arms wrapped around her knees, her eyes staring at some point on the ground that she didn't see. The dog—wild or stray, by the smell of it—lay on the ground beside her, regarding the vampire with some strange canine fascination.

"We don't have much time," Arthur said, glancing up at the reddening sky. "What happened?"

"Lyle and the others found us," Terry said. "He said they have Jennings, and they'll trade the Book for him."

Arthur snorted. That wasn't a trade Lyle would *ever* honestly think Arthur would make.

"Where are we, and how did we get here?" the vampire asked.

"We went through all this already," Terry said.

"Did we?" Arthur asked. "I don't remember it."

"You're kidding, right?"

"Why? Did something I said strike you as amusing?"

Terry gave an irritated sigh. "I don't know where we are, exactly," she began. "I'm pretty sure we're still in Spain. We didn't pass a border, or anything. I woke up yesterday morning with you screaming, 'Help me, help me,' into my head. I found you at the Plaza de Mayor after the sun came up. I got you into the trunk of my car and just started driving. This is where we got to before we broke down."

"How did Lyle find us?" Arthur asked.

"Dunno," she said. "Some weird vampire-shit, I imagine. The way you were yelling into my brain, I wouldn't imagine it would be too hard for them." Terry pointed to the dog. "You brought *him* to us."

"With the Influence? the second voice?" Arthur asked. "I very much doubt that. The Influence doesn't work on animals."

"So I've heard," Terry said. "You gave me this same argument last night, and you were wrong then, too. I know what I saw. If you don't believe me, why don't you just use the fucking Voice on me again?"

Arthur ignored this comment in favor of another question. "How did you manage to kill four vampires while I was incapacitated? Did I ... "

"The wolf did it," she interrupted. "He got them all—except Lyle. Lyle must have gotten away."

Arthur could not suppress a little chuckle. "No wolf could do *that* to four vampires. It's impossible."

Terry stood. "Whatever. I'm hungry. I'm hitching someplace I can get something to eat. You have any money on you?"

The vampire reached into the pocket of his tattered pants, producing a money clip holding the equivalent of a couple hundred dollars. "Take it all," he said, tossing it to her. "It should be enough to get you back, and fed."

Terry barely regarded the money as she stuffed it into the pocket of her jeans.

"I'm sorry ... we're running out of time," Arthur said. "Obviously, we're going to need to talk about this a bit more."

"Obviously," Terry said dryly.

"Find me in Tito's tomorrow night, and we'll see if we can sort this through."

"Sure," she said, "so long as you tell the wolf to come with me."

Arthur considered debating the point, but Terry was clearly in no mood for rational thought. "Dog, go with Terry," he said.

To his surprise, the wolf stood and followed Terry as she stormed off.

It didn't take Arthur more than a few hours to get back to Salamanca. A Push here, a Push there, and he was being dropped at his doorstep by a mortal who was only too glad to help.

He had several flats in the city—both because it made him more difficult to trace, and because dawn sometimes had a way of sneaking up on you. All were decorated tastefully (by others) and looked like perfectly normal mortal dwellings—save for rather thick window coverings and somewhat advanced security systems—and each portrayed a slightly different style of living depending upon the lie he was telling that night. Although he still had a few hours before daylight, he headed straight for the seediest one he owned to gather his thoughts and attempt to form some kind of plan.

Lyle claimed to have Jennings. Okay. He wouldn't have made the claim unless they'd either captured or killed him. The question was, was Jennings dead or alive? Hmm. Actually, that wasn't the question at all. The question was, was Jennings dead or undead?

What purpose would his destruction serve? Another demonstration of power? Another fuck-you from Lyle, like the Gypsy girl? Perhaps. It would also halve Arthur's number in Salamanca. Jennings offered no new facet of vampiric power, but he was valuable nonetheless. He had Intelligence Training that dated back to World War II, and working for Arthur had kept him in training ever since. He could do things like trace credit cards and phone calls, obtain false birth certificates and passports, ask the right questions to get the right answers from just about anyone. He was a valuable, clever bastard, and he would be impossible to replace.

What purpose would his life serve? Information? That would be impossible. Arthur had complete faith Jennings could resist any method of questioning they put to him. Even if one of Lyle's number had the Gift of Telepathy, it wouldn't work on Jennings. Not even Raymond could read Jennings' mind. Of course, Lyle didn't know this. It had only been two nights—Lyle might still believe that he could get information from him, so that would be a valid reason to keep him alive. Jennings could also be used as a bargaining chip.

Terry'd said that Lyle had mentioned a trade: the Book for Jennings. If Lyle was clever enough to set up that devastating ambush at the plaza, then he was clever enough to know that Arthur would never make such a trade; and if Arthur agreed to trade Jennings for the Book, it would be a matter of whose ambush was better thought out. Without Jennings, that contest wouldn't be as one-sided as Arthur would have liked.

That's what Lyle would most likely do. He would keep Jennings alive. Lyle didn't have any way of knowing whether he and Jennings had some kind of psychic link. Gifts were unpredictable that way—you never knew what your enemy might be capable of. Using the Influence on the deaf girl had been a mistake on Arthur's part. He'd revealed a strength, and had perhaps given Lyle the edge he'd needed for the ambush at the plaza. *Never reveal all of your strength for a mere demonstration*, he'd been told once by the leader of the Society of Vampires. *For a demonstration, reveal some of your strength. Allow your enemy to be surprised by your real power when you move to destroy him.*

Then the only question left concerned his course of action.

Should he find the Book, or rescue Jennings? He knew what Jennings would do, could hear his voice in his head as though they really did share a link of minds.

'Part of the reason they're keeping me is to distract you. They want you to search for me, instead of the Book. Imagine worst-cases in each scenario: they kill me, or they get their hands on the Book. My death won't alter the history of humanity—same can't be said of the other.'

Yes, that was true. Arthur had to find that Book, and leave Jennings until it was secured. If he was alive, he would remain alive for a time. And Arthur couldn't very well find the Book if he was concentrating all of his efforts on finding Jennings, could he? It was clear. Arthur's impulse would be to use Stephanie to find Jennings, destroying as many of Lyle's cabal as possible in the process. But he had to play this smarter than that. He was no longer in a position of power in Salamanca. He was just another vampire in a city full of vampires. What would their number be by now? Better than a hundred? For the first time in a long time, he was going to have to use the night, use the shadows. He was going to have to be a vampire again—a Prince of Darkness, instead of a King.

The Book. Where the hell could that accursed thing have gotten to? He and Jennings had examined all the angles, followed up on all the leads. It hadn't just up and walked out of the library. Someone had it, most likely someone who didn't even know ...

... someone who didn't even know what they had.

That was it. That was the answer.

The full moon lit up the flat countryside east of Salamanca. Arthur was tempted to drive his Volvo without the headlights, but knew it was a foolish temptation. He couldn't afford to waste time being pulled over for something as trivial as headlights.

It was just past nine as he pulled into Dr. Del Rio's driveway—not an unreasonable time to expect to find a mortal awake, unless one took into account that this mortal was better than eighty years old. Not that it mattered. For this, he would wake the doctor, regardless of his age.

Arthur put the car in park, cut the lights, killed the ignition. He smelled pipe-smoke before the door of the car was even closed behind him, and looked to the porch to see a wrinkled face in the cherry glow of tobacco.

"Hello," the man said in Spanish. *Hola.*

"Good evening," Arthur replied. "I have been told you speak English."

"*Sí.*"

"I apologize for the hour. I would have called, but I am also told you have no phone. Are you Dr. Del Rio?"

"*Sí.*"

"I spoke with an antique dealer earlier this evening. I asked him about a book, and he referred me to you."

"What sort of book?"

"Very old—centuries old. It was stolen from the library at the University of Salamanca. I was told that if someone were asking questions about such a book, he might eventually be sent to you."

"Are you from the university?" the doctor asked.

"No."

The old man took a puff from his pipe. "Then what is your interest in this book?"

"It belongs to me."

"Did you write it?"

Arthur tried to laugh nonchalantly. "This book is over eight hundred years old," he answered.

"I see," the doctor said. "Did you write it?"

The old man's English wasn't as good as he'd hoped. "Do I look old enough to write an eight hundred year old book?" Arthur asked patiently.

"You could be," he replied. "With your kind, it's hard to tell."

So, *that* was how it was. Dr. Del Rio knew about more than just the Book. He knew about vampires.

"No, I didn't write it," Arthur said. "The Book is even older than I am. But I have a special interest in keeping the Book out of the wrong hands."

"I don't want to know any more," the doctor said. "I'm too old to take a side in your fight."

"Has anyone come to you about this book?" Arthur asked.

The old man laughed, taking another drought of smoke. "You are the *third*," he said.

"Who were the other two?"

"The first was a girl. *Negro*, pretty black girl but a little heavy. She wanted to know what I knew about the book, and about you."

"About me?" Arthur asked.

"Not about you, personally—about your kind. One

moment," he said calmly, taking another puff while he thought. "One moment. No, the black girl was someone else. This one was short, dark hair, nice legs. I didn't like her voice, though. Too squeaky, like Minnie Mouse."

"What did you tell her about 'my kind?'" Arthur asked patiently.

"When I was younger, I was approached. He wanted me to join him, I refused. She wanted to know why I refused, and I told her."

"And why did you refuse?"

The old man smiled, lowering his pipe to his lap. "You have to ask?" he said.

"No, not really," Arthur replied. "Who else came and saw you?"

"After she left, I called my friend. He's in London now—we stay in touch, but not really. We stay in touch well enough for me to find him, and that's all."

"I thought you said you didn't have a phone?" Arthur asked.

"*You* said I didn't have a phone. I said nothing. I called this friend, and he told another friend—someone who took the offer that I did not. He asked me about the book and I told him about the girl. That is all."

"What about the girl? Do you remember her name?"

"Yes, Anna. No, Anne. Anne Rice. That's it."

Anne Rice. *Wonderful.* "Did she tell you how she stumbled on the Book?"

"I didn't ask. I assumed she was a student at the university," the doctor said, lifting his pipe to his mouth for another drag.

"You say she was short with dark hair. Is that all you can remember about her?" Arthur asked.

"Yes, short with dark hair. Or, tall."

Great. *Beautiful.* So he had a physical description—either black or white, tall or short, with a voice that may or may not sound like Minnie Mouse—and a false name. What a productive night this was turning out to be. Perhaps if he Converted this old man, it would clear his mind. No option was beyond consideration at this point.

The doctor sucked another puff of smoke from his pipe. "Tell me something. If you had the choice to make over again, what would *you* do?"

"I wasn't given a choice," Arthur replied.

"You know what I mean," the old man snapped. "If you'd been given the choice, knowing what you know now, what would you have done?"

"I can't answer that," he confessed. "I don't know. Sometimes I wish the whole thing had never happened—but if it hadn't, I wouldn't be here to regret it. Why? Do you regret your choice?"

Dr. Del Rio's lips tightened. He held his hand up at chin-level, watching the quiver of age there, before he closed it into a fist and dropped it. "Of course I regret it," he answered. "I've regretted it every day for the last twenty years. But if I was given the choice over again, I probably would have chosen the same. Does that make any sense?"

"It makes a lot of sense," Arthur said.

Arthur sat in Tito's, wetting his lips with a nice gin and tonic. He wanted to drink it—he envied Jennings that talent so badly right now he could spit blood. The hunting was pretty good in here tonight, but Arthur wasn't interested. After the vampire blood he'd had two nights ago, it would be another week before he needed to feed. Besides, the thought of the incident with Terry was still turning his stomach.

The large man who watched the door walked up to his barstool. "*Señor*, there is a woman at the door looking for you," he said in Spanish.

Arthur set his glass down. It had to be either Terry or Stephanie, but complex orders like the ones he'd given Stephanie required reinforcement and she'd had three days for the Influence to wear off. Unless she had an extraordinarily weak will, he could no longer count her as an unwilling ally. It had to be Terry. "Why doesn't she come inside?" Arthur asked the other man.

"I told her, no dogs," he replied.

No dogs? Then the wolf *had* gone with her. Arthur sighed as he rolled his eyes. "Thank you," he said to the bouncer, sliding down from his stool to follow him back to the door.

Terry was waiting there, her pet wolf on a nylon leash. "I see you brought the thing back with you after all," Arthur said disdainfully as the two of them began walking.

"Bear in mind that this thing saved your life," Terry retorted. "And his name is Iago."

"Really? Did he tell you that?"

"Arthur ..." she began sharply before he cut her off.

"It's a wild animal, Terry," he said. "Do you think it *likes* being in the middle of Salamanca?"

"He hasn't minded so far," she snapped back. "I had second thoughts after we left you that night, and I was going to leave him behind. But he started chasing us when we drove away, and the guy who picked me up looked at me like I was abandoning my dog. Iago didn't *want* to be left behind."

Arthur didn't know why, but Terry seemed angry for some reason. Ah well, it wasn't important. "You aren't going to be able to house-train it, you know," he said.

"For your information, I already did. It was the first thing I trained him to do."

"In a day?" Arthur asked incredulously. "I don't think so. Maybe it was someone's pet before we found it."

"No, I *trained* him," Terry said. "He comes when I call him, too."

"Great. Well, he'd better be house-trained, because the two of you are staying at one of my flats until this thing is resolved."

"Why?" Terry demanded. "They aren't coming after me."

"You argue everything, don't you? You don't even give thought to whether you may be right or wrong, it's just a knee-jerk reflex. If they didn't come for you last night, they'll come for you tonight. They'll trace the license plate on your car and they'll find you."

"It was a friend's car," she said.

Arthur threw his hands into the air. "Fine. You're right. I'm sure you're perfectly safe. Forget the whole thing. Go back to your dorm or apartment or whatever you're living in. I'm sure you'll live through the night."

Arthur turned around, walking the other way. "Iago, no!" he

heard her saying behind him. "Iago, heel! Stay! STOP!"

The wolf was suddenly in front of him, dragging Terry along by his leash. Its posture was curious—not at all threatening—as he seated himself in Arthur's path and stared at the vampire.

"Your animal has more sense than you do," he mumbled to Terry.

"Fine," she said angrily. "I'll stay with you. Let's just go back to my place so I can get some things, okay?"

"Very well," Arthur replied.

They climbed five flights of stairs to reach Terry's apartment. It wasn't that different from Arthur's own low-scale flat. Her couch was secondhand, dusty, and faded; her coffee table was scratched and abused; her tiny television sat on top of a wooden crate. Posters adorned the walls: one proclaiming that there was no city like Salamanca (*Salamanca—Hay no Mejores*), and another with streaking lights and fast boats that said 'Miami Vice.'

"You said before you had a roommate," Arthur said. "Where is she?"

"At her boyfriend's, I guess," Terry answered, unhooking Iago's collar from his leash. The unnaturalness of blue nylon against the wolf's golden coat turned down the corners of Arthur's mouth. "Do you think she's in danger, too?" she asked.

"Yes," Arthur answered flatly. "Any idea where she might be?"

"None," Terry answered. "Should I leave a note?"

"Pack your things," Arthur said. "I'll come back once you're safe, and if she returns tonight, I'll collect her."

"Like she's just going to come with you? She doesn't even know you." Arthur answered her with a hard look. "Right. Forget I said anything," she said as she headed into the bathroom.

Iago was acting strangely, as though nervous. His ears were flat against his head as he cautiously smelled the floor, his massive head slowly swinging back and forth. Arthur watched as the wolf walked around the room with his head down, searching for an invisible trail.

Suspicious, Arthur went to his hands and knees, smelling the floor. His sense of smell was keener than a human's, but he wasn't sure if it measured up to Iago's. He could smell nothing.

Terry reentered the room, seeing the two of them sniffing the floor. "What are you doing?" she asked, trying to sound sarcastic but not quite pulling it off.

Arthur gestured to the wolf. "I don't know what he's so disturbed about, but I can't smell it. We should get the hell out of ... here."

"What?" she demanded. "What is it?"

"Vampires," Arthur answered. "Lyle's fledglings—*lots* of them—down on the street."

Iago turned his head towards the glass door of the balcony—his lips drawn away from his teeth—and uttered a long, low growl.

"Can you handle them?" she asked, unable to keep her voice steady. "You're at full strength now, right?"

The number of vampires in Arthur's perception continued to increase, until the street below glowed with their presence in his mind's eye. "Do you have any weapons here?" he asked.

"There are knives in the kitchen," she answered.

"Get two, in case any get by me," he instructed. "If it comes down to it, go for the heart. Stay up here until I come for you."

Arthur slid opened the glass door and stepped onto the stone balcony, into the crisp night. The street below him looked deserted, but they were there all right—in numbers so large, he could smell them. Lyle had his entire army down there.

Get two, in case any get by me, he repeated in his mind. As though that would help. If any got by him, she was dead—unless that wolf got lucky again, and Arthur could not count on luck. He was going to have to be careful—more than careful. He was going to have to be flawless.

Arthur leapt over the balustrade. Alternating hands grabbed balusters to control his fall, and he was on the sidewalk in seconds. There were too many for him to sense individuals, he knew only that he was more than surrounded.

"Come out, come out, wherever you are," he Influenced. No response. Lyle's entire army was deaf, and he couldn't Push someone who was deaf unless he could see them—or at least perceive them. Lyle was getting smarter all the time.

The sound of shattering glass cut the night as a fledgling dove through a window across the street. He landed on his feet and rushed him in what would have been a blur of motion to human eyes. A clawed hand found empty air where Arthur had been standing, as he ducked beneath it with speed that far surpassed that of his foe. More glass shattered as he circled behind the fledgling, grabbing his face to stare into his eyes.

"Kill them," Arthur commanded. "Kill them all."

The unnatural creature—who had once been a human boy of perhaps fourteen years—streaked towards those who had once been his allies. He took out three before he was put down, his head wrenched from his body; and in that time Arthur incapacitated one—reaching into his body to pull out his heart—and Influenced another. It was a ballet of death. A scant fourteen seconds after Arthur had opened that glass door five stories above, no less than twenty downed vampires littered the street. He ducked and he wove and he Influenced and undead bodies continued to drop. Then Terry's scream came.

Arthur focused. None had gotten past him; he was certain of that. She could have screamed for a dozen reasons, a dozen reasons Arthur dared not consider. He had to kill and think of nothing else—a moment wasted on thought could mean the end of his own un-life. He was a machine, a machine whose only purpose was to destroy vampires. Arthur allowed himself to be consumed with an instinct he'd spent seven centuries suppressing. Thought was a commodity beyond his means. There was only the Killer within.

Forty seconds after he'd left the balcony, he stopped. Five Influenced fledglings surrounded him, looking for someone else to tear into. The street was dense with bodies, body parts, broken glass, splintered wood. And blood. Plenty of blood. Muscles in Arthur's shoulder had been torn—rendering his left arm useless—and a tendon on the back of his knee was rapidly re-bonding from where it had been bitten through, but he was otherwise unharmed. He quickly estimated the count of bodies around him at seventy or more. Arthur hobbled over to one of his slaves, uttered the words, "Don't resist," and fed on the fledgling.

More glass shattered—Terry's balcony door. Arthur looked up in time to watch the slow plummet of two bodies.

The one on the bottom was Lyle. It was easy to identify him, even though he'd never seen a look of terror like that on Lyle's face. That look gave Arthur no small amount of pleasure.

The form on top was another matter entirely. It was vaguely shaped like a man: arms, torso, head. But Arthur had plenty of time to study it in its slow fall towards the street, and it was definitely not a man—nor any creature he'd ever encountered.

First of all, it was big. Bigger than a modern basketball player—bigger than any man he'd ever seen. It was big like a bear was big—a *big* bear. Monstrous. As-big-as-a-small-car big.

Second, its appearance was wolfen. It had a large, canine head, and the air rushing past it in its fall pushed back its snarling lips to reveal bloody, canine teeth. Ears like a wolf, a ruff around the neck, hocked hind legs. The two of them plummeted towards the street, Lyle struggling in the creature's clawed hands, trying to get himself out from beneath the thing. It did him no good.

They landed with a force that shook the ground beneath Arthur's feet, and would knock pictures from walls three blocks away. Five enslaved vampires converged on it, following their vague orders—this thing was one of 'them.' Arthur's body was healing quickly, but he was still robbed of the speed to intervene. It proved to be unnecessary.

Even lying on the ground, its arms were long enough to grab one by the throat. It slowly got to its feet as one fledgling clamped her jaws onto its immense neck and another attached himself to its back. It threw the body of the first one it grabbed, and the vampire's back broke against the iron-wrought balustrade of a third-story balcony. The girl on his neck was torn free unceremoniously and thrown in a similar manner, as was the one on his back, until it seemed bodies were flying everywhere.

Lyle crawled out of arms reach of the fighting creature, and got his feet on the far side of Arthur. He attempted a pursuit, but his tendon hadn't healed and Lyle's miraculously undamaged legs quickly carried him away.

Arthur's five enslaved fledglings were down by the time Terry burst out of the building door, stopping on the sidewalk to scream the word, "Iago!"

"Iago?" Arthur questioned aloud, staring at the formidable creature before him.

He stood at his full height for only a second before crouching down and facing Arthur. It was difficult to tell just how large the creature was—eight feet? nine? He seemed to continue to crouch, but the truth was, he was shrinking. Arthur's mind reeled. Iago's shoulders hunched forward with the sound of muscles popping and bone sliding on bone, until Arthur was facing the animal that had walked at the end of Terry's leash not half an hour ago. He seemed tiny now, even though he was still one hundred and fifty pounds of wolf.

"Jesus Christ," Terry whispered, staring up at her balcony. Arthur followed her eyes—the railing was folded over where their bodies had slammed through it. "Tell me I didn't just see that."

"Pretty strong evidence for the existence of werewolves, isn't he?" Arthur asked.

"Marta is dead," she said coldly. Too coldly. Something disturbing had happened up there, something that Terry was blocking so completely it was as though she didn't even hear herself speak the words 'Marta is dead.' But Arthur didn't have time to deal with that right now.

"I have to go after Lyle," Arthur said.

Terry nodded, vaguely understanding.

"You'll be safe enough with Iago, I think. Call a cab and get yourself to this address," he said, handing her a business card and a key. "I'll be there before dawn."

She was in a bad way. Arthur knew he'd be lucky to find her at his flat when he returned. He sometimes forgot just how disturbing a routine thing like death could be if you'd never been exposed to it. Something in Terry was dying, just like something had died in him when Charlotte had been killed before his eyes seven hundred years ago.

The hardest thing for the dead to feel was sympathy for the dying. The pain is forgotten, and the dead feel, *Well, I got through it, didn't I? This dying person will be all right, just like I am now.* It isn't so much that the pain is forgotten—it merely goes to a place that isn't pain anymore, but is instead dull memory. That was where Charlotte lived now. In dull memory.

Arthur ran off after Lyle, leaving Terry in Iago's care.

Lyle's trail was not difficult to follow. It was similar to the Mark, in that it wasn't precisely a scent, or any other mortal sense. It was a path he could see, a humming of latent power he could hear, a knot in his stomach he could feel, a metallic tang he could taste ... without being any of these things. It was that which the Society had called *Le Sens*. The Sense.

Arthur followed this Sense through the dark streets. He smelled blood as he ran past a young man, lying on his back on the sidewalk. His heart was still beating and the man would live. Lyle had briefly fed here, but he knew that Arthur would be coming after him, and hadn't taken more than a few pints. Lyle would be at full strength when Arthur caught up to him—not that it would make any difference. Lyle would die the Final Death tonight.

The path circled around, taking him through the Plaza de Mayor, towards—then past—the Roman Bridge. Lyle was thrashing about in a clearing beside the bridge when Arthur caught up to him. He could feel that Lyle was in pain, but its source was unclear. Arthur pushed his Presence, making himself noticed—the vampiric equivalent to clearing one's throat.

"Kill me, and Jennings dies," Lyle shouted, too loud for the thirty feet that separated them. He held a bloody ice-pick in his hand, and streams of blood flowed from either ear. Lyle had punctured his own eardrums.

"Where is Jennings?" Arthur demanded.

"I'm not a fledgling," he said, still shouting. "You can't affect me if I can't hear you." The ice-pick dropped to the grass. "And I can't hear you."

"I can still run you through with my fist, can't I?" Arthur asked. "Where is Jennings?"

"Why don't you just give me what I want?" Lyle cried, stamping his feet in a tantrum of frustration. "Is it a sin to want more than you have?"

"You already have more than you should have ever been given," Arthur replied. "You endanger us all with your reckless use of your powers. Tonight, I correct Drew's mistake."

"And what about Jennings?" Lyle taunted. "Dawn is only a few minutes away. If I don't get to him in time, he will burn. Do you want that?"

Arthur could see that Lyle was telling the truth. Such a thing would be simple to arrange. Stake him down in the open somewhere—somewhere like this field—where the rising sun would kill him unless someone intervened. "What is it exactly you think I'm going to do?" Arthur asked. "Just walk away?"

"If you want Jennings to live, yes," was Lyle's reply. "Otherwise, we'll stand in this field and die together when day breaks. What do you say? Does Jennings live one more day?"

Arthur considered carefully. The sky in the east was red with the coming of his deadliest weakness. The opportunity to kill Lyle would come again, while the opportunity to save Jennings might not. And why would Lyle allow Jennings to die, when it gave him this incredible advantage? No, he would have to rescue Jennings before he could destroy Lyle.

"Go," Arthur ordered.

Lyle smiled, executing a grandiose bow before fleeing into the trees. Arthur turned, finding the old Gypsy woman standing behind him, backed up by a small group of strong-looking men. Perhaps they'd heard Lyle's deaf shouting, or his own

Influencing voice. Or, perhaps the old woman really was a mystic. Whatever the reason, they were here—and they'd seen the entire thing.

Arthur approached them, a cold look in his eyes and a sick feeling in his stomach. *"No es acabó,"* he said to them. *This isn't over.*

Terry

Massachusetts, 1975

Eight-year-old Theresa Ann Butler woke in the middle of the night. Voices were coming from downstairs. She thought at first her mother must be talking on the phone—her father was away at some kind of cop convention—but she could hear a man's voice as well. They were both whispering, but a heating vent that connected her room to the living room of the old house carried those whispers to her young ears. Besides, she never slept well when her father was away.

Theresa had always had nightmares, ever since they'd moved into this house. She dreamt something terrible would happen to her and Mommy while Daddy was working one night. Daddy didn't work nights anymore, because Theresa had nightmares. But he'd gone to this convention.

She climbed out of bed. If Daddy was home she wanted to see him, just so she would be able to sleep. But before she reached her bedroom door, she heard something strange about the whispers. Something frightening. A sob had escaped her mother's mouth. She'd heard some of Daddy's stories through that vent—stories of rape and murder and other worse things. Something was going on downstairs. Something very bad.

Theresa silently opened her bedroom door and slipped into her parents' room. She went down to her knees on the carpet, reaching under the bed through the draping comforter. Her fingers groped blindly for a second, before they found the case that had been forbidden to her from a very early age. She grasped the handle and pulled it out through the comforter, stopping to listen intently. There were no vents to the living room from here, and she heard nothing.

She popped the clasps on either side of the case and opened it. The revolver inside was huge and heavy. She'd fired it once or twice, and had been nearly knocked over by it. But she knew how to hold it, and how to aim it. Her tiny hand took the stock, and she lifted it out of the case.

She held it with both hands—at the side of her face and pointed towards the ceiling, like she'd seen Daddy do—as she padded out of the room, towards the stairs. The steps creaked in spots, but Theresa knew those spots well enough to walk down the stairs quietly. She'd been practicing for this, for the time when something bad would happen and she'd have to get the gun from her parents' room and save her mother and herself. Theresa cocked back the hammer of the revolver with both thumbs, and began down the stairs.

Her mother's crying grew louder and louder with every step. They were on the couch—Theresa could tell by their shadows. A single creak of wood would reveal her, so each step was slow and careful. The man would see her legs long before she could see him, she just had to hope he didn't look.

She was four steps from the bottom by the time she could see them. Her mother's back was to her, the man was beside her, facing her. Theresa recognized the profile.

It was Brian Higgins, a friend of her father's, but he wasn't wearing his uniform. His hair was messy, and he was in a T-shirt.

He caught her out of the corner of his eye, and turned towards her. She saw pity in his face and tears in his eyes—tears that blurred his vision and kept him from seeing the gun. Her mother noticed Brian, and turned about to face Theresa.

It all made sense—too much sense. Her mother's crying, Brian's messy appearance. Theresa knew without anyone having to tell her. "Daddy's dead, isn't he?" she asked, her voice deceptively steady and calm.

Theresa's mother broke into a new volley of sobs, and Brian looked away for a second. "There was an accident, Punkin," were all the words he got out.

The cocked gun fell out of her hands, discharging when it hit the stairs. The round passed through the step, ricocheting from the basement floor and wall before embedding in a beam. It was the sound that did the most damage, as it startled the adult out of Theresa and reduced her to a little girl—a little girl who couldn't bear what she was hearing.

Eight-year-old Theresa Ann Butler covered her ears with her hands and began to scream.

Spain, 1986

Terry walked through the campus of the University of Salamanca, sorry she'd ever allowed herself to be dragged into this project.

At first, the idea of it had seemed kind of cool. The University of Salamanca was slowly being dragged into the Information Age, and one of the first things they wanted to do was catalog all of the manuscripts in the old library and put them onto a database. Being a thorough man, Dr. Marcus wanted all of these books confirmed by hand, which was turning out to be one hell of a chore even for fifteen graduate students.

Terry had been brought into it because she was an American, and because all Americans are intimately familiar with computers. *Yeah.* She hadn't even taken any computer classes in high school, and this was the first time she'd ever actually worked on one. It was no time at all before she'd learned that she did not *like* computers, and that the old manuscripts weren't nearly as charming as she thought they'd be.

Vaguely, she wondered what Doug was doing right now. It would be ... around noon Eastern Standard Time. Noon on a Friday. Tough call. Maybe in a class. Maybe having lunch with another woman. He probably had a gig tonight—or tomorrow night. The work had been pretty steady when she'd left the States.

Terry thought about the last time they'd spoken, that time in the apartment. She thought about the deliberate trips back up the stairs for paper bags of her stuff, neither one of them saying anything. She'd been thinking the entire time, *When he finally does stop me, he'd better help me carry this stuff back upstairs.* But he hadn't stopped her.

The thing with Dominic hadn't worked out, either. He wouldn't leave his fiancée, blah, blah, blah. He'd turned out to be a jerk, just like Doug had always said he was. Terry'd had three relationships since then. But although she'd fawned over them and made them believe she was in love with them, she never stopped missing Doug.

They had a few mutual friends, and she would hear things from time to time. Apparently, he hadn't had any relationships—any *real* relationships—since then. He probably still missed her too. That was why he couldn't commit to anyone else. He was waiting for the day when she would call. But she'd be damned before that day came. *He* would call *her*, or they would never speak to each other again.

She'd gone to see one of his gigs after she'd broken off with Dominic, thinking that maybe they could finally talk. It hadn't worked out. He'd been singing to another girl in the audience; not just any song, but *Unchained Melody*—*their* song. She'd left before he'd even known she was there. Well, if the song didn't mean anything to him, it didn't mean anything to her either. So she'd intentionally fucked Keith while listening to it—and had thought of Doug the whole time. Bastard.

He was such a stubborn asshole. Sure, it was wrong of

her to sleep with Dominic. She would tell him she was sorry if she ever got the chance to, and she would mean it. Terry had taken the opportunity to study at the University of Salamanca, hoping it would get back to him and he would call ... he would stop her. But he'd let her go, and now here she was. An American computer whiz, cataloging old books in a dusty library.

Sometimes she fantasized he would come here, to Salamanca, and track her down—take her into his arms and tell her he was sorry, that he couldn't live without her. She'd stand in the Limón y Menta or the Numero Uno or Tito's and she'd look around the bar to see if he was there, across the room, staring at her. But Doug wasn't ever going to come. Doug didn't care. Jesus, they hadn't seen each other in over a year. How long was it going to take her to get it through her thick head?

She walked into the library, passing the guard at the door who recognized her by now, and headed straight for her section (Doug wasn't waiting for her in the library, she noticed—cursing herself for the thought moments later). She hadn't even picked up a book yet and already the smell of dust and decaying paper was giving her a headache.

"Hi, Stranger," Stan said as she passed him. He was an American like herself, and took no great pains to hide the fact that he was more than interested in her. Not that it mattered; Terry made it a strict policy not to date men shorter than she was—which ruled out quite a few men considering her five foot eleven frame. "Haven't seen you in here in a while," he added.

"I was in here yesterday," she replied, as though shooing an insect.

"I must have missed you," Stan said, putting his book down to follow her to her section. "Are you going to Tito's tonight?"

Tito's. She'd gone a total of two times, and had made the mistake of mentioning it to Stan, who had clung to the idea like a bull terrier. "I don't know," Terry answered. "Marta hasn't been feeling well. I think maybe I'll just stay in." The part about Marta, the girl she shared a flat with, was true—the part about staying in was not.

"Oh," he said, a little disappointed. "Because I was thinking about going."

"Why don't you?" she suggested. At least if she knew where he was going to be, she could go someplace else.

"I don't want to go alone," Stan said. "I won't know anyone there if you're not there."

Terry had felt bad for Stan at first, but that was four months ago. She'd tried to let him down easy, but apparently she was letting him down too easy because he wasn't getting the message. "Well, if Marta isn't going, I'm not going," she said as she slipped on a pair of plastic gloves. "Tito's is her place, not mine."

"What's your place?" Stan asked, as Terry took the next manuscript—marked with an index card from yesterday—from the shelf.

"I don't have a place," Terry sighed, growing annoyed. "I go wherever."

"Oh," he said.

Terry was no longer hearing him. If she was going to finish this project while she was still young, she had to get through the portion of books that had been assigned to her, and she wasn't even halfway there. The one in her hands, like so many others, had no title on the outside—meaning it would be cataloged by the first few words of text. She opened it carefully, and hissed, "Shit!" at what she found.

"What?" Stan asked.

"Look at this, someone has torn out the first few pages of this book. It's hundreds of years old! Some people have *no* respect."

"Maybe it was done a while ago, before the last time they cataloged," he offered. "What are the first words there?"

"'*Nulla somniant.*'"

"'Never dream.'" Stan translated. "That's interesting. Let me see." He took the book from Terry's hands, and Terry resisted the urge to snatch it back. This job was going to take forever with Stan looking over her shoulder all the time.

"It's the last two words of a sentence begun on a missing page," Stan said redundantly. "Listen: 'We don't eat, we don't *aetate conficimus*, we don't die. We ... we *sangeum bibimus* and *vitemus* the sun and 'all is' ... and that's all. Do you think he's describing angels?"

"What else would he be describing?" Terry said, flipping through the ream of computer paper. "'*Nulla somniant*' isn't here."

"Really?" Stan said. "You mean you found a book that isn't cataloged?"

"This is the third one I've found," Terry snapped. "Whoever made this list did a sloppy job, that's all. That's why we're going through them one at a time."

"You want me to enter it in for you?" he asked.

"No," she answered, taking the book and setting it sideways in the shelf. "I'll do it later, in case I find others."

"'*Aetate comficimus*,'" he repeated. "I going to look those words up and see what they mean."

"You do that," Terry said, taking the next book from the shelf.

"I should be getting back to my own section," Stan said. "I'll see you later?"

"Yeah," she replied. *Looking forward to it.*

Stan meandered off, and Terry resumed her work.

Six hours later, Terry walked through the door of her flat like a beaten dog. Eight books. That was all she'd been able to accomplish today: the verification of eight books. The rest of that time was spent trying to find a file on a disk that some moron (probably Stan) had wiped the directory from. She was never going to get her section done if she had to play computer guru for five hours a day.

She dropped her backpack near the door and was dragging herself towards the bedroom when Marta came out of the bathroom. Terry didn't envy many women for their beauty, but Marta was an exception. She'd poured herself into a tight red dress that just about reached her thighs; her brown, Spanish legs didn't need nylons, and the heels of her red pumps brought her to exactly the height Terry had always wished for: five foot seven. But with Marta's thick, dark hair and big brown eyes, she would have been gorgeous in jeans and a T-shirt. Terry hated her.

"Are we going out?" Marta asked in English. That was their deal: when they spoke to each other, Marta would practice her English and Terry would practice her Spanish.

"*Muy caliente*," Terry replied. *Caliente*? Terry had just

told Marta that she was very hot—she was too tired for Spanish.

"*Cansado*," Marta corrected. "Is okay. You speak English and I understand."

"I'm too tired to go out," Terry slurred in English. "Another time, okay?"

"You sick like me?" Marta asked with concern.

"No, I'm not sick; I'm just tired."

"*Vamanos*. If you no sick, you go out." Marta grabbed her arm, and dragged her into the bathroom. "You sleep later. You see, you have good time."

A shower had helped, and in fact, Terry had very badly wanted to go out—she just needed a little convincing. By ten o'clock they had reached Tito's and were muscling their way to the bar for the first round of drinks.

"Is good, no?" Marta shouted over the music.

"Yes," Terry shouted back. "Let's find some seats."

Finding a table in Tito's at ten on a Friday night would usually have been a futile endeavor, but they were lucky tonight. They sat down, and Terry noticed someone across the room. "Look," she said, discreetly pointing out a man to Marta. "Your friend's here."

Marta glanced over at him, but there was no recognition. "I don't know him," she replied, shrugging her shoulders.

Terry examined him closely: dark blonde hair, styled immaculately; designer suit; Marta's height in heels; young face, old eyes. "Sure you do," Terry insisted. "You were dancing with him last Friday night."

Marta's response was a bit of a laugh. "I never see him before. I wasn't so drunk to forget."

She was *sure* Marta had been dancing with him. Maybe Marta had some reason to keep it secret, or maybe the mysterious illness she'd suffered since last Saturday was actually a brain tumor and she was forgetting things.

Or maybe Terry *was* mistaken. Ah well, it wasn't that important anyway.

They started dancing halfway through their second round of drinks, together at first, until two guys they knew from the University got up to dance with them. She didn't watch Marta very closely after that; she was too busy watching her dancing partner—the Spanish Mel Gibson named Benja—to pay much attention. Mel excused himself to go the the bathroom, and Terry returned to their table. Only then did she find Marta again.

She was still dancing—and goddamn if she wasn't dancing with that same guy from last week. Terry smiled; there was something going on there that Marta didn't want her to know about. That was fine, Marta was a big girl, but Terry watched them closely all the same.

It was strange to watch—although Terry couldn't exactly put her finger on why. He wasn't a bad-looking guy, but she'd seen Marta act aloof to men much better looking. She was simply reserved by nature, but she was being very obvious about the fact that she was turned-on by this stranger. Her hands were all over him, and her eyes were full of lust. She *wanted* this man.

But that wasn't all that was strange about it. His reaction wasn't at all what it should have been. He was far too casual, as though women as beautiful as Marta always found him this attractive. Having spent as much time with

Marta as she had, the entire scene was just ... bizarre.

He leaned over, and whispered something into her ear. Her arms went around him passionately, and he forced her back and walked into the Men's Room. Marta continued to dance as her eyes followed him, and she watched the door as though waiting for him to emerge. Half a minute went by before she walked over to the Men's Room door and walked right in.

Terry could scarcely believe her eyes. Marta was going to get laid in the bathroom. Marta, whom to the best of Terry's knowledge had only slept with one man in her life. There was something *definitely* not right here.

She waited, watching the door. The song ended, and another began. Still nothing. Terry was beginning to think something might really be wrong when the bathroom door opened and Marta came stumbling out, as though she'd had much more to drink than she actually had. She was pale and her eyes weren't quite focusing, and Terry was instantly on her feet and nearly running towards her when she recognized the symptoms of the illness Marta had felt all week.

"Marta!" she shouted into her ear as she took her by the arms. "Marta, are you all right?"

"What?" Marta answered weakly. "Terry?"

"Come on, we're getting you out of here."

Terry nearly dragged her up the stairs that led out. She glanced back to the bathroom door just in time to see the man step out—not a hair out of place. All the same, the look on his face was somewhat ... satisfied.

The whole thing was very bizarre.

The Spanish word for her translated to 'witch,' but the American students who had first told Terry about her had called her the Healing Woman. Even that was a bit of a misnomer because she didn't actually heal—she diagnosed. The stories were endless. The Healing Woman told this-one's-mother her cholesterol count to within four points of what the doctor told her three days later. The Healing Woman found a lump of fat between the vertebrae of this-one's-cousin's spine, and ended four years of back pain with a hard blow from a very small hammer. The Healing Woman congratulated this-one's-girlfriend on her pregnancy, three weeks after the child had been conceived and before the girl had even been late with her period. She touched your hand and she saw things, things the ordinary doctors of Salamanca sometimes missed. Then she would either prescribe some herbal cure, or send the patient to a real doctor with advice on what he should be looking for. It was all very Old World and superstitious, but in modern day Salamanca, they still believed in the Evil Eye—no doubt they considered themselves 'forward thinkers' for not burning *la Bruja* at the stake.

Terry had heard of psychometry. She'd seen *The Dead Zone*. As far as whether she believed in it or not, she was undecided. But Marta believed in it, and the conventional doctors had been unable to explain her mysterious illness. 'Stress,' they had called it, which was just another way of saying, 'We have no fucking clue.' That Marta was being levelheaded about this whole thing was evidenced by the fact she had gone to see the doctor first. But Marta was frightened now. She wanted to see the Healing Woman.

Terry had never been before, and she had to admit she was more than curious. Besides, Marta had wanted her to come—in case she was hit with another spell on the way. Saturday morning found them walking the tawny streets of Salamanca, heading for the Healing Woman.

"I yam afraid," Marta said as the two of them walked.

"Of what?" Terry asked. "You've been to see her before, haven't you?"

"I yam no afraid of *la Bruja*," she responded. "I yam afraid of what she tells me. Or what she no tells me."

"You mean she might not tell you if something is wrong with you?" Terry asked.

"One time, a man went to see *la Bruja* because he was feeling bad. She said to him that he was fine, and then told his brother after he left that he would be dead in three days, and that they should try to make him ... *como se dice 'cómodo?'*"

"Comfortable," Terry translated.

"Sí, 'comfortable.' That man, he die three days later. What if I yam so sick, she no want to say to me that I yam sick?"

"You're not *that* sick," Terry said authoritatively. This seemed to calm Marta a little—Americans not only knew computers, they knew medicine too.

Terry hadn't quite known what to expect of the Healing Woman's home—perhaps a Gypsy wagon, or even a darkened basement. What she didn't expect was a well-lit, well-kept, thoroughly unremarkable flat. There were crosses on the walls (the Healing Woman was apparently a devout Catholic) and framed family photos on the end tables (her oldest grandchild was high-school age). The only thing that marked it as different from any other flat was the smell. It was similar to a doctor's office, but not—a house that was so clean it was nearly sterile, with a slight scent of medicinal herbs that, although not unpleasant, didn't smell like anything you'd want to drink unless you had a hell of a lot of faith.

The Healing Woman herself was a dark haired little lady with a kind face and a generous smile. She invited them inside and took them through her home, to a study she used to examine superstitious Spaniards, and sat Marta on a table while inviting Terry to sit across the tiny room. The Healing Woman pulled a stool up to Marta and sat. As was customary, no mention of the specifics of Marta's problem were given and none were asked. There was no showmanship, no bells or whistles; she simply took Marta's hand for a few seconds, and then released it, a perplexed look on her face.

"What is it?" Marta asked in Spanish.

The Healing Woman nodded her head back and forth. "It is an allergic reaction," she mumbled distractedly. "Something in Tito's disagrees with you. Don't go back there. The reaction is very bad. If you go back, you could get very ill." The Healing Woman stood from the stool and crossed the room, opening a tiny drawer full of pills, and counting a few into a paper bag. "Drink lots of fluids over the next few days, and take these with every meal until they're gone."

"What are they?" Marta asked.

"It's just iron," she replied. "You aren't eating enough liver. If you get dizzy again, come back and see me."

What a bunch of bullshit, Terry thought to herself. *Everyone* went to Tito's. And iron for allergies? What the hell kind of allergy made you dizzy in a bar? She'd never heard of such a thing.

The Healing Woman approached Terry, tentatively requesting her hand. Terry complied. What harm could it do?

As with Marta, she held it for just a second and released it. "You're fine," she said, "but you're susceptible to the same sickness. You shouldn't go to Tito's either, I think."

"Really?" Terry asked, unimpressed. This woman was a complete fake.

"Yes," she replied. "Also, you spend much time thinking about the *cantante*."

Yeah, right. If this woman were any more ... any more ... *cantante*?

"It's over between the two of you," the Healing Woman continued. "Learn from your mistakes, and get on with your life."

There was a rational explanation for this. The Healing

Woman had heard about Doug from Marta. Or maybe she'd just picked it out of the air—at any given time, half of the population of the world was getting over an ex.

Except that she'd used that word. The '*cantante*.'

The singer.

It was then that Terry's world began to change.

The two of them made it all the way back to their flat before they finally spoke. "Do you feel better now?" Terry asked.

"Yes," Marta answered. "I know I yam not dying, or else she would no have given me pills. Beside, she say that you might get same thing."

"Maybe you're allergic to that guy you didn't dance with last week," Terry said with a slight smile.

"What guy?" she asked.

"You know, the blonde in the suit. The one you went into the bathroom with last night, for Christ's sake. Do you want to talk about it?"

"I no go into the bathroom with no guy last night," Marta said.

Marta's denial of this whole thing had been cute at first, but now it was beginning to get irritating. "You were just coming out of the bathroom when I grabbed you," Terry said. "You don't remember?"

"Only a little, I was drunk," Marta said, fear beginning to creep into her voice.

"So drunk you would go into the Men's Room?" Terry demanded. "Look, if it's none of my business, tell me it's none of my business—but don't tell me you don't even know the guy because I saw you dancing with him and I saw you go into the bathroom with him."

"I don't know him!" Marta yelled in frantic Spanish. "I don't remember dancing with him, and if this is a joke I wish you would stop because you are making me think I might have a brain tumor and the Healing Woman was afraid to tell me!"

"All right, all right," Terry calmed. "You don't have a brain tumor. Why would the Healing Woman give you pills if you had a brain tumor?"

"Because she wants to make me think there's some hope," Marta said, crying now, "and I go to sleep tonight or tomorrow night and I don't wake up ..."

"Then why would she tell *me* not to go to Tito's?" Terry interrupted. "Listen, you're fine. Maybe I saw someone else dancing with him, and I thought it was you. I was pretty drunk too. I'm going to the library to try and get some more of this cataloging done, why don't you take your pills and relax for a while? I'll be back later, maybe we can do something if you feel up to it. Okay?"

"Okay," Marta said, switching back to English now that she was a little calmer. "I yam very tired, I think I take a nap."

"Good idea," she said, suddenly realizing how tired *she* was. But she knew even if she tried, sleep would not come—her mind was racing in too many directions.

Terry sat in the Plaza de Mayor, drinking coffee and thinking thoughts she didn't like.

The *cantante*. That Healing Woman had been for real, and what was more, she could see a lot more than just what was wrong with you medically. She could see Doug. So there had to be some logical reason why she would call a sickness 'allergies' and prescribe iron. There had to be some logical reason why she would tell both Marta and herself not to go to Tito's anymore. But what was it? What did she see there?

Then there was Marta. She really didn't remember the man in the suit. Terry no longer saw inebriation as an option to explain this away, and she no longer believed that Marta was trying to keep something from her. Hypnotism was not a feasible explanation—she'd gone through enough therapy after the death of her father to know that. But what was?

"Hi, Stranger," an American said as he sat down at her table, startling her from her thoughts. It was Stan, from the library. Stan the Man. "Did you go to Tito's last night?"

"Yes," she answered. "Marta got sick again and it was this whole big thing. A good time was had by none."

"Is she all right?"

"Yeah, she's fine. We went to see the Healing Woman

this morning, and she told her that it was an allergy and that she shouldn't go back there—and that I shouldn't either."

"That's strange," Stan said. "She's allergic to Tito's?"

"That's what the Healing Woman said. Stan, do you know what iron is prescribed for?"

"Iron?" Stan asked. "Anemia, maybe?"

"Maybe," Terry said. "When Marta first went to the doctor, he told her he thought it might be anemia—but decided it wasn't after a blood test."

"I don't know much about Spanish medicine, or medicine in general," he said. "This is a bit of a coincidence, though."

"What?" she asked.

"I wrote down those words from 'Never Dream,' and one of them was 'blood.'"

"'Never dream?'"

"You know, that uncataloged book you found last night," he said, searching his pockets until he found a slip of paper. "Here we go: the we-form of 'acquire oldness,' the we-form of 'drink blood,' the we-form of 'avoid.' Those are all the words I looked up, but I can't remember the rest of the text now."

"'Never dream,'" she struggled to remember. "'We don't eat and we don't ...'"

"... 'acquire oldness' ... age," Stan substituted.

"'We don't eat and we don't age and we don't die. We ...'"

"'Drink blood,'" Stan continued. "It could be a poetic description of a monk."

"A blood-drinking monk?" Terry questioned skeptically.

"Sure, the Blood of Christ. Communion. Either that, or a vampire. Considering Bram Stoker wasn't born yet, I think Dr. Marcus would more readily accept the monk-theory."

"Where did you find these words?" Terry asked.

"I have a Latin-English Dictionary in my room," he answered. "Do you want to borrow it?"

"How long would it take you to get it?" she asked.

"Come with me, I can give it to you right now."

"Let's go," she said as she stood, throwing too much strange money on the table as they left.

"'Never dream,'" Stan translated aloud while Terry looked over his shoulder—the only two in the library. "'We don't eat and we don't age and we don't die. We drink blood and we avoid the sun and nothing more.'"

"Jesus," Terry said. "It's sounding less and less like a monk."

"'Avoiding the sun' could be a metaphor for the fact that they never leave the monastery," Stan countered.

"What else does it say?" Terry urged.

"'They say we are evil,'" he continued. "'They say we are of the devil. How can this be, I still love our Lord Jesus Christ. But Jesus Christ does not prevent me from committing evil acts. I pray to him, and he does not hear me. Why do you not hear my prayers, Lord?' Oh shit, what time is it?"

"It says that?"

"No," Stan said, checking his watch. "I'm supposed to tutor at noon. I have to go." He closed the book and set it back on the shelf, before handing her the Latin-English Dictionary. "Here," he said. "Take this for as long as you need it."

He lifted his knapsack onto his shoulder as he was heading out, Terry distractedly taking the book from the shelf as his sneakered footsteps receded. This was another piece of the puzzle she was trying to solve—suddenly, she was certain of it. No one would notice it if it was missing, would they? It wasn't cataloged, and only Stan and herself knew it was even here.

It took some cramming to get it into her book bag, but it fit. She would have to study this at length. There was an answer hidden here somewhere.

Terry never thought she'd find herself missing Stan.

The last hour and a half had been spent in the flat she shared with Marta—finding a word, looking it up, finding the next one, looking it up, trying to guess at a verb conjugation by its context, moving on to the next word. The sentence structure was vaguely similar to Spanish, if somewhat archaic, but this chore was still a bitch.

Terry closed both books and rubbed her eyes. She needed a nap, just a few hours of sleep. She opened her eyes and read the sheet of notebook paper where she'd written her translation.

> *Perhaps we are of the Devil. Perhaps Hell is the well (source?) of my gifts. I have killed many men. I will kill many more men. I curse this life and I murder for it to continue. I speak to them and they do what I command. They come willingly to their deaths or they forget they ever saw me. I convince myself that this is because it is their true desire, to die that I may live. Sometimes that makes the killing bearable. But other times I know that this is not the truth.*

Terry read the words again.

> *they forget they ever saw me*

Terry

"Sweet Jesus Christ," Terry said aloud.

Terry climbed the stairs to the Healing Woman's flat, hoisting her bag higher onto her shoulder as she reached the door. She'd intended to knock, but her fear made her shaking hand pound on the door incessantly until a man answered. She'd seen him in the pictures on the wall—short, on the thin-side of plump, balding—and recognized the Healing Woman's husband.

"I need to see the Healing Woman," Terry said in Spanish.

"She's not here," he replied. "Come back later."

Terry shoved her hand into the door. "It's important ... please."

"Let her in," the Healing Woman said from behind the door. Her husband's eyes dropped, ashamed of his lie, as he opened the door and allowed her in.

"There's no allergy in the world that iron will treat," Terry bluffed as she stepped through the door, uncertain whether it was true or not. "And there's no reason for me to stay out of Tito's because I have no allergies. You know that, don't you?"

The Healing Woman nodded her head.

"You see much more than just someone's sickness. You saw the singer. Can you read objects the same way you read people?"

"Not always," she replied. "But sometimes, I can."

Terry took the ancient book from her book bag. "Read this," she commanded, holding it out to her.

"I do not wish to," the Healing Woman said.

"Why not?" Terry asked coldly.

"When I read you this morning, I saw that you had touched the book. It is an evil book. It has been touched by evil hands. It has been touched by the one who touched Marta. You must return it and forget you ever saw it."

"Why?" she asked.

"Because if you do not, others will come. Others more dangerous than the man you know."

"Other vampires?" Terry asked.

"Do not say that word!" the Healing Woman hissed. "They can hear you. Sometimes the mention of the word is all it takes to arouse their interest, and you do not want to arouse their interest."

"Marta already has."

"No, she hasn't," she said, turning her back on Terry as she slowly paced the hallway. "Not really. To the man you've seen, she is only a vessel of blood. He does not know her name. You do not want him to learn your name."

"How do you know so much about them?" Terry asked suspiciously.

"My mother was a Healing Woman, as was my grandmother before her. My grandmother told me of a man who came to her, a teacher at the University. Dr. Del Rio was his name. He suffered the same illness as Marta. It was not the same man who afflicts Marta, but it was the same *kind* of man."

"The word you cannot say."

"Yes. My grandmother knew the moment she touched

him what his affliction was, and she told him."

"What happened?"

"He was lucky. The man gave him a choice, and Dr. Del Rio declined. But the man was very angry. In three days, twenty-four young men disappeared. The man left after that and never returned."

"Dr. Del Rio used to be very social," her husband said. "Now he lives out in the middle of nowhere, and never sees anyone."

"He's still alive?" Terry blurted anxiously.

The Healing Woman shot her husband a dark look. "Yes," she answered. "He's an old man, but he's still alive."

"Where does he live?" Terry asked.

"Why do you want to know that?" the Healing Woman asked, stepping towards Terry. "Why do you want to see him?"

"I don't know," Terry confessed. "To learn more about whatever it is that threatens Marta, perhaps."

"As long as Marta stays out of Tito's, she's safe. Tito's is where he hunts. I *know* why you seek this creature. When I saw into your heart this morning, I thought you might if you knew the truth. You are curious—curious in a bad way. You've read books about him and his kind. You want to join them, eh? But you do not know. You do not want to know. The danger isn't just to you, but to many others. *Many* others. I'm begging you, in the name of the Host, return that book to the library and forget you ever saw it."

Terry put the book back in her bag. "In a way, I wish I could," she said. "Maybe after I talk to the doctor, I'll do just that. But I have to at least talk to him. If you don't tell me where I can find him, someone else will. It may take weeks, and I'll be holding onto the book the entire time. It seems to me that's a lousy way to avoid drawing attention to myself. Wouldn't you agree?"

The Healing Woman stared at her, nodding her head. "No," she finally said. "I cannot help you in good conscience." She turned and left the room, leaving Terry alone with the woman's husband.

Terry sighed. In truth, she wasn't sure how she would find this Dr. Del Rio. She'd have to ask some of her teachers, find out who the old-timers were, and see if any of them knew this doctor. She might not be able to find him at all.

"I do not often go against my wife's judgment," the little Spaniard finally said. "But I think perhaps you should talk to the doctor. He was given a choice of lives, and he chose well. He made the choice both Carmen and I hope you choose. Perhaps if he tells you why he made that choice, you will make the same one. Do you have a pen?"

Marta was still sleeping when she got back to the flat, and Terry didn't figure she'd mind if she borrowed her car. Terry wrote her a short note, grabbed the keys from a hook by the door, and left.

The drive to Dr. Del Rio's gave her time to think. She hadn't really had that time since this whole thing started. She'd set about on a relentless pursuit, without a thought to what she was doing or why she was doing it.

Why *was* she doing this? What was she going to do if she succeeded? Back up—how did she even define 'success' in this?

Terry's world had always been black and white. Wrong and right. Even when she was lying to Doug and screwing Dominic, she'd known it was wrong. What she'd done to Doug had been wrong. Perhaps if she'd been totally in the right, she would have been able to stop thinking about him. Now she had to deal not just with the fact that she missed him but with the fact that she wanted to make amends, to do right by him somehow. If she were back in the States she would have gone to him, right now, and apologized for everything. Fuck pride—she was wrong and she still loved him and that's all there was to it.

The funny part was, she hadn't seen it that way until the Healing Woman had told her to forget the *cantante* and get on with her life.

What intrigued her about *this* was the fact that it wasn't black and white. A huge white part of her life had been abruptly spray-painted gray. The line that separated Truth from Myth had shifted the moment the Healing Woman had told her to forget the *cantante*, and it hadn't stopped shifting since. Terry had to follow this through, and see how far the Truth-line would move before it was over.

Back to the other question: how did she define success? She'd never given any thought to vampires before. Vampires were movie monsters, along with the Werewolf, Frankenstein's Monster, and the Mummy. At Doug's insistence, she'd read *Interview with the Vampire*. It was a great book, but it was a book. Vampires were fictitious creatures, period. But the Truth-line was moving. Were they really just fiction? Or did the genesis of the legend lay somewhere this side of the Truth-line?

The Healing Woman believed Terry would try to become a vampire. That wasn't completely outside the scope of possibility, was it? Anne Rice painted a beautiful world—monstrous and Gothic, but beautiful. No more aging. No more mortal concerns. Just feeding and living. *We drink blood and avoid the sun and nothing more.* It certainly wasn't without appeal, was it?

Maybe that's what she wanted. Maybe that's what this whole thing was about. Maybe she just wanted to live forever.

She wondered what Doug would think of her coming back to the States as a vampire.

Dr. Del Rio's place wasn't hard to find. Just as she'd been told, it was out in the middle of nowhere, with nothing surrounding it but a vast green expanse. The house itself was reasonably well maintained, but far from immaculate.

Terry pulled the tiny car into the driveway, yanked up the parking brake, cut the ignition. The engine gave a reluctant sputter before dying and she was abruptly surrounded by a silence so complete it was almost tangible. The creak of the car door, the groan of the seat as she stood, the slamming of the door behind her, each violated the silence in a way that was almost sacrilegious. Dust kicked up from her sneakers as she walked up to the fragile looking porch, and she rapped lightly on the door for fear of knocking it from its frame.

A tiny, ancient Spaniard, wrinkled with time and sun and dry air, appeared behind the screen. He looked disoriented, and his thinning gray hair protruded at odd angles, contributing to the impression that he had just awakened.

"Dr. Del Rio?" Terry asked.

"Sí," he answered in a voice that was gravelly from lack of use.

"The husband of the Healing Woman told me where I

could glue you," she said, her nervousness mangling her Spanish. "May I speak without you?"

"Only if you speak in English," he replied in her language. "You're raping my mother tongue like a three dollar whore."

Terry laughed, despite her slighted language skills. 'Three dollar whore.' It wasn't just an English saying, it was American. "You speak English very well," she commented.

Dr. Del Rio turned and walked away from the door, yelling out behind him as he wandered back inside. "I ought to—I lived in your country for fifteen years. Fifteen years? No, it was closer to twenty." He returned to the door and came out onto the porch, holding a pipe and a pouch of tobacco. "We'll talk out here."

"They didn't mention that you'd lived in America," she said to him.

"They probably didn't know," he replied, ambling to a wooden chair and sitting. "What was it you wanted to talk to me about?"

Terry thought about what she was going to say, realizing how crazy it was. *I want to talk to you about vampires*, she heard in her mind. *Yeah.*

"I want to talk to you about the supernatural," she said.

"I see," Dr. Del Rio said. "And the Healing Woman sent you. You want to talk about vampires."

Busted, she thought to herself. She took a minute to compose what she was going to say before giving up and asking, "Are vampires real?"

"Yes."

Terry stopped to digest this. But that an old man believed in vampires didn't really *prove* anything. "Tell me about them," she said.

"What about them?" the old man asked in response.

"I don't know. What are they, really?"

"Do you want the long answer, or the short one?"

"I didn't drive all the way out here for the short answer," Terry said. She walked in front of him, taking a chair beside the doctor and setting the book bag on her lap.

Dr. Del Rio took a deep breath. "All right. Let's begin by discussing the Fury."

"The Fury?" Terry repeated.

"Yes. It is a virus. The English translation is the Fury. In Spanish, it's *rabia*."

"*Rabia*," Terry considered carefully. "Are you talking about rabies?"

"That's it," the old man said. "Do you know what it is that makes this virus so insidious?"

"The fact that it's transmitted by bite?" Terry offered.

"No, no. A great number of viruses can be transmitted during an exchange of saliva and blood. No, what makes the Fury so ingenious is that it actually alters the behavior of the doomed host animal, to make it more likely another animal will be infected. You see? It's as though the virus knows where to go in the body to produce a desired effect, in this case, hostility. For a few days—days critical to the propagation of the virus—the parasite is in charge of the host."

"All right," Terry said, nodding her head as she tried to grasp his point. "Are you saying that's what vampires are? Humans with rabies?"

"No, no," Dr. Del Rio laughed. "You caught the ball, but you ran the wrong direction. I believe there is a sister virus, far more insidious than the Fury, and vampires are the remains of men killed by that virus."

"'The remains?'" Terry asked. "Wouldn't that make

them dead?"

"They are dead," he replied.

"I don't understand," she said.

"What's your background in medicine?"

"I know what an aspirin is," Terry replied dryly.

"Do you know how a virus works?" the doctor asked.

"Yeah. It gets into your body and makes you sick."

Dr. Del Rio sighed impatiently. "Your body is made up of millions of cells, and each of these cells performs a certain function. Most cells work together to form an organ, and most organs work together to form a system."

"Wait a minute," Terry interrupted. "I *did* pass tenth grade Biology."

"Do you want to learn about vampires or not?" Terry said nothing, and he continued. "Every cell is basically a tiny living creature. Your body is basically a colony of little, tiny animals, all working together to sustain a larger organism. Each cell performs a certain function, and each cell is told what function to perform by its DNA. Left alone, a cell grows, takes food, passes waste, reproduces, and eventually dies.

"And then we have viruses. Strictly speaking, a virus is not a living entity. A virus is a piece of microscopic dust—a strip of either DNA or RNA covered with a layer of proteins. A virus is like a letter—a letter signed by the President. A virus gets into a cell, and the cell reads the letter, and the letter says 'Dear Cell: You are to commence writing letters until you die. Best Wishes, President Eisenhower.' That's how they reproduce themselves.

"So the cell stops doing what it was doing and starts writing letters, usually destroying itself in the process. Every virus likes a certain kind of cell, depending on the layer of proteins that surrounds it. The virus that causes Parkinson's Disease likes nerve cells, while the virus that causes warts likes skin cells. The kind of cell a virus likes, and how the virus affects the other functions of a cell, govern how it affects the organism as a whole. A virus can cause a cold, or it can give you polio. Are you with me so far?"

Surprisingly enough, she was. If Mr. Burchell had been this good, she might not have forgotten this stuff in the first place.

"The second cleverest virus I know of is the Fury. We're talking about a letter that says: 'Dear Cell: If you're a cell in the salivary glands, write more letters. If you're a nerve cell, write more letters. If you're a brain cell, tell this animal to bite something, will you?' It's clever even by human standards, and by viral standards it's absolutely brilliant. It's the best-written letter your cells have ever read. We're talking about a piece of RNA that's not only going to tell your cells what to do to further its existence, but tell *you* as well. It would be comparable to your giving orders to God."

"All right," Terry said. "So rabies is a clever virus. What does that have to do with vampires?"

"Imagine a virus even smarter than rabies. Imagine a virus that kills the host and then alters and animates the remains to further its existence."

"That's something I don't get," Terry said, leaning forward in her chair to better face him. "How can they be dead? They're still up and walking around, right?"

The doctor smiled around the pipe clenched in his teeth. "Part of the definition of life is the ability to reproduce. Vampires can't do this—not like we can. A vampire can't make a baby. They can, however, spread the virus. They consider this reproduction, but it's not. It's merely the corruption—the murder—of an already existing organism."

"But they can remember their lives before, right?"

"Not always. And when they can, it's only because the virus has obtained access to the memories in the deceased host's brain—the better to survive. But it also changes the thought processes. The hunger instincts combine with the sex drive, to create a passion for blood you and I cannot even imagine. I'm sure to them, it doesn't feel as though they've died. I'm sure it only feels as though they've been changed. I'm equally sure their souls have passed on."

Terry leaned back in her chair. "So, this virus kills the body and animates it. But why doesn't the body decay away?"

"When the virus gets into you it changes everything ... every aspect about the way your body works. It begins—naturally—with the blood. The heart stops beating, and the red blood cells form loose bonds with each other. The circulatory system becomes a secondary nervous system, and the energy that was once circulated around the body by the movement of blood is instead conducted as chemo-electrical pulses, as in the nervous system. The newly altered cells in the body use these pulses to feed itself—but it also uses them as instructions on how to rebuild itself."

"You're losing me, Doc," Terry admitted.

"Vampires have an incredible healing ability. Given time, a vampire can even re-grow a lost limb. But the new muscular-skeletal system needs instructions to do that. The blueprints to your entire body live in every single one of your cells, but by now the virus has already changed those blueprints throughout the entire body. That is, except for one organ. An organ that no longer beats."

"The heart."

"The heart. It doesn't have the same function as when the organism was alive, but it is equally important. The virus grabs a single cell of the heart and uses the blueprints it finds there to first 'rebuild' the heart by those blueprints, and then rebuild the body."

Terry absently stroked the book bag in her lap. "But all of those blueprints should be the same, right?"

"No," the doctor said, searching for a match to re-light his now extinguished pipe. "Your cells are constantly aging and being replaced by other cells. As the body ages, the blueprints become more and more flawed. It's part of our design. If every creature on this planet didn't eventually grow old and die, we would not evolve. The ends of the DNA chain fray like the tip of a shoelace. The master plan is corrupted."

He struck the match against the leg of his chair, and re-lit the pipe with puffs of thick, fragrant smoke. "The muscles grow weak ..." Puff, puff. "... the skin wrinkles ..." Puff, puff. "... the bones become brittle." He shook out the match with an unsteady hand and dropped it into a can beside his chair. "Since each and every cell in your heart carries a blueprint in a varying stage of perfection, the apparent age of a vampire can vary wildly. A man who was killed by the virus in his twenties can age to sixty within a few days and stay there, and a man who was killed in his fifties can suddenly be eighteen again. The end of the shoelace is taped up, and the blueprint is cast in stone."

"But cells that don't age ... that's not possible, is it?" Terry asked.

"There are trees two thousand years old, using a chain of DNA not so different from your own to continue to reproduce cells. There are single-celled animals reproducing asexually right now, using a strand of DNA that hasn't broken down for millions of years. Aging is merely part of our design. Change that design—correct that flaw—and aging stops."

Terry absorbed this for a moment, while the doctor puffed. Each tiny cloud was accompanied by a wheeze that sounded painful, but it didn't slow him in the least.

"What about a stake through the heart?" she finally asked. "Does that work?"

"A stake through the heart won't kill a vampire, all by itself," he replied. "But it *will* immobilize it. Damage to the heart will stop a vampire from doing anything until that damage is healed. Generally, it only takes a few seconds—but if there's something lodged in the tissue and the heart can't heal, the vampire can't move or think until it is removed."

"And sunlight?"

Dr. Del Rio shuddered, as though reliving something in his memory. Whatever it was, he didn't share it—instead he continued with his clinical explanation. "Every cell of a vampire stores an incredible amount of energy, and those cells are highly reactive. Exposure to sunlight releases this energy all at once."

"You've seen this happen?" Terry asked.

The doctor focused an unsettling gaze on her. "I've seen it happen. When it's over, nothing remains—and it's over quickly, believe me."

"I don't think anyone with decent knowledge of modern medicine would accept these ideas of yours," Terry said candidly. "A vampire-virus ... it's just too wild to be real."

"Read a description of the Fury," the doctor said. "By my way of thinking, that virus is also too 'wild' to be real. But you're right, I myself have difficulty believing in such nonsense. The vampire-virus theory is just my attempt at a rational explanation."

"Wouldn't a more rational explanation be that vampires don't exist?" she asked.

The old man again leveled his gaze at Terry.

"Considering what I've seen," he said, "that explanation is not an option."

Dr. Del Rio removed a pinch of tobacco from his pouch, and began packing his pipe. Terry leaned her head back against the house, staring out at the horizon. A faint glow was all that remained of the day—it was time for the vampires to rise.

The doctor struck another safety match against his chair and lit his pipe again. He blew out a mouthful of smoke, watching it waft away from his face in the still night air. "Was it worth the trip out here, to hear a crazy old man's theories on the walking dead?"

"The Healing Woman told me you had the chance to become one of them," Terry said. "Why didn't you take it?"

He took another drag of smoke and exhaled, smiling bitterly. "I could tell you I was afraid the virus wouldn't leave any of my mind. I could tell you the lifestyle didn't appeal to me, or the entire thing seemed unnatural. But the truth of the matter is much more mundane."

Terry stared at him, wordlessly urging him to answer. The bitterness left his smile as he spoke. "I like sunshine," he said. "I always have. It's a foolish reason to give up a chance to live forever, I suppose. But that's my reason. I never gave a reason to the man who wanted to infect me. It didn't seem in good taste to tell him how much I loved the daytime—a bit like telling a man without legs how good it feels to run. But that was my only reason."

"Do you read Latin?" Terry asked.

The unexpected question surprised the doctor. "I used to," he answered. "Why?"

She repositioned the book bag in her lap. "I brought this with me in case you were reluctant to talk about vampires—to prove I knew something about them. I want you to take a look at this and tell me what you think it is."

Terry unzipped the bag, removing the book with both hands to place it on his lap. He eyed her questioningly as he took reading glasses from his shirt pocket, carefully placing them on the end of his nose. He opened it, examining the first, painted page, the expression on his face quickly going from doubt to awe. "Where did you get this?" he asked breathlessly.

"I took it from the library at the University," she answered.

"Young lady, you cannot simply *take* something like this!" he reprimanded. "It's hundreds of years old! This book is more important and more valuable than ..."

"Read it," she instructed, cutting him off. "Just the first few sentences."

He did as he was told, but not before scowling at her one last time. His lips mumbled the Latin as his incredulous eyes passed over the words. Soon, he was flipping excitedly through the pages, skimming phrases as he went along. He went through half of the book this way, before closing it with shaking hands.

"This is quite a find you have here," he said, barely containing himself. But Terry could see it wasn't enthusiasm alone he was trying to keep suppressed. "This book has been hidden for centuries," he continued. "How did you stumble across it?"

Terry considering telling him the whole story, but now that he was holding back, she wasn't sure she trusted him. "I think I'd rather keep that to myself," she replied, taking the book from his hands and returning it to her bag.

"What do you intend to do with it?" he asked guardedly.

"I don't know yet. I wanted to show it to someone, so I brought it here."

"Would you be interested in selling it?"

Terry was feeling increasingly uncomfortable with the doctor, and she regretted showing him the book at all. "How much would you be willing to give me for it?" she asked.

"I'm not talking about buying it myself," he said. "But I know someone who would be *very* interested in this. You should talk to him."

"I don't know," Terry repeated. It seemed like a safe thing to say, considering she suddenly had the feeling she was in way over her head. "I was thinking about just returning it to the library and pretending I never saw it."

"*Don't* do that!" he blurted. He took a breath, composing himself. "When I say this book is worth a great deal to certain people, it's no exaggeration. Leave me a phone number where I can find you—it's really very urgent you talk to this friend of mine before you do *anything* with this book."

"I don't have a phone," Terry lied.

"Then come back here in a week," he said. "I'm sure he would make the trip for this. What day is this?"

"Saturday," she replied.

"Come back next Saturday, after dark," he instructed. "I'm sure my friend would make it worth your time."

'After dark?' So, he wanted her to meet with his vampire friend. She didn't like it one bit—Dr. Del Rio was too desperate. She wanted to get the hell out of here, but realized the old man wouldn't take 'no' for an answer. "All right," she said, uncertain of whether she meant it or not. "I'll come back in a week and talk to your friend."

"Good," the doctor said, immensely relieved. "*Very* good. I promise you won't regret it."

"It's getting late," Terry said, standing. "I should get back."

Dr. Del Rio stood as she did, walking her to the edge of the porch. "Don't forget, next Saturday," he said. "What did you say your name was again?"

"Anne," she said. "Anne Rice."

"Anne Rice," he repeated, fixing the name in his memory. "Very good. I'll see you next Saturday, then."

"Next Saturday," she repeated as she was walking towards Marta's car. She tried not to give the appearance she was bolting with fear as she got into the car, turned the key in the ignition, and slammed it into reverse. She gave a polite little wave as she was backing out, but Dr. Del Rio didn't notice. He seemed lost in his thoughts, staring at the front end of Maria's car.

Shit, she thought to herself. *He's reading the license plate.* She fumbled for the headlight-switch and flicked on her high-beams, hoping to blind him before he caught all the numbers.

It was a long drive back to Salamanca. Too long. It gave her too much time to think about what she'd gotten herself into.

The book. *Never Dream*. She was convinced now that it *was* something important. It had certainly been important to the old man. But why? Not because it was proof vampires existed. Dr. Del Rio was already certain they did. Besides, it wasn't really scientific, empirical proof—it was just an old book, written by someone who *believed* he was a vampire. Big deal.

There had to be something else within those painted pages, something really important. She could spend the next few days translating random passages, to see if there was anything there that made any sense to her. But after the grueling few hours she'd spent with it for the first two paragraphs, that wasn't a particularly attractive option. She could show it to Stan again, and see what he was able to make out, but she didn't like that either. He probably still believed it was written by a monk, and it was perhaps better to leave him thinking that. She wasn't sure what was going on here, but she strongly felt that the fewer people who knew about the book, the better. No, she wouldn't drag Stan into this any further than she already had.

Then there was Dr. Del Rio's vampire-friend. He would be here in a week, and if she didn't show up at the doctor's house on Saturday night, he would begin searching for her. Depending upon how much of the license plate he'd gotten, it might not be a difficult search—despite the lie about her name. *Anne Rice*, she repeated in her mind. Terry had been damn lucky the doctor didn't keep up on his popular fiction. She would probably not be so lucky with the doctor's friend—any true vampire would know the name immediately. She should have chosen a name at random. Jesus, what if she'd given Marta's name instead? That would make their search pretty easy, wouldn't it?

Finally, there was the vampire from Tito's. How did he figure into all this? Hell, for all she knew, *that* vampire was Dr. Del Rio's friend. Somehow that leap in logic didn't feel right. Wouldn't the Healing Woman have known? Perhaps, but that wasn't the only reason it didn't feel true. All she had to go on was intuition, but her intuition was telling her that Marta's vampire was not the same creature who had killed twenty-odd men in a temper tantrum.

Of course, she could be wrong.

Information. *That's* what she needed. Terry didn't have enough right now to choose a course of action. So, how did she get more information? She could talk to Dr. Del Rio's friend next week, but something about that didn't feel very safe. All right, what else did she have? Nothing. She'd pursued every avenue, and hadn't found anyone she could trust. Unless she wanted to talk to the vampire from Tito's.

She laughed at the thought of it. '*Hi, you don't know me, but you sucked blood from a friend of mine.*' Yeah. But the more she thought about it, the more logical it seemed. She really *didn't* have anywhere else to turn. Besides, what was the worst that could happen?

He could kill you and dump your body in the alley, the voice of reason said in her mind.

Well, yeah, that could happen, she conceded. *Or*, he could bail me out of this little mess I've gotten myself into. All right, it wasn't a mess yet, but she could see the signs. Within a few days of the skipped-meeting with Dr. Del Rio's friend, it would turn into a huge, whompum-stompum knock-down-drag-out Gonzo of a messity mess-mess-mess. So what was to be done?

First, there were the others. Marta, Stan, the Healing Woman and her husband—they had to be kept as far away from this as possible. That meant not turning to them for any more help. God only knew what kind of danger she'd already put them in.

Second, there was her own life. It had its ups and downs, and sometimes she missed Doug, but Terry *liked* her life. She didn't want to lose it just because she'd been a little too curious about an old book. If she could focus on those two priorities, everything would be fine.

Terry would talk to Marta's vampire. She wouldn't tell him about the book—she'd made that mistake one too many times already. She would talk to him, find out a little about him. If she could just get a little more information, maybe she could get enough to figure out how the hell she was going to get out of this.

Marta was on the couch watching TV when Terry finally got back to the flat. She hung the keys by the door, shuffled over the couch, and threw herself down beside her roommate. She was physically and mentally exhausted—it had been a long day.

"Where were you?" Marta asked casually, without looking away from the set.

Protect Marta, she inwardly repeated the resolve. So, the lies would begin already. "I went to the library for a while, then I went back to talk to the Healing Woman."

That got Marta's attention away from the television. "About what?" she asked. "About me?"

"No, *not* about you," Terry snapped, abruptly cutting off Marta's fear of dying before it could build a good head of steam. "About me. About the *cantante*. Did you tell her anything about Doug?"

"No," she answered. "I no tell her nothing about you. You believe now, no?"

"Yes," Terry confessed. "I believe. But that doesn't mean I think she was right about Doug."

"That you should forget him?" Marta asked. "Why no?"

"I guess I keep thinking of that story you told me, about the guy who had three days to live?" she said. "Maybe she looked deep inside me and saw I should try to contact him, and she also saw the only way she was going to get me to do that was if she told me not to."

Marta laughed. "And you calling me crazy."

"I'm serious, Marta," Terry said, standing from the couch to pace over to the table. She'd intended to start with a lie, but she'd instead begun foraging into thoughts she'd been too preoccupied to think. Maybe it was all the other confusion in her life, but right now she missed Doug more than she ever had.

Marta stood from the couch, crossing the room to turn off the television. "If this is how you are feeling, why no you write him a letter?" she asked. "Forget the Healing Woman—she good at what wrong with your body, no your heart."

"You really think I should?" Terry asked.

"What could you lose? He already no in your life, is he going to be *more* no in your life? Jus' write him, and tell him how you feeling."

"You're right," Terry said, taking a notebook and a pen from the clutter on the kitchen counter. "I'm going to do just that."

"I'm going back to bed," Marta said, yawning. "I'm still very *caliente*."

"*Cansado*," Terry corrected distractedly, before realizing the joke. A few days ago, she'd told Marta in Spanish that she was too *hot* to go out. *Shit*, she thought as it suddenly dawned on her: *That wasn't a few days ago. That was only last night.*

Terry sat at their table. The only light on in the apartment was the one over her head. She'd wrestled over this letter for long enough. She was going to write it. She didn't have to send it if she didn't want to, but she would at least write it.

Dear Doug,

Bet you never thought you'd hear from me again, did you?

I don't know how much you know about what I've been up to lately, but I'm studying at the University in Salamanca now. (I guess you could probably figure that out from the postmark, huh?) Things are fine out here. It's getting close to the end of the spring semester (one more year to go!) and I'm thinking about staying here for the summer. I've got a lot of friends here, and I think I could find a job to keep me fed for a few months until school starts again. Or, I might transfer back to the States. I haven't decided yet, but I guess I'll have to figure it out soon.

You're probably wondering why I bothered to write you. I'm not quite sure myself. All right, that's not exactly true. I know why I'm writing you. I miss you so much. I can't go anyplace or do anything without thinking how much I'd like to be doing it with you. I'm always wondering what you're up to, how you are, if you're all right. I know you're thinking that I'm only writing this because I'm far from home, but I'm not. I missed you for a long time before I even came out here. Hell, I only came out here because I missed you so much, if that makes any sense. Probably not.

This may be coming way too late, but I'm sorry about Dominic. You don't know how sorry. If I start to tell you why I did it, it'll sound like I'm blaming you, and I don't blame you. What happened with Dominic is all on me, it's all my fault. Maybe enough time has passed that you can forgive me, or maybe you'll never forgive me. Maybe, in some way, it doesn't matter whether you forgive me or not. I probably don't deserve it. The only thing that's important is that you know how truly and deeply sorry I am, and if I had it to do all over again, that whole thing never would have happened.

Oh well. I guess you have better things to do than to read about how sorry a stupid ex-girlfriend is. If you have time, write me back and tell me how you're doing. It's important to me to know you're okay. I still consider you the best friend I've ever had, even if we haven't spoken for a year.

All right, I'm going to go for broke. I said that I was considering staying the summer, but that's only true if I don't hear back from you. Maybe we've been apart for long enough that we could give this whole thing a second chance. I'm ashamed for what I did, I really, really am. If you took me back, I swear nothing like it would ever happen again. I love you. I would do anything to get back what I lost with you.

Please, just think about it.

Terry

Over the next few days, Terry managed to keep herself too busy to think about the book. There was schoolwork, classes, the cataloging—that was the most difficult for her, the cataloging. She read every title with a sense of dread, afraid of what she might find. But to her relief, she discovered no more books on vampires.

Overall, her part of the project was going well. She found herself going at odd times so no one could bother her with computer questions, and the drive to keep her mind occupied kept her in the library during most of her free time. Tuesday night found her nearly halfway through the books in her section.

There were only a few others in the library with her that night. Stan was here, but he hadn't noticed her, so she slipped by him hoping to keep it that way. Dr. Marcus was here, which was unusual. Since he'd brought the graduate students and Terry on-board for this project, he hadn't even feigned interest in their progress.

Dr. Marcus was talking to a man she hadn't seen before: on the short-side of average height; dark hair so short it almost looked like a skullcap; round, little, dark-framed glasses. Terry could only catch every other word and she didn't know what they were saying, but she could hear what sounded like an English accent. The stranger was too old to be a student—perhaps in his late thirties—and his accent wasn't uptight and proper enough for him to be a teacher. He sounded like one of the actors from a stage production of *A Christmas Carol* she'd seen a few years ago. Was it called Cockney? She'd done a lot of theater, but accents weren't her thing. He was basically pretty nondescript looking, but in the library of a University in Spain, he stood out.

Terry reached her section and took the next book from the shelf, deciding that it was none of her business. The hair on the back of her neck raised, and she noticed Stan walking over to her. Jesus, it was like he could smell her.

"Hello, Stranger," he said when he reached her.

"Hey," Terry acknowledged, glancing up from her sheaf of computer paper for just a second before returning to it.

"Did you get anywhere with that book?" Stan asked too loudly, searching the shelf for it.

Protect Stan. "I translated a few more sentences after you left," she replied. "You were right—it was just some monk."

"Oh," he said, mercifully believing the lie. "How's Marta doing?"

"She's feeling better. She'll probably be dragging me out drinking in a few more days."

"I guess you won't be going to Tito's anymore."

"Probably not," Terry said, continuing the lie.

"I've been going every night since Saturday," he said. "I took a few friends there, and they fell in love with the place."

"Every night?" she asked, looking away from her printout. *Protect Stan,* she heard again, but she ignored it. "Have you ever seen a short, blonde man in there—designer suit, well-groomed?"

Stan thought about this for a moment. "No, but there's

a lot of people in there. Why, is he a friend of yours?" He hid his jealousy as well as he could, but that wasn't very well.

"No, he's a friend of Marta's," Terry replied. "She lost her spare set of keys Friday night, and she thought he might have them."

"Can't say I remember someone like that, but if I see him I could ask."

"No, don't do that," Terry said quickly. "But could you call me if you see him? We don't live that far from Tito's. Do you have my number?"

Before he could say 'no,' she was writing it on the corner of the printout and tearing it off for him. His hand was nearly shaking as he took it: to Stan, this had to be at least as exciting as getting to second base.

"Remember, don't say anything to him," Terry continued. "Just call me if you see him, and let me handle him."

"Do you think he might be trouble?" Stan asked, standing up to his full height and subtly puffing out his bony chest. Terry had to suppress a laugh.

"No," she answered. "I'd just rather talk to him myself."

"I'll keep an eye open for him," he said as he turned and walked back towards his section. He was staring down at the number in his hand, and nearly bumped into the departing Englishman.

"Oh, sorry," Stan stammered awkwardly.

"No 'arm done," the other replied with distracted cordiality.

Terry sighed, wishing she knew someone to set up with Stan. He'd be an all right guy if he could relax, and he wasn't going to relax unless he got himself laid.

The phone rang the very next night.

"I think your friend is here," Stan said, after the necessary greetings had been exchanged.

"Describe him to me," Terry instructed.

"Short, blonde, nice suit—just like you said. He's sitting alone at the bar. My friends were just leaving, but I'll stick around and wait for you if you want."

Terry was tempted to ask him to stay and wait for her. She'd feel safer with someone watching over her, even if it was just Stan the Man. But she knew it was a selfish thing to ask. *Protect Stan.*

"No, go on home," she said. "I'll be all right."

Forty-five minutes had passed before she reached Tito's. There had been some difficulty deciding what to wear—she'd wanted to look good enough to get his attention, but not so good that he would take her into the men's room. She'd finally decided on her leather miniskirt and a white blouse, hoping it wouldn't be too much.

He was still sitting at the bar when she got there, but he was no longer alone. Another man was with him, and she swore to herself when she recognized the Englishman from the library.

She nearly bolted from Tito's right then and there. The Englishman had been looking for the book. Could he be Dr. Del Rio's friend? It was more than likely. Shit! She'd been trying to get around *that* vampire, and here he was blocking what she'd thought had been her way out.

Terry needed more time to think this through, but she doubted she would get the chance to talk to the Suit before Saturday. She had to take this chance. Terry took a deep breath, summoning her courage, and headed across the bar towards them.

The Englishman noticed her first, and mumbled something to the Suit. The latter didn't respond, but watched her approach. Terry stepped into a character—something she'd learned in theater—completely hiding her fear as she walked right up to them. They weren't vampires right now, just men.

"Buy you a drink?" she asked casually.

"I have one, thank you," the Suit said, gesturing with a conspicuously full glass. "Won't you join us?"

The Englishman jumped from his stool, and Terry realized something: the Suit was in charge. "I've seen you in here before," she said.

"You are a student at the university," the Suit stated.

Terry nearly froze. "How did you know?" she forced herself to ask.

"Because every American in Salamanca is a student at the university," he replied. "What's your name?"

She considered using 'Anne Rice' again, but thought better of it. "Terry," she answered.

"I'm Arthur," he said, before introducing the Englishman. "And this is my associate, Mr. Jennings."

"Nice to meet you," she said to them both, before focusing her attention on Mr. Jennings. There was no hint of recognition in his face—perhaps he hadn't seen her at the library. Terry decided to push it a little further. "Are you a teacher?" she asked the Englishman.

"No," he replied. "Why would you think that?"

"Oh, an Englishman," Terry said, pretending to notice his accent for the first time. "I've seen you at the university, after hours. I thought maybe you taught there."

"What are you studying?" Arthur asked.

"Language and Anthropology." All right, she was doing fine. Everything was going just fine.

"And what do you want to be, when you grow up?" Mr. Jennings asked. He gave a little half-smile as he asked, the intensity of his focus on her suggested he knew something. Just the same, the look wasn't a dangerous one, but mischievous—as though they were playing a game. She nearly played into it and laid all of her cards on the table by answering, 'I want to be a vampire when I grow up,' but it was too early in the game to give away so much. This was no time for her characteristic bluntness.

"I don't know yet," Terry replied. "Maybe a teacher. I'm considering graduate school." Mr. Jennings nodded —apparently the answer had been satisfactory. She turned her attention back to Arthur. "What do you do?" she asked.

"A little of this, a little of that," he replied. "I do some dealing in antiques. Objects of age hold a great fascination for me."

Arthur seemed somewhat oblivious to the little game that was being played, and Terry decided to drag him into it. "And for me," she replied in her most seductive voice.

"Arthur, we still have that meeting with Mr. Wayne tonight," Mr. Jennings interrupted.

'Mr. Wayne,' Terry repeated in her mind. *Bruce Wayne, Batman's alter ego?* Oh yes, he knew she knew all right.

"If you like, I'll tell him you were detained," the Englishman continued. "I'm sure it's nothing I can't handle myself."

"No, I'd better come along," Arthur replied, hopping down from his stool. "I'm sorry I didn't get a chance to talk to you more, Terry. Business, you know."

"I'm sure I'll see you in here again," she said.

"I'm sure you will," Arthur said.

Terry watched the two of them leave Tito's, and turned to the bartender to order a drink. "'I'm sure you will,'" Terry repeated out loud to herself. Score one for Arthur. He might have been in a lower gear, but he certainly wasn't in Park. She reached down to the bar to pick up her vodka and orange juice, only then noticing her shaking hand was causing the ice to rattle against the glass. She drank down the entire glass and returned it unsteadily to the bar.

Terry liked this. Her hand wasn't shaking with fear, but with excitement. Well, maybe there was a little fear involved—but not now. She could deal with this world. She could communicate with these creatures. Terry had always been one for communicating between the lines, and rarely could she find someone who could not only understand her, but communicate back. Doug could talk to her that way—oh shit, she still hadn't bought stamps for his letter. Oh well, she'd remember tomorrow.

Terry replayed the underlying conversation in her mind.

We're vampires, Mr. Jennings had said. *Both Arthur and I.*

I know, Terry had said back. *That's why I came over here.*

That's what I thought, Mr. Jennings had replied, with a knowing smile on his face.

What? Arthur had asked. *Did someone say something?*

Poor Arthur. Still, he *was* in charge. He had to have *something* going for him, besides an excellent tailor.

Terry suspected she would find out soon enough.

It was the next day, and Terry was standing in Dr. Marcus' office at the university, being yelled at in Spanish. Whenever someone yelled at her in Spanish, she felt like Lucille Ball.

"You're leaving the project?"

"Believe me, I wouldn't unless I absolutely had to," Terry explained.

"You're the only one in there doing any work," the doctor continued, exasperated. "*You* might have finished *your* section on time. Now that our deadline has been shortened, I need you more than ever."

"Our deadline has been shortened?" Terry questioned. "Who did that?"

"The order came from upstairs yesterday. They want the entire library finished in two weeks. Can you believe that? I'm between a rock and a hard place, Terry."

She sighed. *This* was why she would never get anywhere in life—because she was a nice girl. "I'll do what I can," Terry said. "Nights are my big problem. I can't be in the library at night anymore, I got a job bartending."

"If money's a problem, the university might be able to arrange something ..."

"It isn't just the money," she said. "I'll give you the time I can offer, which is during the day only and only when I don't have a class. It's the best I can do."

Dr. Marcus rubbed his temples. "I'll take whatever you can give me," he said.

Terry went to Tito's again that night. Arthur was sitting at the bar, intensely reading a newspaper. With Mr. Jennings here, at least she had some competition for her game. She would eat Arthur for lunch.

The place was close to empty, but the music was no less deafening than usual. She decided to sneak up on him, just to see if it was possible to sneak up on a vampire.

"Anything interesting in the news?" she asked at his shoulder. To her dismay, he was already facing her when she spoke—she'd figured it couldn't be done.

"What?" Arthur asked.

She noticed the article he was reading. Everyone at the university had been talking about the murder—the victim was apparently the brother of a student. Back in America, it might not have even been newsworthy. But here in Salamanca, where this sort of thing didn't happen, the horror of the event wasn't lost in its regularity.

"That murder," she said with a glance to the newspaper. "I never thought of Salamanca as a dangerous city. But they say the Gypsies here ..."

"Gypsies didn't do this," Arthur stated with a certainty that was unnerving.

"They didn't?" she asked. "How do you know that?"

"I ... they just didn't," he replied vaguely, his eyes wandering around the room as though he had someplace better to be. "What are you doing here? Don't you know this has become a dangerous neighborhood?"

"It's not dangerous—if you know the right people."

"Really?" he asked, his eyes fixed on nothing. "Who do you know?"

"You and Mr. Jennings," she replied matter-of-factly. "You wouldn't let anything bad happen to me, would you?"

"Not if I could prevent it," Arthur answered, "but I'm not a policeman, I'm just an antiques dealer. I certainly couldn't do anything against the likes of this madman."

This wasn't nearly as fun without Mr. Jennings. Arthur was barely paying attention to her—she felt almost as though she was bothering him.

"They say he was killed somewhere else and carried here," Terry said. "According the newspaper, there's no other way to account for the loss of blood. You're a world traveler, maybe in your experience you've seen something that can account for it."

"Maybe they attached leeches to his body," Arthur responded with a distracted little smile. "They're the only creatures I know of that drink blood."

"What about vampire bats?" she said. *That* would get him. "They drink blood."

"You don't find vampire bats around here," he dismissed. "Maybe it was mosquitoes."

"Maybe it was real vampires," she said. "Do you believe in vampires?"

She'd done it. She'd spoken the word.

"Do *you*?" Arthur countered, staring past her.

"I don't know," she said. "I think I do."

"I think modern science would have discovered them by now, if they did exist," Arthur said.

"Modern science?" she asked incredulously. Dammit! What was it going to take? "Modern science is too caught up with finding rational explanations for everything. Their minds are shut off to the reality—that there are things out there that don't follow their laws. Look at UFOs. How many thousands of sightings have there been over the last forty years? Photographs? Video tapes? Yet, modern science rejects their existence because there is no proof. An alien could walk up to a scientist and slap him in the face, and they'd say it was a man in a costume."

"So you believe in aliens?" Arthur asked, checking his watch.

"Do you believe in vampires?" she asked again.

"I asked you first."

"No, I believe *I* asked *you* first."

Arthur sighed as if irritated—she'd backed him into a corner. "Perhaps," he said "But if they do exist, they aren't what your contemporary fiction would have you believe. They're ordinary men, thrust into an extraordinary circumstances. Some are bad, some are good—just like ordinary men."

"Would a good vampire have killed that guy?" she asked.

"No, a good vampire wouldn't have," he said steadily.

So Arthur hadn't done it—and Mr. Jennings probably hadn't done it either. It was probably safe to say Dr. Del Rio's friend was here.

"Then maybe I should be concerned about the danger," she said.

"Maybe you should," he replied.

"Maybe I need a good vampire around to protect me."

A strange look suddenly crossed Arthur's face. It wasn't a reaction to anything she'd said but to something else, something she couldn't perceive. Whatever it was, it rattled him pretty badly.

"I have to go," Arthur said hurriedly, getting up from the bar.

"Hey," she said, trying to stop him. "I was hoping I wouldn't have to walk home alone tonight."

"You'll be safe enough. Can you meet me here tomorrow night?"

"Yes, I think so," she answered. Whatever was happening, it was urgent. That much she could tell.

"I'll see you tomorrow, then," he said as he turned and left.

Terry turned back to the bar, disappointed in the entire exchange. Arthur had given her nothing. Hell, he'd barely even given her notice. But why would he? What was she to him, but food? Maybe a conversation with Mr. Jennings would go better ... if she could find him.

"Hello, Stranger," Stan the Man said as he sat on Arthur's barstool. "I see you found your friend."

"Yeah," she replied. *Protect Stan.* "Thanks for calling me last night, I really do appreciate it."

"For you, anything," he said, smiling. Stan was a little looser than normal—either he'd gotten laid, or he had a few beers in him. Either way, Terry was grateful for the change.

"Did he have Marta's keys?" Stan asked.

Terry had to think for a minute before remembering the lie of the previous night. "No, she found them at the flat," she said. "But thanks for calling me just the same."

"So, are you, like, dating him now or something?" he asked.

Terry would have laughed if Stan wasn't so pathetic. Put a few beers in a nerd, and all you got was a drunk nerd. "No, he's too short," Terry said, sending a signal that she hoped was loud and clear. "He's just a nice guy." *He's just a nice vampire.*

"Oh," he said. "So, you wanna dance or something?"

"No," she replied. "Marta's still not feeling well. I have to be getting back to the flat."

"You wanna invite me up for a nightcap?" he asked, smiling a smile that would have been alluring from any other human being on the planet.

Terry patted his hand consolingly. "Goodnight, Stan," she said dryly.

"I'll take a raincheck, then," he said, standing as she stood, wavering a bit. "Maybe I'll see you in here tomorrow night?"

"Maybe," Terry said as she left.

"All right, then," she heard him say to himself as she headed for the door.

Arthur didn't show on Friday night.

Terry waited all night for him, from sundown until Tito's closed. Stan the Man and his crew of nerds spotted her early on, and she spent five hours alternately engaging in incredibly dull conversation and warding off inept advances. But Arthur never made an appearance.

Terry's anger grew exponentially every half-hour. She needed to talk to Arthur *tonight*, so she could make a decision about Dr. Del Rio's friend before tomorrow, and he was off sucking blood from Spaniards. Well then, *fuck* him. If he couldn't be counted on to keep one lousy appointment, how could he be counted on to protect her? How could he be counted on for anything?

Bastard.

Terry slept late the next morning. When she was finally up and about she headed over to the library, anxious to finish her part of the project. It seemed like the only things she had in her life anymore were sleep, the library, and vampires. She'd forgotten to buy a stamp for Doug's letter all week, and now it would have to wait until Monday. She still managed to get all of her classes in, but she knew she had at least two term papers due next week and she'd yet to write a word of either.

Hours passed in the library. Terry spoke to no one, thinking only of vampires as she cataloged book after book. If someone dropped a romance novel on her shelf right now, she'd check the list for it, find it missing, and catalog it without breaking stride. Oddly, Stan didn't come to the library all day; but he'd had a lot to drink the night before, and she didn't suppose he was used to that sort of thing.

All she thought about was tonight: the choice between Dr. Del Rio's friend and Arthur. She was fairly certain the former was responsible for the recent rash of deaths in Salamanca. If he was, and Terry went to meet him tonight, she might not see morning. She could easily skip the meeting, but if she did he would definitely come after her. No question. At least if she went to the meeting and left the book at home, she might be able to buy herself another week. Of course, if this other vampire could do what Arthur could do—force people to do things against their will, like he had with Marta—then it would be all over tonight no matter where she hid it.

And then there was Arthur and Mr. Jennings. She didn't feel she was in any danger with them, she just didn't know if they could be counted on to protect her. Terry couldn't make this decision based on the fact that she liked the two of them, she had to make this decision based on what would keep her alive. Damn Arthur for not showing up last night. The only excuse she would accept for his absence was death, which Terry supposed Arthur could use as an ongoing excuse. *Sorry I couldn't make it. I was dead.*

Maybe Arthur would be at Tito's tonight. It was a shot in the dark, and if she blew off Dr. Del Rio, the consequences might be severe. She wondered how long it would take them to find her, with only a physical description and a license number to go by. Probably not very long.

Terry checked her watch and swore to herself—it was past seven. She had to get out of the library before Mr. Jennings showed up, and this was cutting it a little close. She marked her place on the shelf of books, packed her things into her book bag, and scrambled out of the library.

She realized on the way back to the flat that what she really wanted to do was go home and go to sleep, but that was hardly a very wise option. Some action had to be taken, whether it was towards Arthur or the doctor's friend. Terry considered the choice all the way home, and was no closer to a solution when she closed the door of the flat behind her and dropped her book bag on the kitchen counter.

She simply didn't have enough information to be able to make this decision based on facts. People were disappearing, but she didn't know who was responsible. She didn't know anything at all about Dr. Del Rio's friend, except that he'd supposedly killed twenty people during a temper tantrum when the doctor was a young man. Terry felt she could trust Arthur, but again, she didn't *know* anything. This decision could not be based on intellect: it had to be based on intuition. But Terry's intuition wasn't telling her a damn thing.

There was only one thing to do: flip a coin. Heads, she would go to see the doctor tonight. Tails, she would wait at Tito's and see if Arthur showed up. Terry dug in her pocket for a coin and flipped the one she found into the air, catching it and slapping it to the back of her opposite hand. Heads. The doctor won.

All right, Terry thought to herself. *I made the choice to let the coin decide, and it decided. Now I have to live by that decision.*

Terry sat in Tito's two hours later, anxiously hoping Arthur would come. But neither he nor Mr. Jennings made an appearance that night.

Bastards.

By Sunday night, Terry had moved from nervous to terrified.

The day had been a wasted effort. She'd gone to the library (the 'new' library, with the 'new' books), surrounded herself with research material for one of her term papers, sat down with pen in hand and thought about vampires.

It wouldn't take a week for them to find her. How long could it take to run a license number? If they had any connections at all with the Spanish authorities, it would take a day, two at the very most. She walked to Tito's just as the sun was setting, checking to make sure she wasn't being followed the entire way.

Arthur wasn't there when she got there. Dammit! Would it have been so much fucking trouble to leave her a phone number? Now she had to decide if she was going to wait in here until closing, like she had the past two nights, or find someplace to hide. If Stan made it to Tito's tonight, she would go back to his place and screw him just to stay out of her own apartment.

"So glad you could make it."

Terry was so startled at the voice in her ear, she nearly screamed. She turned and found Arthur standing behind her, a slight smile on his face as though nothing had happened. The very *first* words out of his mouth should have been, 'I'm sorry'—at least then, she only would have been angry. As it was, she was way beyond that.

"What?" she began. "I was here Friday night. Where were you?"

Arthur seemed to think about this for a moment, before remembering. "I'm sorry, something rather important came up," he said dismissively as he took a seat to her left. "We need to talk. That is, if you're still interested."

"Maybe," she said, somewhat aloof. She should have listened to the coin Saturday night. "What do you want to talk about?"

"You attend the university," Arthur said. "Do your studies ever take you into the library—the library where the old books are kept?"

That got her attention, and she forgot her anger. Had Mr. Jennings seen her in there that day? or had he seen a list of students working on Dr. Marcus' project? Terry reminded herself that she needed Arthur. She couldn't let pride get in her way, as it had been known to do.

Shit, she thought to herself. *I forgot to buy stamps again.*

"I go into the old library sometimes," she answered nonchalantly. "Why?"

Arthur sighed impatiently. "I can see this is going to require a more direct approach," he said. "So be it. Jennings and I are part of an organization—a cabal, if you will. I consider you a potential member of that cabal. Jennings believes you know the truth about us, but you've got to prove that to me. I cannot be the first to say it. Tell me what you believe—prove Jennings is right—and perhaps we can begin being honest with each other."

Terry took a deep breath, studying his eyes, searching

for some hidden truth, finding nothing. It was silly; she didn't need any more hints. She hadn't stayed awake the night before thinking all of this wasn't real—but the act of speaking the words would make it real in a way she wasn't sure she was ready for. The Truth-line was on the move. "I think you're a vampire," she finally said.

A happy shadow flashed in Arthur's eyes at the mention of the word. Terry shuddered. There was something about that dark expression that Terry *really* didn't like. "What makes you think so?" he asked with a cool smile.

'*What makes you think so?*' Terry repeated in her mind. *Jesus Christ, just fucking come clean, already.* Terry was nearly overcome with the urge to slap him. "Am I right?" she demanded.

"I'll answer that question momentarily," Arthur said in a voice that was almost a purr. "Now tell me what makes you think I'm a vampire."

"I saw you take a friend of mine to the bathroom, and when she came out, she was lightheaded," she replied. "When I asked her what happened, she couldn't remember anything."

Arthur's eyes assumed a distant look, and the dark expression that persisted on his face gave him the appearance of someone who was reliving the pleasant memory of a rape he'd once committed. Then his eyes regained their focus, and rational thought seemed to return. "That's all you had to go on?" he asked. "A lightheaded friend?"

"That, and the fact that you tend to nurse your drinks all night long."

Arthur sighed. He was irritated, but not at her.

"Tell me if it's true," Terry insisted, resisting another urge to grab the little man by the lapels of his designer suit and shake him.

"Let us pretend for a moment it is. Ask yourself: if there are vampires running loose in the world, do you want to know about it? Most mortals live perfectly happy lives because they don't believe there are creatures who stalk the night, feeding on their daughters or their sisters or their mothers. How would you sleep?"

"I would sleep just fine if I *were* one," she answered.

Arthur chuckled at this, then laughed. "Anne Rice, right?"

Terry's mouth went dry. Had Arthur spoken to Dr. Del Rio? Was Arthur the 'friend' she'd been trying to avoid all along?

"You've read Anne Rice?" Arthur asked again, completing the question.

"Yeah, but what's ..." she began, still recovering, before she was interrupted by his laughter.

"Tell me," he began, "what your mortal fiction has taught you about being a vampire."

"You still haven't answered my question." she said.

"Answer mine first."

"This makes two of mine to one of yours."

"You may get fifty more before I'm finished," Arthur said coldly. "Now tell me what you think being a vampire means."

"It means never growing old," she said.

"And what else?"

"It means being stronger and faster than a regular person."

"And what else?"

Terry stopped and considered. What the hell did he want to hear? She carefully looked inside herself, trying to find just why she'd been so intrigued by this from the very beginning.

"It means being in on the biggest secret that's ever been," Terry said. "It means really knowing what's going on in the world, instead of believing the same lie as everyone else on the planet."

Arthur nodded ... that answer seemed to satisfy him. "Let's say all that is true," he began. "But what if it also means never being able to see the light of day? What if it means being a slave to desires you're ashamed of? What if it means spending half your time in a stupor because the sun is up, and spending the other half trying to find enough blood to continue an existence you despise?"

"You think too much, Arthur," Terry said. "Besides, you don't seem to have a problem with that."

"With the shame?" he asked. "There you're wrong. I have a big problem with the shame."

"No—you don't seem to have a problem finding blood."

"Most vampires don't have the ability to make mortals forget things, or do things they wouldn't ordinarily do—assuming they exist, of course."

"I can already make men do things they wouldn't ordinarily do," Terry said, thinking to herself after she said it, *Not too stuck on ourselves, are we?*

"Perhaps now you can, but what if your looks go out of style?" he asked. "What if—in fifty years—heavy women come back? Sure, in this day and age, anyone can feed. But wait ten or twenty years, after this AIDS thing has changed everyone's sexual attitudes, and see how easy it will be."

"Are you a vampire?" she asked for the last time.

Arthur sighed. "Yes," he answered. "I am a vampire."

Terry took a few moments to soak this in. *I was right*, she thought to herself. *God damned if I wasn't right.* "You know," she said, "I've got about a million questions I want to ask you, and my mind is blank."

"That's all right," Arthur said. "We don't have time for questions now anyway ..."

"Have you ever seen a ghost?" she interrupted.

"What?"

"You know," she explained, "a ghost—a spirit."

"Do you think I belong to some Undead Club?" he said sarcastically. "No, I've never seen a ghost."

"How about a werewolf?" she continued.

"I don't understand the point to these questions," he stated flatly.

"Something I've spent all my life believing was a legend just turned out to be real," Terry said. "I want to know what other legends are real. Have you ever seen a werewolf?"

"No," Arthur answered. "I've met those who swear they have, but then, I've met those who swear they're Napoleon. I place little credence in either."

"Did you know Napoleon?" she asked.

"I knew *of* him, just like everyone else at the time. But I never met him. Listen ..."

"Have you ever seen the Loch Ness Monster?" she barreled on.

"No."

"How about Bigfoot?"

"I've never even been to America."

"What can vampires do? What are your powers?"

"We call them 'Gifts,'" Arthur explained. "And they're just as varied for vampires as they are for mortals. Some mortals are good at mathematics, others can fix motorcars. My gift is the Influence—you've seen what that can do."

"What is Mr. Jennings' Gift?"

"That's a personal question," Arthur huffed. "Rather like my asking you whether you're a virgin ..."

"I'm not," Terry said. "I lost my virginity when I was fifteen."

Terry's candor stunned Arthur—and it pleased her that she could stun a man of Arthur's experience.

"Be that as it may," Arthur said, frowning with disapproval, "it's a personal question. I wouldn't have told you *my* Gift, if you hadn't already seen it. Ask Jennings once you get to know him better, perhaps he'll tell you."

"Do you get stronger with age, like Anne Rice says?" she asked.

"Anne Rice says that?" he asked.

"Yes," Terry answered. "Is it true?"

Arthur stared into space, wearing a concerned look. "Yes," he answered. "That's true."

"How old is Mr. Jennings?" A stern look was her answer. "Too personal. How old are you?"

"Why is *that* less personal?"

"Come on," Terry protested. "I told you how old I was when I lost my virginity."

"Look," Arthur finally said. "As fascinating as this is, I have a problem to deal with."

"Tell me how old you are, and I won't ask another question," Terry promised.

"Ever?" Arthur asked hopefully.

"No, just tonight," she said.

"I'm over twenty-one."

"If you were around during Napoleon's time, I'd say you were at least two hundred years over twenty-one," Terry persisted.

"Actually, it's more like seven hundred," Arthur said.

"Seven hundred years?" she repeated breathlessly. "You're older than my country."

"Enough," Arthur said firmly. "As I started to say, I have a bit of a problem. Mr. Jennings believes you would be willing to help us. I need to know if that is true."

"Tell me what seems to be the problem," she said.

"There is another group of vampires in Salamanca," Arthur began. "Their leader is a fledgling named Lyle. He has four women with him—three are vampires, one is a mortal. They are all young, beautiful, and foolish—including Lyle. Lyle's the dumbest of the lot. Against mortals, they are very dangerous. Against the likes of Jennings and myself, they're a bunch of children."

"Then why don't you just spank them and send them home, Arty?"

She suddenly felt his hand on the back of her neck and his lips at her right ear. He'd stood and moved to her far side without Terry even having seen him move.

People were not supposed to be able to do *that*. It was impossible. As ready as Terry had been for proof, she wasn't ready for proof to vanish before her eyes, reappear behind her, and whisper into her ear.

This was not a fun game anymore.

"Be ... very ... careful, Mortal," he whispered. Terry could hear the smile in his voice, and knew that if she could see that smile, she would not find a smile of the friendly variety. Her entire body shook with terror.

"What is it with the young?" he continued. "Is respect *so* difficult a concept? Perhaps you *want* me to feed, right here in public." He brushed her hair back, and moved his lips down to her trembling neck. "Social mores aren't what they used to be, you know. I doubt anyone would even look twice. What do you say? Would you like to see if it's everything you've read about?"

"No," Terry said in a whisper that was barely audible. Tears welled up in her eyes. "Please don't."

"I can make you say, 'Yes,' you know," the vampire said, his lips brushing her neck. "That's my special power.

Your friend ... she begged me to take her. She was actually quite delicious. Will *you* be that delicious, I wonder?"

"Please, Arthur," Terry pleaded. The tears in her eyes spilled down her cheeks. "Please ... I'm sorry ... whatever I did, I won't do it again ... just please don't do this ... I didn't mean any disrespect ... please ..."

Arthur released her hair and stood up straight. Terry could barely hear an oath whispered in French, *Sacre Merde*. When he returned to his seat, he was changed. The lines in his face seemed to have deepened, his skin had grayed, and his red-rimmed eyes were full of remorse.

"I'm ..." he began, before directing his gaze down at his own hands. He seemed unable to meet Terry's eyes. "I'm sorry," the vampire said. "That was ... I'm afraid I haven't been myself, lately. What I ... I was ... I can't even begin to ask forgiveness for what I just did."

In that, he was correct—he couldn't. She angrily wiped the tears from her cheeks.

"We can't talk any more, tonight," Arthur said. "You're in ... it isn't safe. If you still want to help us, meet me here tomorrow. I promise I'll be more myself."

Terry stood, took her purse from the bar, and left Tito's without another word.

She paced the floor of her flat for the rest of the night, waiting for Dr. Del Rio's friend to find her, and trying to figure out what she would do if he did. Garlic, holy water, crosses—did any of those things really work? Somehow, she doubted it. Besides, if this vampire could move as fast as Arthur, she probably wouldn't get the chance to use them anyway.

The experience at Tito's had rattled her quite a bit. She'd been considering her options under the assumption that there would be 'good guy' vampires and 'bad guy' vampires, and that it would just be a matter of determining who was who. On one hand, she had the doctor's friend, who had killed twenty men in a temper tantrum; and on the other, she had Arthur who—she felt confident—had come close to killing her tonight because she'd called him 'Arty.'

Sure, he'd apologized after, but it didn't feel like an apology. It felt more like a salesman's pitch. It felt like he was trying to win her over, to convince her to join his 'cabal.' It felt like one of her fights with Doug (*Stamps*, she reminded herself). If they were out in public, he would say anything to calm her and prevent a scene, but once they were alone, that story changed. When would that story change with Arthur? Once she was a part of his organization?

Terry noticed with a strong sense of relief that the sun was coming up. She slid opened the glass door to the balcony, and stood in the dry Spanish air, watching night slowly turn to day. It began with a glow in the eastern sky that spread almost imperceptibly. Black sky turned blue, black streets turned gray. She couldn't see the sun on the horizon for the buildings, but she could see its light on the orange stone of Salamanca.

She sat on the balcony until full light, wondering what it would be like to never see this again. *That was nice*, she thought to herself as she went back inside. *But not spectacular.*

Terry woke feeling as though she hadn't slept at all. She checked the clock beside her bed, afraid she would find it was close to noon. The red LED numbers maliciously told her it was 3:58 PM. She stared at the clock, thinking, *No, I didn't just sleep through a day's worth of classes WHEN I HAVE TWO TERM PAPERS DUE I HAVEN'T EVEN STARTED!* She'd had this college-anxiety nightmare before. If she just stared at the clock long enough, PM would turn into AM. It had to.

NOPE, the clock said to her. IT'S 3:58 PM ... OOO, NOW IT'S 3:59 PM. IF YOU STICK AROUND LONG ENOUGH, I'LL SHOW YOU THE COOL CHANGE FROM 3:59 TO 4:00. IT MAY NOT BE AS SPECTACULAR AS THE 12:59-TO-1:00, BUT IT'S WORTH WATCHING.

"Fuck," Terry said aloud as she ambled into the bathroom. "I haven't even been bitten yet and I'm turning into a vampire."

Enough. Enough was enough, and this was *enough*.

Terry stormed to the old library, her book bag full of the book. This thing was ruining her life. She couldn't sleep nights, she spent all of her spare time playing word-games with psychos who thought they were vampires, and today she'd *really* fucked-up. If she lost her scholarships because her grades dropped off, there was no way she'd be able to afford to finish school. This had to end, and it had to end Today. She would slide the book into someone else's section, and forget she'd ever seen the damn thing.

Her anger stayed at an even keel, right up until she reached the hall outside the library. Something was wrong. There were teachers and students and *policías* milling about the library's entrance, asking questions, answering questions, shouting angrily. Dr. Marcus was there, shaking like a leaf and white as a ghost. Stan was in the crowd, and he noticed Terry and walked right to her.

"What the hell is going on?" she asked, clutching nervously at the strap of her book bag.

"Someone broke into the library last night," Stan said. "The damage is ... I've never seen anything like it. It looks like twenty of the biggest, strongest three-year-olds you've ever seen got in there and just went to town."

Terry walked towards the library door, as if in a trance. Stan was right with her, hissing in her ear. "I wouldn't go up there," he said. "They'll just grab you and ask a million questions like they have everyone else. Take my word for it, it's probably nothing you want to see anyway."

But Terry could not stop her feet from moving her towards the door. She wanted to see—she *had* to see. She moved through the crowd of people as though in a dream, moved to the door, and then into the library.

The shelves along the walls, once full of books, were now empty. Instead, torn covers and painted pages lay heaped into piles around the room. Not one of the ancient manuscripts was left intact—except the one she carried in her bag.

A page at her feet caught her eye, and she slowly stooped to pick it up from the floor. She examined it without rising. The hair on the back of her neck was already standing, but now she felt her face flush, her stomach knot, her legs weaken.

Terry saw the scene clearly. She saw it as though it was happening right before her eyes. Three beautiful women with fangs for teeth and claws for hands, taking book after book from the shelves, rending them apart with preternatural strength while they laughed insanely. One beautiful man, dancing about the room while bindings and paper fly around him. They make a game out of destroying irreplaceable manuscripts, because they hate anything older than they are. Because they hate Arthur.

The beautiful man takes one of the thick sheets of parchment, and while the others watch, bites down on an edge, leaving two clear puncture marks where the fangs penetrate. He cries out in exultation, celebrating the fact that he will not age and he will not die. He will drink blood and avoid the sun and nothing more.

"You can't touch anything in there," Terry heard a man's voice order in Spanish from the door. "All of that mess is evidence."

A parchment—two clean holes on its edge—slipped out of Terry's shaking hand as she stood, turned, and walked towards the door. She returned to the hall, ignoring a barrage of questions from a *policía*, and leaned one hand against the wall.

This was too real. She'd thought about the danger she was in, wondered what she should do to get out of it, but the whole thing had still been like a fantasy ... like a book she was reading. You set the book down and you go about your life. If the book is really good, you think about it even when you aren't reading it. Later on, you pick it up again to see what happened. But it's just a book. It's not real. *This* was really, really real.

Terry threw up.

She rushed into her flat, closing and locking the door behind her. She grasped the book, allowing the bag to slip to the floor, and threw the manuscript onto the couch. She found a photo album she'd brought with her from America and ripped the cover from it, pages of pictures falling unceremoniously to the floor. She took up the book, wrapped the cover of the album over it, and put it directly on the center of the coffee table. Then she was on her knees, picking up the guts of the photo album. Pictures of her mother, her friends; pictures of Doug, a single picture of her father—all went into the bag before it found its way under the couch.

Perfect, she voiced within her muddled mind. *No one will ever find it.*

Terry took a seat in a booth instead of at the bar. Barstools were for being seen. Tonight, she wanted to hide. She also wanted to have no less than three drinks in her for the meeting with Arthur. She wasn't halfway through her second when Mr. Jennings slid into the booth across from her.

"Hello," he said in his Cockney accent. "Come here often?"

The knot in her stomach eased ... after last night, she had very little desire to see Arthur again. She felt much safer with Mr. Jennings, but who was to say the exact same thing wouldn't happen again? Or, worse?

"Arthur sends his apologies," the vampire said.

Terry nodded, shivering involuntarily at the sound of the name. "S'okay," she mumbled.

Jennings said nothing for a while. A waitress came, and he ordered a *cervesa* with an accent so thick it was a small miracle she understood what he was saying. When he sipped it, Terry's curiosity piqued.

"You can drink beer?" she asked.

"I can, yes," he replied. "But I can't digest it. It sits in my stomach until I ... get rid of it."

"And how do you do that?"

"The regular way," he said with a little grin, "back up

the way it came."

"Oh," she said, before tentatively adding, "Is that why Arthur never drinks?"

"Nope," Jennings replied. "Arthur never drinks because he can't. You see, with most of us, it comes right back up as soon as it's drunk. We're not designed for it anymore, and our bodies seem to know that. I'm an exception to that rule."

"Is that your Gift?" she asked.

Jennings mouth trembled a little bit. It must have sounded strange to him, Terry thought, to hear one of their secret words spoken aloud in a bar by someone who wasn't *one* of them. "I'm not sure I'd call it a 'Gift,'" he finally said. "It's more of a peculiarity, really."

"Then what *is* your Gift?" Terry continued.

"Can't really say as I've got one, to be honest," he replied. "What's yours?"

"Huh? What do you mean? I'm not a ... " she cut herself off, afraid to say the word.

"I know you're 'not a ... ', but you aren't really so different from us. You've all got Gifts, too. A few of *your* Gifts are obvious," he said, giving her an exaggerated look up and down, "but I'm wondering if that's where it ends."

"I've got a gift for fucking up my life ... does that count?"

Jennings chuckled a bit. "I think you and I *share* that Gift, Terry," he said.

"How'd it happen with you? I mean ... did Arthur ... "

"Did Arthur Make me? No, he didn't. Arthur ... Arthur saved me from the one who Made me."

"Oh, I see," Terry said, nodding knowledgeably. She began to laugh—at herself, mostly—for her awkward attempts to make this conversation seem more ... normal. "Okay ... no ... " she began, her laughter usurping her speech in tiny increments. "I guess I really have no idea what you're talking about," she managed to eek out before falling into a fit of giggling.

Jennings shared her amusement with a broad grin. "Am I safe assuming that this is the strangest conversation you've ever had?"

"It's definitely high on the list," she said, giggling uncontrollably, now. "Very, very, very high on the list. Someone ransacked the library last night. Damn, my drink's empty."

The vampire's grin suddenly disappeared. "What did you say?"

"My drink," she repeated. "It's empty."

"No-no ... before that."

"Oh ... that thing about the library? Damnedest thing, really. I'm talking ran-*sacked*. Nothing subtle about it. *At all!* I mean, one of them even left two neat-little puncture marks on the edge of one of the pages! Why not just spray-paint, 'Vampire!' on the fuckin' wall?"

Jennings' eyes quickly darted around the room to see if anyone had heard the word. Terry was making him nervous with this little outburst. Terry didn't care. Her hysteria had moved away from giggling/amused hysteria, right into hysterical hysteria.

"And *last* night, your little friend decides he's gonna scare the be*jee*sus outta me!" Terry continued. "He was all breathin' on me like I'm a fucking appetizer!"

Somewhere deep inside Terry—in a part that was still rational—she wondered if this was a normal reaction to lack of sleep, too much alcohol, and stark terror.

"I mean, *damn*," the rest of Terry continued. "If the man doesn't like to be called 'Arty,' all he has to do is tell me so! Ya know? Jesus *Christ!*"

Suddenly, the tirade was over. She reeled in the echo

of her words in her mind. Had she really just said all of that? To a vampire? Oh well ... it was out there now, and Terry felt much better.

"Feel better?" Jennings asked.

Terry nodded dumbly that Yes, she felt much better.

"Good," the vampire said. "First of all, why did you just bring up the library, out-of-the-blue?"

Terry thought about this for a moment ... why *had* she brought up the library? Had she just overplayed her hand and given herself away? No ... no, she remembered ... Arthur had brought it up last night. The library. He hadn't said anything about the book, but he'd asked, 'Do your studies ever take you into the library—the library where the old books are kept?' He'd said that. She wasn't fucked. Yet.

"Arthur mentioned the library last night," she explained hastily. "He specifically mentioned the *old* library. He didn't say more." Terry's throat tightened to a tiny pinhole, as a question came to mind that she absolutely did *not* want to ask.

"That wasn't you guys, was it? In the library? You and Arthur didn't do that, did you?"

Hello, my name is Terry, and my head is a fucking gumball machine. A question comes to mind and WHOOP! suddenly it just falls right out.

Jennings reached across the table and gently took her hand. It wasn't a warm hand—which was creepy, because she knew it wasn't warm for all the wrong reasons—but there was an integrity in the gesture, and in his eyes, that she couldn't deny.

"No," he said evenly. "That wasn't us."

Terry wanted to believe him. She really, really did. She liked Jennings—she didn't know why, but she did. Maybe it was that goofy accent, or the fact that he really seemed to be trying not to take himself or any of this vampire stuff too seriously despite the fact that it *was* serious and he *clearly* knew that. Terry *wanted* to believe him.

But by the same token, Terry wanted to be the person she was last week, back when there was no such thing as vampires. She wanted to meet Jennings as a regular person, so the two of them could hang out and drink together. He could keep the whole vampire-thing a secret, and she would suspect there was something strange about him, but he'd never give her enough to really give her suspicions a firm handhold, because that was what he did. Because Jennings had been around for a long time, and that was what he had done for ... for ...

"How long have you been a vampire?" Terry asked.

"In two years, I'll be celebrating my centennial as a member of the undead," Jennings replied.

"Wow." It wasn't particularly insightful on Terry's part, nor particularly eloquent. But it was the best she could come up with. "Wow," she repeated. "I'll bet you've seen some shit."

"Yes," he answered. "I've seen some shit." Jennings took another sip from his beer and checked his watch.

"Wow," Terry said again, in case Jennings had missed it the first two times.

"Arthur will be here in a few minutes," Jennings said. "By the time he arrives, there are some things I need to have explained to you."

"Okay, shoot."

"Two hundred years ago, Arthur hid a book in the library," Jennings began "A small group of vampires somehow learned that the book was there, and came all the way from London to get it. Arthur and I have to make sure that they *don't*. Since you're in this now, we want to know if you're willing to help us."

"'Help you?'" Terry repeated. "How the Hell could *I* help *you?*"

"You can do something very important," he replied, "something Arthur and I can't do anymore—you can walk around in the daylight. They brought a mortal with them when they came, which gives them twelve more hours a day more than *we* have to search for this book. If you'd be willing to join us, it could even those odds a little."

Terry said nothing for a moment, instead staring into space, wondering what might be considered a 'bad' question under these circumstances. She'd come to no firm conclusions when she finally spoke. "Um ... when you say, 'join us,' what does that involve, exactly?"

"Arthur has a cabal of vampires spread across the globe. We have one purpose and one purpose only: we enforce the Vampire Code."

"And that is?" she asked.

"The Vampire Code forbids vampires from revealing themselves to mainstream human society, and from interfering in human history in any way," Jennings explained. "We must keep ourselves separate from the mortals—to protect the mortals, and to protect *us*. The roles taken by the members of the cabal depends upon the members. If you want to help us with this and be forgotten, you can do that. If you decide to take a larger role in the struggle—and you're capable enough—you can do that too."

"What's the pay scale like?" Terry asked.

Jennings chuckled a little. "It's less like an actual salary, and more like having your every need taken care of forever. I guess from your perspective, it would be a bit like military service—only with better uniforms. On the one hand, you never have to worry about anything financial, ever again. On the other, you can never be sure what part of the world you'll be waking up in."

"Will you make me ... one of you?" she asked.

Jennings rubbed his chin, and squarely met her eyes. "Well," he said, "there's the official answer, and there's the truth."

"Could I have both, please?"

Jennings checked his watch again. Judging by the pacing of his speech, Arthur was expected shortly. The near-forgotten knot in Terry's stomach gave a little tug at her insides.

"The official answer," Jennings began, "is that if you decide to take that step, we'll consider it. We'll all weigh it out together, and decide what's best for you and the cabal."

"And the truth?" she asked.

"The *truth* is that I've never known anyone to choose natural death over eternal life," he said. "When your beauty fades and your body doesn't work like it's supposed to, you'll ask us to be Made. And you'll work *very* hard for the cabal to ensure that you'll be too indispensable to be let go, when that time comes. I've never seen it happen any other way." Jennings checked his watch again. "I need an answer, Terry."

"You mean, right now?" she exclaimed. "I need to tell you for certain what I want to do with the rest of my life, right this second?"

"No ... no," Jennings corrected calmly. "I just need to know if you're willing to help us find this book. You won't be expected to decide about the rest of your life until tomorrow, at the very soonest."

There was no question about joining Arthur's cabal. She didn't know exactly when she'd given up that choice, but she knew it was no longer hers to make. The only question was how honest to be with them. The only question was the book. If she gave that up, would he still have a reason to protect her? And could he be counted on to protect her if he suddenly had no need to? It was true she had no choice but to join his little club, but she still had to look out for her own interests. No, the book would stay hidden, for now.

"Tell me what you need, and I'll do what I can," Terry said.

Jennings smiled. "You made the right decision," he said.

Terry fleshed out a brief fantasy with different circumstances—a fantasy where she'd actually had a choice. It was a good fantasy, if perhaps a somewhat-unlikely fantasy. But Jennings interrupted that fantasy with what he said next.

"One problem down. One to go."

"And what problem's that?" she asked.

"Well ... when you get right down to it, we don't really know if you can be trusted, do we?"

This was too fucking unbelievable.

"Wait ... what? *You* guys don't know who you can trust? Are you fucking for *real*?"

"Why is that so difficult to believe?" Jennings asked.

"Oh ... I don't know ... maybe because Arthur can make my roommate go into the men's bathroom with him and donate a couple of pints to the cause whenever he wants. Maybe *that's* why."

"Oh ... *that*," Jennings said, rolling his eyes.

"Yes ... *that*," Terry snorted definitively.

"That's something you'll have to bring up with Arthur," he said. "He's got weird rules, when it comes to that."

"How so?"

"The Voice—that's what *I* call it ... *he* calls it the Influence—the Voice is for food only, unless necessity dictates otherwise. Or, something like that. What it boils down to is, since he considers you a potential member of his cabal, he's not going to want to use that on you."

"That's a little stupid, don't you think?" Terry said, desperation bringing a certain trace of anger to her tone. She *needed* Arthur and Jennings to trust her. If things went poorly with the book, and they discovered that she had it all along, she needed them to at least know that she wasn't working for this other group of vampires.

As if on cue, Arthur chose that moment to slide in beside Jennings. "Good evening," he said, his eyes not quite meeting Terry's. "What are we talking about?"

Terry's bowels turned to water. She began to bury her fear to keep from showing it to them, remembering too late that fear was one of the few things she *didn't* have to keep from them. All the same, her words carried more fear and anger than she'd intended.

"We're talking about the fact that you have a magical way to tell whether or not I can be trusted, and the fact that you won't use it for some dumb reason."

Her attitude seemed to set Arthur at ease a bit, to release him from a small part of his shame. When he spoke this time, he was able to meet her eyes. "You don't understand," he said. "It's not a pleasant experience. I don't know for certain that we're all going to end up friends when this is over, but we may—and assuming complete control of someone isn't something one does to friends."

"No, *you* don't understand," Terry said. She scrambled for a lie that wasn't quite a lie ... some series of half-truths that would convince Arthur to do this thing, to get him to trust her completely. She needed that, and she didn't care about the rest.

"You're right," she began. "I don't know if we're all

going to end up friends when this thing is over, either. But I want to help, and I don't want you two watching me for a knife in the back the entire time. I *need* you to do this, Arthur. It's important to me."

Arthur stared at the surface of the table, again avoiding her eyes. "You don't know what you're asking," he said.

"Then show me."

Arthur glanced at Jennings, and seemed to find there some unspoken approval. When he finally spoke, it was with a great deal of reluctance and resignation.

"Are you working for Lyle?"

"No," Terry answered. She hadn't thought about her answer, she just heard it as she was saying it.

"Have you ever met Lyle, or anyone you suspect might be Lyle?"

"No," she answered again.

"Have you met with anyone who has mentioned the book to you, besides myself?"

"No."

Terry wanted this to stop. Arthur had been entirely right about this ... it was awful. She felt as though she was being raped with all her clothes on. What was more, it was dangerous. Her last answer had been true, strictly speaking, but if he'd worded that question just a little differently ...

"Did you have any knowledge of the book, before I ... " Arthur's voice abruptly trailed off, and his eyes assumed a far-off look.

"What is it?" Jennings asked.

Terry held her breath, waiting for the rest of the question that would fuck her.

"One of Lyle's fledglings."

"Where? In here?"

"No. Outside, I think. But close by."

Terry's eyes watered with the effort to stay silent.

"This may be our first real stroke of luck. Is she alone?"

"I believe so."

"Let's go," Jennings said, pulling Arthur out of the booth. "I can't spot her without you."

Mercifully, the two of them were gone by the time Terry spoke the word.

"Yes."

Fuck, Terry thought to herself. *Fuck* fuck FUCK. *That* had been really close. She hadn't liked that *a lot*. There was no way in hell she was going to do *that* voluntarily again. She wanted to go home and shower. She wanted what just happened to have *never* happened. And Arthur hadn't needed all that much convincing, had he? Apparently, he didn't mind as much as he claimed.

Terry wiped the tears from her eyes with a napkin.

When they returned, they had a girl with them. Arthur had been right about Lyle's women—she *was* beautiful. Marta had the same red dress she was wearing, and Marta didn't look like *that* in it. Terry recognized the look on the girl's face—the muscles were relaxed and impassive, the eyes were terrified. She looked like Terry had felt less than a minute ago.

Before they could sit, Terry slid out of the booth. Whatever they were going to do to this girl, she didn't want to watch. She couldn't watch, knowing that had been *her*, in that position. just now.

"Where are you going?" Jennings asked.

Terry didn't answer. She had neither the heart nor the stomach for it. She simply left.

Terry reached the door of her flat feeling no less violated than when she'd left Tito's. She took her keys from her purse, and was fumbling for them loudly when the door suddenly opened in front of her. Terry drew a sharp breath, so startled she dropped her keys.

"What is wrong?" Marta asked.

Jesus, Terry thought as she bent over and picked up her keys. She'd couldn't tell Marta she'd thought she was Lyle or one of his girls. "You just startled me," she said, passing Marta in the doorway. She had her bathrobe and fuzzy slippers on—didn't look like she was going out tonight. Terry had pretty much managed to avoid her since this whole vampire-thing started.

"Why are you angry?" Marta asked. "What happened?"

"Oh, just some asshole at Tito's," Terry replied, flopping down on the couch.

"You went to Tito's?" Marta asked, sitting beside her, facing her. Ooops. "What about your allergy? The Healing Woman ..."

"The Healing Woman worries too much," Terry said. Actually, it occurred to her that the Healing Woman had been right.

"You have been out very much," she said. "I thought about waking you before I left today, but I did not because you seem very tired. If you're going to pass your classes, you should no go out so much, I think."

"I know," Terry admitted. "I had two term papers due today I haven't even started, and I slept until four this afternoon."

"Mmm," Marta said, nodding disapprovingly. "That is very bad." She pointed her chin at the photo album on the table. "You've been looking at pictures, no? You are still thinking about Doug?"

"Shit," Terry said. "I still haven't sent him that letter."

"Why no?"

"I keep forgetting to buy stamps," she said. "I'm just too busy."

"*I* have stamps," Marta said excitedly, leaping from the couch.

"Marta, wait," Terry said, stopping her with her hand in her purse. "I'm not going to send the letter."

"Why no?"

"Because ... it's over. It's *been* over. It was stupid of me to write the letter and it would be even more stupid to send it. We already know it doesn't work. We should just leave it at that. Besides, the Healing Woman told me to forget the *cantante*."

"If you want to send the letter, you should send the letter," Marta argued. "The Healing Woman doesn't know everything."

Terry stared at the album, thinking about the pictures that had been inside. "I don't want to send the letter. He never loved me, Marta."

Terry took the mangled envelope from her purse, about to tear it in half. "Wait!" Marta cried, stopping Terry. "You are very tired, I think," she continued. "Here, take the stamps and put them in your purse. Tonight, you sleep. Tomorrow when you wake up, you see things better. If you still want to rip up the letter tomorrow, rip up the letter. But wait until tomorrow. You still feel something, or else you would no have written the letter."

She considered this, the letter poised between her fingers. She would still feel the same way tomorrow—but there was no harm in putting off trashing it until then. Terry took the stamps from Marta, folding them inside the letter before putting it back in her purse. "Why are you so up on love tonight?" Terry asked.

Marta smiled as she sat back down. "I don't know," she answered, smiling coyly.

"You met someone, didn't you?" Terry said. "Oh, you bitch, I hate you. What's his name?"

"Roberto," Marta began. "I met him at Pirri's on Friday ..."

This felt good. *This* was real. It seemed like an eternity since she'd lost herself in the mundanity of girl talk. For an hour and a half, there was no Lyle, no Arthur, no Jennings—and no book. There was just Marta, in love for the third time in her life and excited and bubbling and optimistic about everything. It wasn't sleep Terry needed to recharge her tired mind, it was this—a return to her normal life.

The vampires would still be there tomorrow at sunset.

Help me.

Terry woke with a start, sitting up in her bed. Arthur. She fumbled for the light and turned it on, expecting to find him in the room with her, but she was alone. Her alarm clock politely informed her that it was 7:13 AM.

Someone ... anyone ... please help me.

Terry checked under the bed. No, Arthur was definitely not here. It was an odd sensation. After last night, she knew Arthur by two voices: the one she heard, and the one that clawed directly into her mind. When he combined them, he could make people do things—what had Jennings called it? the Influence? But this was the unheard voice without the spoken one. If not for the incident last night, she might have mistaken it for one of her own idle thoughts.

The voice carried images with it, images that came to her like the aftertaste of a cheap beer. A cocktail party? No, he was lying wounded in the Plaza de Mayor.

Terry leapt from her bed and snapped the blind from the window, finding the sky was already bright blue.

"Shit," Terry said aloud, bolting away from the window, scrambling for a pair of jeans. She hastily pulled them on, tucking in the T-shirt she'd worn to bed, and threw on a pair of sneakers.

7:20 AM, the clock told her. THE SUN'S BEEN UP FOR OVER AN HOUR. YOU'LL NEVER MAKE IT.

Help me ... please.

She was about to run out of the room when she stopped, grabbing the blanket from her bed on an impulse.

'Every cell of a vampire stores an incredible amount of energy, and those cells are highly reactive,' Dr. Del Rio had said. 'Exposure to sunlight releases this energy all at once. I've seen it happen. When it's over, nothing remains—and it's over quickly, believe me.'

Terry had no intention of seeing that happen. She ran out of the door, grabbing the car keys from the hook. "Hope you didn't have to drive anywhere today, Marti," she mumbled to herself as she closed the door behind her.

The sun was already peeking into the plaza by the time she got there. The Plaza de Mayor was not a small place. Running at full speed, it could take her as long as ten minutes to find him—and ten minutes from now, the sun would be that much higher in the sky.

Please ... anyone ... help me.

She backed the car into the shadow of the western wall, until her bumper hit the barrier of steel poles that prevented her from driving right into the plaza. Terry jerked up the parking brake, popped the trunk, slung her purse over her shoulder, grabbed the blanket, and bolted from the car.

It took her twenty seconds to get through the alley into the plaza. Within, things were definitely not business as usual. Bodies were being carried out of the plaza two and three at a time, in some cases, by girls who didn't look strong enough to lift a typewriter. The biggest, buffest bitch Terry had ever seen was running around the section of the courtyard the sun already touched, picking up empty clothes and putting them into a huge garbage bag. The entire plaza smelled faintly like ... burned ... something.

I'm dying ... help me.

Arthur was lying near the center of the courtyard, at

the edge of the wall's shadow. A small group of vampires stood ten feet away, safe within the shade, waiting for the sun to take him. Quickly, Terry stepped into the sun, walking deliberately towards Arthur's prone figure. It didn't take long for the group to notice her. One of them shouted, "Connie!" and the half-woman/half-ape with the garbage bag stopped what she was doing and ran over to Arthur.

"This doesn't concern you. Turn around and walk away," a female vampire said to Terry from the shade. She was using the Influence, but compared to the driving force of Arthur's voice, it was a gentle gust of wind.

"Fuck off," Terry replied, her hand in her purse. "I'm walking out of here, and I'm taking him with me." She did a quick count—seven vampires and one mortal. One big mortal.

"Connie, bring her into the shade where we can talk," the same one said.

"Gladly," Connie replied in a voice that could have been a man's as she walked towards the other mortal. Terry's hand came out of her purse holding a can of mace, and a fog of chemicals hissed from the canister. She felt the can cool in her hand as Connie began screaming, rubbing her eyes and face furiously. She was bent over as Terry walked up to her and hit her full in the face with everything she had. After Connie was down, Terry gave her a few good kicks in the ribs, just because she could.

"You're dead," the leader of the group said. "You can't leave the plaza without coming into the shadow."

"You're right," Terry said, her hand returning to her purse. "I guess I'll have to kill you all."

She fumbled about for a minute, unable to find what she was looking for. Seven vampires stood waiting confidently. Long moments passed, and Terry noticed that the edge of the shadow was even closer to Arthur. "I am seriously going to have to clean out this purse," she mumbled.

"What have you got?" the vampire asked. "A little gun? Maybe a .22?"

"You'll see," Terry said, still searching. "And boy, will you be sorry."

Please help me ... please.

"I'm right here, Arthur," Terry whispered, hoping he could hear her.

"It's not a cross, is it? Or maybe some garlic—a little something to sprinkle into your blood for flavor."

Marta picked a hell of a time to go rifling through my purse without asking, Terry thought. "Oh," she said aloud. "Here it is."

She took the mirror out of her purse, reflecting the sunlight into the face of the leader first. She was able to sweep the reflection across three of them before the others turned and ran. They didn't get far.

Dr. Del Rio's description of what happened to vampires touched by the sun had been accurate. The reaction wasn't at all slow, like she'd seen in movies. Once the light touched their skin, a glow like the cherry of a cigarette quickly spread through their bodies with a dry, crackling sound. Terry could feel the heat coming off of them from where she stood, but the cellular reaction happened so quickly, their clothing was hardly singed.

The other vampires were already clear of the courtyard, and she was alone with the Arthur's body. It was no mystery why he wasn't moving—she could plainly see a huge gash in the side of his head. There was no blood, and if she looked real close, she could probably see his brain. Terry didn't care to look that close.

Please help me.

"I'm here, Arthur," Terry said, as she carefully wrapped the blanket around him. She noticed the sun on her hands as she worked—another half an inch, and Arthur would have burned just like the others. His hands and his head were the important part—with luck, his clothes would protect him somewhat. With luck.

She threw his arm over her shoulder and lifted him from the stone pavement. "All right," she said. It was a good thing he wasn't a big guy. "Let's go, Arty. You don't mind if I call you Arty, do you?"

Help me ... please help me.

"I didn't think so."

I'm dying ... please ...

"I *am* helping you, Dumbass," Terry managed. "Please stop screaming into my brain." Terry rambled on as she walked, partly because she thought he might be able to hear her through his delirium, and partly because she'd just killed seven vampires and her mind was moving a mile a minute. "Jesus, Arty. What do you weigh, about one-sixty? You really shouldn't snack between meals. I hope I'm not scuffing up your shoes. Maybe if you'd move your legs a little, you know, you might not be such dead weight. Get it? I said dead weight. You're dead, and I called you 'dead weight.' That's funny."

It hurts ... the fire hurts.

Terry noticed with some alarm that smoke was seeping from beneath the blanket, and they weren't even halfway to the alcove at the edge of the plaza.

"Oh shit," Terry mumbled. Impossibly, she picked up speed. "Don't do this, Arty. Arty! I mind if you smoke! This is a nonsmoking section!"

Halfway there, and the smoke was pouring off of Arthur.

I'm burning! Please help me! I'm burning!

"I can't go any faster, Arthur! Hold on ... we're close to the shade now!"

I'm burning! I'M BURNING!

"I know, Baby," Terry managed. She wished she had some water, but she knew it wouldn't stop the chemical reaction taking place beneath the blanket.

IT ... HURTS! I ... AM ... BURNING! SOMEBODY ... HELP ... ME!

Suddenly, the weight was less. Terry thought for a moment Arthur was supporting some of his own weight, but when she looked, a complete stranger had taken Arthur's other arm, and was helping her carry him to the shade. She could barely see him for the smoke that came from Arthur, but he was there.

There were no longer words to Arthur's mental scream—it had become an anguished, thoughtless, agonized wail. There was a wetness on Terry's upper lip, and she realized her nose was bleeding.

Twenty more feet to the shade. Fifteen. Terry's ears began to bleed as well—and she realized what was happening. Arthur's cries were causing her to hemorrhage. She could only hope the tears in her eyes weren't blood as well. Ten feet. She wondered if that happened when the brain hemorrhaged—if the eyes bled. Six feet.

The three of them reached the shade. The urgency of Arthur's cries abated, but the cries themselves did not. "Don't stop," Terry ordered the stranger in Spanish. "We have to get him to my car." The two of them carried Arthur the length of the alcove to Marta's car, and loaded him into the tiny trunk. It took just a second for Terry's shaking hands to get the rest of the blanket in, before she slammed the trunk shut.

Terry turned and sat on the back of the car, wiping the

blood from her lip with the back of her hand. She got a good look at her benefactor for the first time—an older man dressed in rags, probably a Gypsy. He was staring at the trunk with vacuous eyes as blood dripped from his nose, and Terry realized he hadn't helped her out of the kindness of his heart. He'd helped her because Arthur had Influenced him, without even opening his mouth. She thanked him in Spanish, but he turned in a daze and walked away without hearing.

"Fuck, that was close," Terry mumbled, watching the Gypsy walk away. Ahead of him, from deeper in the alley, a red-faced, red-eyed, plenty-pissed-off-looking Ape-woman came running towards her. Terry's right hand went back into her purse, but instead of slowing Ape-woman down, it sped her up. The distance between them was rapidly closing, and the nearer she got, the more pissed-off she looked.

Terry's right hand came out of her purse, and her left hand went in. Five feet separated them when Terry yanked her left hand out of the purse, holding it out in front of her, and made a sharp hissing sound with her teeth. Ape-woman stopped in her tracks and turned away, throwing her arms up over her head. Terry quickly backed towards the driver's side door.

The other lowered her arms, slowly realizing that she hadn't been maced. Terry jangled her keys at the massive woman. "Fooled ya," she taunted, and Ape-woman dropped her arms and charged.

Terry's right hand came up, already holding the can of mace, and Ape-woman was completely unprepared for the face-full of noxious mist. "Fooled ya twice," Terry said as she jumped into the car, jammed the keys into the ignition, started it up, and drove off as fast as the whining little engine would allow.

Help me, Arthur said into her mind. The cry had less urgency than before—and less strength. Arthur was pretty bad-off, but he was alive, and the sun wasn't getting to him in the trunk.

"You're going to be all right, Arthur," Terry whispered. "You're going to be all right."

Please help me.

Five hours.

Someone please help me.

Terry had been driving for five hours, and Arthur would not shut-the-fuck up.

Anyone ... please ... help me.

She hadn't known where to go. Where could she go? She'd chosen northeast, towards France, simply because any other direction would had trapped her against a body of water.

Help me ... please.

The car hadn't been running right for the last hour and a half, but Terry had kept on driving. She'd decided to drive until at least five o'clock, and then stop at the first town she found with a garage. When the temperature light had begun coming on intermittently, she'd changed her decision to four o'clock. Then three-thirty.

Please help me ... someone.

Now, with the temperature light staring her down unblinkingly, her plan was to stop at the first garage she could find ...

... anyone ... please ...

... which had seemed like a good plan, until steam began billowing from beneath the car's hood. She didn't know much about cars, but knew the possibilities would be along the lines of 'seized engine' or 'blown engine.'

Help me.

Terry pulled the car off to the side of the road. One o'clock. She could leave the car on the road, and hope someone passing by would see her and stop to help, or she could try to pull the car off the road to hide it. Her lips tightened grimly as she realized there would be no hiding the car. It simply wasn't an option. The trees were too sparse, there were no ditches, no conveniently placed billboards, nothing.

Someone.

Once the car was stopped, she got out and opened the hood for no particular reason. A fog of steam poured out of the engine like smoke had poured off of Arthur. At least the car wasn't repeating 'Help me,' into her brain every ten seconds.

Help me.

Yeah, like that. There was no traffic on the road, no farmhouses or houses of any kind in sight. Except for the cadaver in the trunk, she was alone.

Please ... anyone.

Terry wondered if Arthur would have any money on him. When you dressed like he did, you kind of had to carry money around, didn't you? Unless he was a tightwad who let the magic voice cover his expenses and leave his tips. Not that it mattered right now—she wouldn't be able to open the trunk until sundown.

Someone please help me.

She'd passed through the last town about forty-five minutes ago. She could walk back there, but she probably wouldn't even be there by dark. Or she could walk on ahead. There could be a town a half-hour away, or dark could come and she could be stranded out in the middle of nowhere. Ooo! What an attractive option!

Please help me.

"PLEASE SHUT-THE-FUCK UP!" Terry screamed at the lid of the trunk. "SOME OF US ARE TRYING TO THINK OUT HERE!" She punched the lid once for emphasis, and resumed her pacing in the road.

No cars. No towns. No people.

No thoughts from the trunk.

Terry walked back to trunk, waiting for something. She stared at her watch, timing the silence. Thirty seconds, then a minute. Still nothing.

"Arthur?" Terry said warily. "Arthur, are you okay?"

Still, nothing. At least his incessant pleading had let her know that he was still alive—so to speak. The silence made her nervous. Very, very nervous.

Someone please help me.

Terry breathed a sigh of relief, resting her hand on the trunk as though she could touch him. "Jesus, Arthur," she whispered. "Don't do that to me."

Help me ... please.

Terry registered movement out of the corner of her eye. She turned and stared across the road, into the sparse wood. High on the gentle slope, perhaps sixty feet away, a dog stared at her through the trees. From this distance, it could have been a German Shepherd.

The idea that the animal might be dangerous never occurred to her. She was from suburbia, where a dog was something to pet and feed and sometimes cleanup after—not something to be afraid of.

"C'mere, boy," Terry shouted to it, patting her leg.

The dog didn't move.

Please help me.

The dog moved towards the car cautiously, stopping about twenty feet away. She'd never seen a dog move that way before. It wasn't the trot she was used to seeing, but more of a lope, its massive head bobbing up and down with each step. Its coat was golden, with a very slight darkening of the fur on its head, its face, its back. It had a beautiful ruff around its neck that Terry wanted to grab with both hands like the cheeks of chubby child.

She went down to one knee. "C'mere," she repeated. It didn't respond at all, but just stared at her, and she noticed for the first time that the dog had yellow eyes.

Help me ... someone.

The dog took a few loping steps closer, seeming to stare right at the trunk. "Do you hear Arthur, boy?" she asked. "Hmm? Do you hear Arthur? He's okay." She patted the lid of the trunk. "C'mon ... it's all right, I'm not gonna hurt you."

She stood as the animal walked right up to the trunk—close enough for her to touch, but it was too nervous and she didn't dare. From a distance, she hadn't been able to tell just how big this dog was. Its shoulder was as high as her waist, and it wasn't lean like a Great Dane or husky like a Saint Bernard. This dog was all muscle. This dog would eat a Pit Bull for lunch. She had visions of it grabbing the bumper in its massive jaws and dragging the car off the road. This dog could put a serious hurting on someone.

It sniffed the trunk. She backed away from it a little—not out of fear, but out of respect for the dog's trepidation. Its tail was lowered and she couldn't see its sex, but she guessed from its size that this was a boy-dog.

"Hey, boy," she said reassuringly, returning to one knee. Terry made a kissing sound with her lips, which got his attention. She held her hand out for him to sniff, and gently repeated, "Hey, boy." Hesitantly, the dog approached her, smelling the tips of her outstretched fingers while it stared into her eyes. Terry found herself staring back, fascinated by his yellow eyes—she'd never seen a dog with yellow eyes before. There were things going on behind those eyes.

He moved a little closer, and a little closer, until he was sniffing her face. Terry touched his fur gently, finding it coarse under her fingers. When he licked her face, she knew she'd passed his doggie-test.

Terry woke shivering in the driver's seat of the car. She checked her watch—it was after six—and she checked the sky. They had to have an hour of daylight left, but it was getting cold. She'd driven into the mountains, and the altitude had cooled the dry air considerably.

She opened the door and got out of the car, stretching. The dog was lying down behind the car, still staring at the trunk.

"Hey, boy," she said, talking more to herself than to the dog. "You hungry? I hope not, because there's nothing here for you to eat but me." She walked back to him, and sat down on the shoulder of the road beside him. "I can't believe we've been here for five hours and not a single car has passed. Or maybe they did, and they saw you and kept driving." She patted his head, and he regarded her solemnly before returning his attention to the trunk.

Terry abruptly realized she was no longer hearing Arthur's voice in her head. She hoped that wasn't a bad sign. She stood and paced a bit, trying to get warm, "I wish I could build a fire," she said aloud, before laughing at herself. "I'm in the middle of nowhere, freezing to death, and I'm not going to start a fire because I'm afraid I'll get into trouble. Yeah."

She set into the sparse trees, looking for wood.

Terry sat by her fire, watching the sun set. If Arthur converted her, this was something else she wouldn't be able to see. Of course if she opened the trunk and Arthur was dead—really dead—and Lyle and his little buddies came and found them, then she probably wouldn't see another sunset anyway.

The dog was growing anxious as well. He paced to the trunk, stared at it, paced over to her, stared at her. He was waiting for something to happen. It made Terry think of a mother hen, waiting for an egg to hatch. The moment the sun dipped below the horizon, she was on her feet with the keys in her hand, heading for the back of the car.

She put the key into the lock and looked down at the dog, who looked back up at her expectantly. "Don't be dead, Arthur," she whispered to herself, before turning the key and opening the lid.

In the light of the trunk lamp, Arthur looked like a prop from a bad vampire movie. The only part of him she could readily see was his head, but that was enough. His skin was blackened and burned, and drawn tight across his skull. His lips were pulled away from his teeth, showing his canines, and his eyelids were either burned away or simply incapable of closing. Terry's empty stomach churned threateningly, but she couldn't take her eyes from the ghastly scene in the trunk.

Arthur stirred, trying to move in the tiny area of the trunk. *This is what it means to be immortal*, Terry thought to herself. *To be hurt this badly, and still be able to feel everything.* The dog nudged her hand, bringing her back to the present.

Arthur wasn't having any luck getting himself out of the trunk. "Here," she said, trying to help him, unsure of where to grab him for fear that his flesh would fall apart in her hands. To her surprise, his arms felt firm under her grasp.

"Come on," she said, extracting him from the trunk. The blanket she'd used to cover him fell to the road, and she let it go. "Can you stand?" He didn't even seem to remember how, let alone seem able. Not that it mattered—he probably didn't weigh a hundred pounds at this point.

Terry carried him over to the fire, more for herself than for him.

Not too close.

"I won't," she replied, only then realizing that her ears hadn't heard the words. No big deal—she'd been hearing him in her mind the entire day, and his lips were in no condition to form words. "There," she grunted as she lowered him to the ground.

Where are we? What happened?

"I was hoping you could tell *me* that," Terry replied. "I woke up this morning with your voice in my head. You were saying, 'Help me, help me,' over and over again. I found you in the middle of the plaza about to become a crispy-critter, so I wrapped a blanket around you, put you in my car, and drove until it stopped working."

Do I know you?

For a brief moment, Terry was speechless. "You mean,

you don't know who I am?" She grasped her head with both hands, trying to think. "I can't believe what a day I'm having," she mumbled.

I've had better days myself.

She took another look at him—no doubt he had. "My name is Terry," she said. "We met a few nights ago."

And I told you I was a vampire?

"I'd already sort of guessed it by the time you told me."

The dog came out of the darkness and seated himself next to Terry, staring at Arthur the entire time.

Your dog?

"Actually, no," she said. "I think it's *your* dog."

I don't have a dog.

"I think you called it the same way you called me," she said. "It just sort of ambled up after the car broke down. He seems friendly enough."

I can't call animals. Arthur moved, pushing himself up onto his elbows.

"Apparently, you can," Terry said. "He's not acting like a stray. He's been staring at the trunk all day. Don't worry, he's not going to hurt you."

How do you know? Arthur asked.

"Because I know dogs," she answered. "Look at him. He isn't threatened by us, just curious. I can tell he's smart, too. He doesn't understand what's going on, but he's intelligent enough to know he doesn't know what's going on."

That's not a dog.

"Oh? What is it then? A bird?"

It's a wolf.

Terry suddenly felt very stupid. Of course it was a wolf. "Well then, it's a smart *wolf*," she said. "If you don't like it here, tell it to go away."

I told you, I can't. After seven hundred years, I think I would know my own limitations. Some vampires can speak to animals. I'm not one of them.

Terry sighed, forgetting about the wolf for a moment. "Are you going to be able to fight when they get here?" she asked.

When who gets here? he asked.

"Lyle and his little friends," Terry said. "Do you remember Lyle?"

Vaguely, he answered. How would they know where to find us?

"You've been moaning 'Help me' into my mind for ten hours. If this wolf—whom you supposedly can't communicate with—could hear you, I'm sure they could. Can you fight?"

A slight smile cracked his burned lips. I can't even speak. I need blood.

The wolf suddenly turned and bolted into the darkness.

"Hey!" Terry cried out after it. "He didn't mean you! HEY!" She looked down at Arthur, "Tell him to come back!"

I never told him to leave. Maybe he had important wolf-business to attend to.

"Dammit. I was beginning to like having him around." Terry threw herself back to the ground. "What are we going to do?"

You're going to walk until you reach a town, and get yourself back to Salamanca. Then, you can either find Jennings, have him convert you, and help him find the book, or you can return to your mortal life and forget any of this ever happened.

"What a shitty idea! How did you get to be seven hundred years old with such shitty ideas?"

I must bury myself, stay underground until I've healed ...

"You know, when you lie right into my mind, it sounds

like every other word you say is 'lie.' You won't heal
without blood. Don't ask me how I know that—I think you
spoke it into my mind on some other level."

So what is your plan? You want to stay and die with me?

"Can't you take some blood from me?" she asked, not
particularly liking the idea, but liking the other options
even less.

You don't have enough blood in your body to heal my wounds.
Besides, whether you stay or go, you're going to need your strength.

"I'm staying," she said decidedly.

Arthur met her eyes. If I had the strength to Influence you
to go, I would.

"You said you wouldn't do that," Terry said.

Did I? Then I lied. I'm a liar. I'm a liar and I'm not worth dying
for.

"I don't intend to die for you," she replied. "I intend to
keep both of us from dying."

How?

"I don't know yet."

How long do we have? How far did we get before the car broke
down?

"About five hours."

Then we might have three before they get here. Jesus, I can't
even think clearly. I need blood.

At that moment, the wolf reappeared at the far side of
the fire, a bleating sheep struggling in its jaws.

"Oh my God—I can't watch this." She stood and
walked away, trying not to hear the pathetic sounds of the
animal. Terry was thankful they didn't last very long.

She stood in the silence and the darkness, realizing
what the wolf had just done. Arthur had said he needed
blood, and the wolf had run off to find him some. Terry
didn't care what Arthur said; he could talk to animals. Or
at least, he could talk to this one.

Arthur stopped speaking into her mind after that, and what she did pick up didn't make any sense. She had unnerving flashes from him—not speech, but tiny segments of memories encompassing every sense.

She saw Jennings in a stolen Nazi uniform. They were standing in a wooden building, like a barracks, in the midst of a horde of baldheaded, skinny men. Arthur had come to a decision—what the decision was wasn't clear—and he spoke the words, 'Go ahead.'

She saw iron bars, and felt agonizing, unending Hunger.

She blearily saw a dark, stone room; felt a throbbing pain in the back of Arthur's head; looked up to see a sword standing perpendicular to a cot. Charlotte!

She walked through a village at night, smelling death and decay, realizing that every man, woman, and child here was dead, and knowing it was the Black Death.

Terry thought she would go mad. Arthur had seen so many ugly, ugly things in his seven hundred years, and now he was showing them to her. She sat across the fire from him, tears running down her face, rocking herself. She wanted her father to come and make this all better.

She saw Marta in the men's bathroom, allowing Arthur to feed on her. She felt the throbbing in his gums, and the intense pleasure it gave him to feed. And she felt the Shame.

Back to the stone room. The sword. The woman.

Iron bars, the key lying across the room where he'd thrown it. The Hunger.

She saw a cocktail party. 'Met her? She just fucked me in the plaza.'

Arthur's thoughts cleared for an instant, but he was still in her head. She saw, with senses that were beyond mortal, that Lyle was coming. He was still hours away, but he was coming. She also saw in his thoughts that although he wasn't enjoying the nightmare any more than she was, it brought him a sense of relief. All of his memories weren't gone, and the damaged tissue of his brain was healing. Then, he slipped back into the delirium.

She saw herself through Arthur's eyes the first time she approached him, heard Jennings say, 'My, she looks good enough to eat,' and understood what he was asking.

She felt the wood of the ax handle in Arthur's hands as he brought the blade down on the neck of his first fiancé, a neck he'd kissed many times. She experienced the anguish of watching the woman he loved die a second—and final—time, and the anguish of knowing he'd done it by his own hand.

Decades and decades of self-imposed Hunger. The Lion must triumph over the Dragon ...

The wolf howled at the sky. She was thankful for it, because it brought her out of Arthur's memories, even if just for a moment. But it was the saddest, most baleful sound she'd ever heard in her life. Was the wolf was catching Arthur's thoughts, too? Terry wanted to grab the animal and hold him like a child, to somehow make the entire experience more bearable for the both of them. But the wolf would not understand that. He understood the howling. That was how he expressed his grief. They could share the howling, and the wolf would understand.

Terry threw back her head and howled. She didn't attempt to sound like a wolf—that would have made it a trite gesture. She simply released the grief of the images she was seeing, and the grief of her own memories. Moving her things out of Doug's apartment. Coming down the stairs with a gun in her hand, and finding her mother crying in the living room with her father's best friend. Leaning into the casket on her tiptoes and kissing her father's forehead, feeling the cold skin beneath her lips and knowing it wasn't her father in the box, but his lifeless body. Her mother telling her her father was in Heaven now. It wasn't difficult to release the power of these images ...

Charlotte!

... to vocalize them into the night sky in a grieving wail she could share with the wolf.

In the distance, other wolves shared their own grief. Lost mates, dead pups, man, hunger—Terry could hear all of those things. For the first time, Terry understood why wolves howled. She shared her pain with them until she had no voice left, and then she lay near the warmth of the fire and listened until the night fell silent.

A small warning bark from the wolf woke Terry. They were coming.

She got to her feet. The fire had died down while she'd slept, and it was freezing out here. She threw some more wood on the fire and waited for it to catch.

The wolf was staring intently into the darkness, growling slightly. They were close. She spared Arthur a glance, but he was staring into the stars, and the random thoughts she was receiving—although not as nightmarish as they'd been earlier—told her he would be no help.

"Good evening," a voice said from beyond the edge of the fire's light. The accent was slight, but this guy was another Brit. "Anne Rice, I presume."

Well, that was a good sign. At least they didn't have her real name yet.

"Connie was very upset with you," the voice continued.

Connie ... Connie ... Ape-woman?

"She wanted to come herself. I was finally able to get her to stay by telling her your death would be a long, painful ordeal. *That* seemed to appease her."

The voice paused, as though waiting for some response. Terry looked down at the wolf. He was sniffing the air, staring into the darkness. Terry was glad the wolf was on her side.

"Arthur's looked better," she heard from the darkness. The wolf gave a low, ominous growl. "Better tell your dog to heel."

"He's a wolf, and he's not trained," Terry replied, finding her voice. She'd been terrified for her life sixty seconds ago, but she was forgetting that and getting irritated. Something about this guy's voice just rubbed her the wrong way. "If he was trained, he'd already be tearing you a new asshole."

"An untrained wolf—how very Walt Disney," the voice said. "Where is the book, Ms. Rice?"

"Book, Lyle?" Terry asked. "What book?"

"There appears to be a misunderstanding. By, 'Where is the book?' I actually meant 'Give me the book or I will kill you.'"

"Then there does appear to be a misunderstanding," she replied. "By 'What book?' I actually meant, 'Fuck right off.'"

"Americans are so vulgar. Are you familiar with Mr. Jennings?"

Terry didn't respond.

"We have him, you know," Lyle said. "He's proving to be quite a lot of fun—much less troublesome after we removed his arms and legs. We could do that to you, you know. Of course, we'd have to Make you first. But this doesn't have to be quite that difficult. I'm offering a simple trade: Jennings for the book. Can you hear me, Arthur?"

Arthur mumbled something unintelligible into their minds.

"Hmm. Interesting. You aren't going to fool me by playing 'possum, Arthur. Do you know that?"

"Let's set him on fire," a female voice said from behind Terry. "That should get his attention."

"I have no doubt that it would—but I have something

else in mind. Arthur may be incapacitated, but I'm certain he's listening to every word, and I'm certain he heard my offer. Jennings for the book, Arthur. Kill the girl and her dog—I did promise Connie after all."

"If you kill me, you'll never find the book," Terry said.

"Oh?" Lyle replied. "And why is that?"

"Because only I know where it is, Lyle."

"Hmm. No, I'm afraid I find that too difficult to believe. Arthur would never trust you with the book."

"Arthur doesn't know I *have* it, dumb ass," Terry said.

"And how is that possible?" Lyle stepped into the light, and Terry saw that Arthur hadn't been lying when he'd said Lyle was beautiful. He reminded her of that guy from 'Wham,' especially his eyes. "I know of Arthur's Gift. If you had the book, he'd know it."

"He said because he considered me a potential member of his cabal, I deserved more respect than that," Terry said.

"Your lie is becoming more and more believable, Ms. Rice." God, he was *gorgeous*. "If that's the case, why shouldn't I allow Victoria to set him on fire? What do I need him for? Or Jennings, for that matter?"

"Because if you don't let Arthur live, *and* free Mr. Jennings, I'll set the fucking thing on fire and watch it burn during the day when you can't touch me." Lyle was a pretty man, but he was *really* irritating.

"You've proved your point—your point being that I can't let you get back to the book before we do. I'm betting we'll find it just fine without your help." To the others with him, he ordered, "Kill Arthur. Anne Rice is mine."

Before Terry could speak, the wolf leapt at Lyle, grabbing a thigh in his massive jaws. The vampire's look of disdain told Terry he'd expected an attack, and he grabbed the wolf's neck with both hands, as though he believed his unnatural strength would make the wild animal an easy kill. Not only did the creature not die, it crushed Lyle's leg as though it were cardboard, and Lyle's expression changed to surprise, and then terror. The creature shook his powerful neck back and forth, flailing Lyle from his feet like a man-sized chew toy and tossing him about. He screamed like a girl until the wolf released his leg, tossing him beyond the fire's light where Terry could no longer see him.

Another vampire charged the wolf, and the creature leapt at him, hitting him in the chest and pushing them both into the darkness. Terry couldn't see what was happening out there, but she could hear it well enough to know what was going on. The fierce snarling of the wolf, the confused screams and cries and curses of the vampires—they didn't know why they couldn't stop this animal, but they couldn't.

Then it was over. No more sounds came from the darkness. Terry waited for something, but nothing came. For long moments, she didn't know if wolf or vampire had survived. When the sound of rustling reached her ears, she moved to Arthur, who still showed no signs of cognizance.

"Arthur," Terry whispered. "If you can wake up, now would be a good time."

I understand the stars.

"Beautiful," Terry mumbled under her breath. "Thanks for your help, Arty."

The wolf backed into the light, and Terry knew before she saw that he was dragging something. It was one of the vampires. She'd probably been a beautiful girl before the wolf got to her, but it was difficult to tell at this point. Her skull was crushed, and the skin of her face was torn and bunched to one side so that one eye was completely closed, and the other stared sightlessly skyward from its nest of exposed bone and bloody muscle. Her arms were mangled, her legs were mangled. Blood collected at the sight of the many wounds, but it didn't pour out of her like it would have if she were a mortal. Terry knew inside that inanimate body, a parasitic virus struggled to heal the abundant damaged tissue, overwhelmed by the enormity of the task, and lacking the blood for energy.

The wolf dragged the body over to Arthur, right up to him, and stared expectantly at Terry. She knew what had to be done, knew the part expected of her. Physically, it was rather simple. Mentally, well, it would have been difficult once. A few days ago, before she'd believed any of this was real, she couldn't have done it. But after all she'd seen and all she'd heard and all she'd felt through Arthur's nightmares—through Arthur's *memories*—it wasn't so hard.

Terry reached over and took the vampire's hand, lifted the arm, and placed an exposed wound on her wrist over Arthur's mouth.

He didn't respond at first. His jaw began to move as the taste reached his tongue, and Terry actually watched as Arthur's canines grew from his gums. He bit down, and he began to suck and swallow like a nursing puppy. His hands came up, and he forced the girl's wrist deeper into his mouth as the parasite in him became aware of the life-giving blood. Terry watched almost impassively—just another horrible scene in a night and a day of horrible scenes. No big deal.

The background noise of images which Terry had grown accustomed to ignoring ceased, and Terry knew Arthur's mind was clearing. His face had even healed somewhat, and he was even able to blink as his eyes found Terry.

"I think there are more where that came from," she said. She felt pretty steady—or maybe she was just numb—but her voice was quivering just the same.

"Bring me the next one," Arthur said.

The next one. Sure. Why not?

The sun was up. Time for all good vampires to bury themselves in the dirt. At least, that's what Arthur had done.

Right now, four lives were ending. Four vampires whose hearts Arthur had staked were burning in the sun.

Terry was good at playing roles. Oh, yes. It had never occurred to her that the role she might be playing would be herself. She cast herself as tough, street smart Terry, when all she really wanted to do was curl up in a ball and suck her thumb.

Whatever. I'm hungry. I'm hitching to someplace I can get something to eat. You have any money on you? she'd said to Arthur. Just as though nothing had happened, as though she was still Tough Terry. But Tough Terry had gone away. Tough Terry didn't live here anymore. She'd moved and she'd left no forwarding address.

Terry and the wolf reached the end of the back road. She didn't remember why she'd left the main road, why she'd made the right turn that had left her in the middle of nowhere. But here was the main road, so she must have left it at some point. Maybe her heading had been too 'north,' and she'd wanted to jog east a little bit. Who could tell? Tough Terry would have known.

"I'm going to have to name you, you know," Terry said

to the wolf as they walked along the main road. A car passed them, and Terry stuck out her thumb, hoping they knew what the thumb meant on this side of the Atlantic. Apparently, *that* driver didn't.

"I know you've gotten through your whole life without a name, but I'm going to have to name you. It's a sign of respect. It gives you an identity. Believe me, it's a great honor to be named."

But what? One name came to mind, but it was from a play she'd done, and to name an animal after a character in a play seemed a little cheesy. Well, perhaps not so cheesy—the play had been *Othello*. Nothing Shakespeare did was trivial. He'd been dead for three centuries, and they were still quoting him. 'Never a borrower nor a lender be.' 'What's in a name?' *'Et tu, Bruté?'* He was The Bard. A name from Shakespeare wouldn't be cheesy.

Paul Jervis had played the part. She hadn't slept with him, but she'd wanted to. He was one of the best actors she'd ever seen, and most definitely the best she'd ever worked with. He had pale-blue eyes you could see from the back of the theater. It was part of what made him so intense on stage, part of what made him so fantastic to work with, part of what made every woman in the audience want him.

"Iago," Terry said aloud. "That's your name. Iago. Iago?"

The wolf looked up at her as he loped at her side.

"That's right," she said. "That's your name. Iago."

A farmer driving a pickup truck finally recognized the international sign-language for 'Hey, I need a ride,' and stopped for them.

He was an older man, perhaps in his sixties. He laboriously rolled down the passenger-side window, and shouted out in Spanish, "Your dog can get in the back."

Terry had thought about this ever since she'd named him. The name itself was a great honor, but to bring him into the city—that wouldn't honor him. Iago had performed a great deed. He'd saved the lives of both herself and Arthur. What sort of thanks was it to drag him out of the wilderness that was his home, into an alien environment? It was no thanks at all.

"The dog isn't coming with us," Terry replied to the man, as she squatted to talk to Iago. She scrunched the ruff of his neck as she talked, and he stared into her eyes as though he understood every word she was speaking. "Thank you, Iago. You're a good dog—a good wolf. I want you to go home now, and make lots of big, healthy puppies with some hot little wolf-chick. I love you, you good dog you. If I had a Milkbone, I'd give it to you."

Iago seemed to understand. *Seemed* to.

Terry kissed him on his nose, and he licked her face. Then she grabbed him around his massive neck and squeezed with all of her might, knowing it wouldn't hurt him.

She stood, scratching his head. "Remember, lots of puppies." It was difficult, but she knew her generous benefactor wouldn't wait forever. The door of the truck creaked loudly as she opened it, and she climbed inside and closed it behind her.

"You are leaving your dog?" the driver asked.

"He's not my dog," Terry replied in his language. "He's just some stray."

The farmer spared a glance at the animal as he shifted into drive. "He sure *acts* like your dog."

Iago stared at her as they drove off, and Terry felt tears well up in her eyes. Goddamn, she really *did* love that dog. If it wasn't for Iago, she'd be dead now—or an arm-less, leg-less vampire laying next to Mr. Jennings. She shuddered at the thought.

"Where are you going?" he asked.

"Salamanca," she said, wrestling the money Arthur had given her from her jeans. "You wouldn't happen to be going to Salamanca, would you?"

The farmer eyed her, eyed the money, and eyed her again. "I could be," he said.

"Glad to hear it," she said, tucking the money into the pocket of his worn, green, cotton shirt.

They'd only driven about one hundred yards before the truck slowed, pulled to the side of the road, and stopped. Terry began to wonder if giving him the money so early on in the trip *might* have been a mistake.

"What's the matter?" Terry asked.

He pointed to the rearview mirror, and Terry turned around to see Iago, chasing the truck.

"He may have been a stray when you found him, but he's your dog now," the driver said.

If Iago wanted to come to Salamanca, who was Terry to deny him? She leapt out of the truck, slamming the door behind her. "Is it okay if we ride in the back?" she asked excitedly.

"Yes," he replied, smiling. "The two of you won't fit up here."

Terry coaxed Iago into the bed of the pickup truck, and the two of them rode back to Salamanca, her arms wrapped around the wolf.

Iago followed her up the stairs of her building, to the flat she shared with Marta.

"This is it," she said aloud to the wolf. "This is my apartment." Terry didn't really think he understood what she was saying, she just wanted him to get used to the sound of her voice. Also, she needed to hear her own voice right now. It was something she was used to—something normal. Killing vampires, or watching Arthur feed on vampires Iago had killed ... that was *not* normal.

"In here, we have the kitchen," she said, "and over there, the living room. I don't think you'll have much use for the kitchen, because you won't be making your own food." She turned to Iago, and noticed the hair on his back was bristling, and he was uttering a low, nearly inaudible growl as he sniffed around the floor of the apartment.

"What is it, Iago?" she asked as though he would answer. He sniffed his way over to the glass, balcony door, and back to the coffee table, then down the hall to their bedrooms—Terry following him. She told herself he was just checking out his new territory, if he really understood that this was his new territory. Giving his new surroundings the once over? *That* she could buy.

Iago led her back up the hall, to the living room, to the closet door, back to the balcony, and back over to the coffee table. The book. Hiding it in plain view had made sense to her at one point, but she really had to find a better place for it—especially after she'd told Lyle *she* had the book. It was just a matter of where ...

She carefully lifted the album, but not carefully enough. Plastic sheets of photographs spilled out of it, onto the floor. Terry's heart jumped into her throat, and she began to sweat.

"Oh ... fuck."

Iago curiously smelled the fallen pages as she dove to her knees and reached under the couch. She pulled out the book bag—the bag where she'd shoved the pages of pictures a few days ago. Too light. There was no book in this bag. She hastily unzipped it anyway. Nope, no manuscript inside. Just a plain white sheet of paper with a note scribbled in red ink.

> Dear Ms. Rice:
>   I can't thank you enough for this. You've saved me an awful lot of trouble and I am truley gratefull. I wish there was some way to repay you. Perhaps we can come to some sort of arrangemant. I'll be in touch.
>
>   L

"Oh fuck oh fuck oh fuck," Terry repeated. 'L.' There was no mistaking it. It certainly wasn't a 'J' or an 'A.' Besides, she was sure Arthur and Jennings were better spellers. Lyle had the book.

She was hearing something through her shock, but it took a moment for the sound to travel from her ears to her stunned mind. At first, she thought the low staccato sound was the tearing of heavy cloth. Then she saw that Iago's leg was lifted to the couch.

"No!" she said sternly. All dogs understood 'No.'
Lyle had the book. Fuck.

Terry didn't want to think about it. The last few days—the last few weeks—had been difficult enough that she didn't want to think about this problem anymore. She cleaned up Iago's urine (Marta would kill her if she returned from her boyfriend's and found urine on the carpet); went out and bought the wolf a leash, some dog-food, flea powder, dog shampoo; returned and took him for a walk; got back from the walk and tried unsuccessfully to feed him; put him into the bathtub and bathed him until the shampoo was gone; and spent half-an-hour pulling hair from the drain. It was mid-afternoon by the time she ran out of errands, and she realized if she was going to get any sleep, now would be the time. She certainly wasn't going to sleep tonight.

Terry lay in her bed for a while, waiting in vain for sleep to come to her racing mind.

Lyle had the book. The note was odd. Lyle had a courteous way of being threatening, but the note hadn't read that way. Maybe Lyle was just an 'aweful' writer. It could be he'd been attempting to be threatening in the note, and had just pulled it off poorly. *Or*, it could be ...

NO. No. She would not think about this anymore. She was going to go to sleep. Period. She jumped out of bed, nearly tripping over Iago's enormous body. "Sorry, boy," she mumbled as she walked into the bathroom, threw open the medicine chest, and removed her bottle of Valium. More than ten years experience with the drug told her she could afford to take two instead of one and still wake for tonight, and she washed them down with water from the sink. *There.* It wouldn't be long now.

She walked back into the bedroom, Iago's yellow eyes following her all the way to bed. Once she was lying down, she reached one arm to the floor and stroked the coarse fur on his head. "This all must be really strange to you, huh?" she said reassuringly. "It's strange to me, too. By the way, thanks for saving my life last night."

Iago stood from the floor, placing his head on the bed to stare at her with sad, yellow eyes. "You want to sleep up here?" she asked, sliding over on the bed to make room, patting the spot beside her with the flat of her hand. He looked at her with complete incomprehension.

After three minutes of cajoling in the International Sign Language of Domestic Dogs, English, and even Spanish, she got out of bed and physically placed his front paws on the bed with a grunt. Jesus, he was a big dog—*wolf.* She pushed him from behind until he climbed onto the bed, and he circled a few times before he laid down, taking up the entire bed.

"Quite the bed-hog, aren't you Iago?" she asked, before attempting to push him to one side. She was sweaty and exhausted by the time there was finally enough room to throw herself down beside him, and the exertion was working the Valium into her bloodstream.

Thoughts of the note returned to her drugged mind, entirely unbidden. Lyle may have intended it to read more cordial than threatening. Or, he may have intended it for Arthur's eyes. It would certainly cause Arthur to question Terry's loyalties, wouldn't it?

"I have to rip up that note," she mumbled as she tried to sit up, but the Valium took hold of her with both hands and dragged her away, kicking and screaming.

Terry dreamed of Doug. They were in the apartment they had once shared, sitting together on the couch.

"I miss you," Doug was saying. "My life hasn't been complete since you left, and I don't think yours has either."

"It hasn't," Terry said. "I missed you every day."

"I missed you more," he said quietly, kissing her lightly, quickly, in Doug's way. "I would give anything for a second chance with you. I never stopped loving you, Terry."

Terry didn't say anything. She'd never had to with Doug. His arm was wrapped beneath her knees, and he was carrying her into the bedroom. She'd always liked that. Every nuance was just as she remembered—the difficulty he always had with her bra, no matter now many times he unsnapped it; how much he enjoyed undressing her with his own hands; the way his fingertips touched every inch of her body before he finally entered her; his gentleness. He stared into her face as he moved inside her, mouthing the words, 'I love you, Terry,' over and over again. Her fingernails drove into his back, leaving scratches they would joke about tomorrow. Even his weight was perfect—not so much that it crushed her, but enough to make her feel feminine despite the fact that she was a tall woman.

She believed everyone had an ideal lover—someone who did exactly what felt good to you without having to be told. Doug was her ideal lover. With Doug, it had never been just intercourse, or just a kiss. With Doug, all of it had been Making Love. Doug could Make Love to her with his eyes, over dinner at a public restaurant.

Terry woke with the orgasm, her mind still bleary from the Valium. It wasn't quite dark yet, but she knew she had to get up before too much longer. It would be Vampire-time soon.

A naked man stood in the arch of her bedroom door. She could make out very little about him in the dusky light, except that he was tall and naked. It was all too dreamlike to be startling.

"Doug?" she asked.

The man didn't answer. She blinked and struggled to focus her eyes, and when she looked again he was gone. Terry heard stirring on the floor, and Iago peered over the edge of the bed in response to her voice.

Now, she was awake—groggy, but awake. She reached over and scratched his head. "Bed too soft for you?" she asked. "It's nothing, Iago. I just had a dream."

The mattress sagged as he leapt up beside her and laid down, and she wrapped her arm around his hairy neck. "Thanks, Iago," she said, giving him a little extra squeeze. "You're a good dog."

Terry drifted peacefully back into sleep.

Her half-sleeping eyes opened just a crack, just enough to read her alarm clock.

10:29 PM. VAMPIRES SHOULD BE HERE ANY MINUTE, DUMBASS.

"Dammit," Terry said aloud, bolting upright in her bed. The wolf lifted his head from the bed to look at her, and she immediately felt better. Iago was looking after her. No one could get to her past Iago, perhaps not even Arthur. She wondered if he'd made his way back to Salamanca yet. One way to find out.

Terry got up and headed for the shower. If she was going to Tito's, she was at least going to smell like a human being.

The fat Spaniard at the door of Tito's wasn't about to admit Iago, but Terry was able to convince him to go looking for a man of Arthur's description. Her eyes darted up and down the street while she waited, nervously trying to spot vampires. Not that she had cause to worry—they had the book now. If they were coming for anyone, it would be Arthur. It wasn't long before he emerged from Tito's. He was wearing a different suit and he was completely healed. There was no sign that twenty-four hours ago, he'd looked like a barbecue briquette.

"I see you brought the thing back with you after all," he said, looking down at Iago.

"Bear in mind this *thing* saved your life," Terry retorted. "And his name is Iago."

"Really? Did he tell you that?"

So that was it. Sarcasm. No 'Thanks for saving my life'—no 'Glad to see you made it back to Salamanca.' And no, 'Sorry I raped your mind the other night.' She was about to give Arthur the verbal reaming he'd had coming to him for days, but only got as far as "Arthur ..." before he cut her off with more of his drivel.

"It's a wild animal, Terry," he said. "Do you think it *likes* being in the middle of Salamanca?"

Terry's anger was instantly redirected to defending

Iago. "He hasn't minded so far," she said. "I had second thoughts after we left you that night, and I was going to leave him behind. But he started chasing us when we drove away, and the guy who picked me up looked at me like I was abandoning my dog. Iago didn't *want* to be left behind."

"You aren't going to be able to house train it, you know."

"For your information, I already did," Terry said, which was almost the truth. "It was the first thing I trained him to do."

"In a day?" Arthur asked incredulously. "I don't think so. Maybe it was someone's pet before we found it."

"No, I *trained* him," Terry said. She'd already told the lie—might as well see it through. "He comes when I call him, too."

"Great. Well, he'd better be house trained, because the two of you are staying at one of my flats until this thing is resolved."

"Why?" Terry demanded. "They aren't coming after me." *No sir-ee, Arty. They're coming after you.*

"You argue everything, don't you?" Arthur shouted. "You don't even give thought to whether you may be right or wrong, it's just a knee-jerk reflex. If they didn't come for you last night, they'll come for you tonight. They'll trace the license plate on your car and they'll find you."

"It was a friend's car." Even as the words came out of her mouth, she realized how stupid they sounded. It wasn't just her friend's car, it was her *roommate's* car. And Lyle had found her just fine, hadn't he?

Arthur threw his hands into the air. "Fine. You're right. I'm sure you're perfectly safe. Forget the whole thing. Go back to your dorm or apartment or whatever you're living in. I'm sure you'll live through the night."

Arthur turned and walked away. Fine. Let him go. She didn't feel good about it, but sometimes you had to do things you didn't feel good about to stay alive. Right?

Somewhere in the middle of that thought, Iago took off after Arthur, dragging Terry along by a strip of blue nylon. "Iago, no!" she ordered. "Iago, heel! Stay! STOP!"

Arthur stopped walking as the wolf sat down in front of him.

"Your animal has more sense than you do," he mumbled to Terry.

So, *that* was how it was. Iago's first loyalties were to Arthur. She'd wanted the wolf to be *hers*, so that if it came down to it, he would protect Terry from Arthur. Stupid fucking dog. But in a way, she was relieved. She didn't really want him to die by Lyle's hand, especially not because of her. Terry wanted Arthur to pull an ace from his sleeve, and somehow get the book and save Jennings—she just didn't feel she could be any help. Then again, she'd been a great help yesterday morning, when Arthur had been lying comatose in the plaza. Maybe she could help again. Even if Arthur was an ungrateful ass, Jennings deserved better.

"Fine," she said to Arthur. "I'll stay with you. Let's just go back to my place so I can get some things, okay?"

"Very well," Arthur replied.

Terry was lost in her thoughts for the entire walk back to her flat.

She was worried about Arthur, about Lyle having the book. The question was: would Arthur do anything differently if he knew Lyle had the book? Probably. Hell, she didn't even know what was in the book. It could be a seven hundred year-old recipe for muffins, or it could be the vampiric equivalent of plans for a nuclear warhead. Oh, shit. What if it was the latter? What if there were things in that book Lyle could use against Arthur? That would make telling Arthur kind of imperative, wouldn't it?

They reached Terry's flat. Arthur entered first, and Terry gave him a few seconds to look around—uncertain whether he was looking for a trap or checking her designing tastes—before following him in.

"You said before you had a roommate," Arthur said. "Where is she?"

"At her boyfriend's, I guess," Terry answered. Iago was pulling at his leash, so Terry unhooked him. "Do you think she's in danger, too?" she asked.

"Yes," Arthur answered flatly. "Any idea where that might be?"

"None," Terry answered. "Should I leave a note?"

"Pack your things," Arthur said. "I'll come back once

you're safe, and if she returns tonight, I'll collect her."

"Like she's just going to come with you? She doesn't even know you." She looked up from emptying her book bag, to see Arthur was giving her a hard look. "Right. Forget I said anything."

Terry headed into the bathroom, systematically grabbing everything she thought she might need, and then into the bedroom for a few changes of clothes. She took only jeans and T-shirts—she doubted she would need dresses and heels for this company.

When she walked back into the living room, Arthur was on his hands and knees, smelling the floor. It was one of those moments you look back on, and think of a thousand clever things you should have said. But Terry was too frightened, and the best she could manage was, "What are you doing?"

Arthur pointed his chin at Iago, and Terry noticed the wolf's ears were flat against his head. "I don't know what he's so disturbed about," Arthur said, "but I can't smell it. We should get the hell out of ..." a strange look came to the vampire's face, "... here."

"What?" she demanded. "What is it?"

"Vampires," Arthur answered. "Lyle's fledglings—*lots* of them—down on the street."

Iago turned his head towards the glass door of the balcony, his lip curled, and uttered a low growl.

"Can you handle them? You're at full strength now, right?" She desperately tried to sound calm, but it wasn't happening. Lyle's vampires gave him a pretty severe beating the other night, and Jennings had been with him then. If they attacked again tonight, he ... *they* ... didn't stand a chance.

"Do you have any weapons here?" he asked.

Terry's mind raced. "There are knives in the kitchen,"

she answered.

"Get two, in case any get by me," he instructed. "If it comes down to it, go for the heart. Stay up here until I come for you."

Arthur slid open the glass door to the balcony and stepped out. Now was the time, Terry decided. She would tell Arthur Lyle had the book. Of course, the mortal assumption was that he would come back inside, leave through the front door of the flat, and take the stairs down—and her intent was to stop him before he left. Arthur shot that plan to hell by leaping over the edge of the balcony.

Terry blinked. "Oh," she said aloud. "Okay." Just like that, her opportunity was gone.

Iago's ears perked up for a second, and he turned to face the hall. Although they were on the inside of the building, the bathrooms of her own flat and the ones below it had windows that opened to a shaft. At the bottom of this shaft was the first floor bathroom window—at the top, it opened onto the roof. Terry remembered thinking that if she needed to get out of the apartment, it wouldn't be too difficult to climb up that shaft to the roof. When she heard the bathroom window sliding opened, she realized the reverse idea had occurred to someone else.

Iago growled slightly, his ears still high on his head as he listened. Terry grabbed him by his collar and backed into the closet with him, pulling the door closed behind her.

She moved to brace herself against the back wall of the closet, noisily rustling plastic as she did. Terry at first thought she'd backed into a dress, still wrapped from the cleaners, but the plastic was too thick. She reached up to touch it, and felt the impression of a face beneath.

Terry's hold on Iago's collar went limp, and the wolf tore free and crashed through the door. There was a hissing sound from without, and Iago yelped in pain, but Terry barely heard these sounds. Light poured into the closet, and Terry stared at Marta's lifeless face beneath a blood-smeared sheet of plastic.

Terry screamed.

A pale hand reached into the closet, grabbed her by the wrist, and pulled her roughly into the living room, flinging her onto the couch.

"You killed three of my favorite girls," Lyle said, anger slipping into his normally polite tone. "I've been forbidden from killing you, but some price had to be paid."

Terry noticed Iago, digging at his face with his front paws.

"I'm told mail-carriers use this," Lyle said, holding up his can of mace, "but *you* were my real inspiration. I have been instructed to offer you an invitation to come to London, to meet someone."

"Who?" Terry barely managed. Marta was dead.

"Someone who has been impressed with your resourcefulness thus far. It shouldn't be a difficult decision—you either come with me or die with Arthur."

Through the open balcony door, she could hear the commotion on the street. "Arthur's not dead yet," Terry said evenly.

Lyle cocked his head as he took a moment to listen. "No, not yet, but soon," he said. "You can be assured of that. What's your answer? Please say 'no.'"

"How about I say, 'What book?'" she replied, her voice seething with hatred. "Do you remember what that means, 'What book?'"

"Of course," Lyle said, smiling wickedly as he approached her. "I'm going to enjoy this more than you can know."

The sound that got their attention was Iago's growl, its pitch an octave lower than any sound any wolf had ever made. It was so low Terry could feel it in her chest, and the couch beneath her vibrated.

The sight that got their attention was of a huge form, standing nearly-upright from the floor on massive canine legs. Even crouched down, the tips of his ears brushed the ceiling, but he was barely there long enough for Terry to see that.

With a feral noise that made Terry's ears ring, he lunged at Lyle, driving him back through the glass door and through the iron railing as the two of them disappeared over the edge of the balcony. A few seconds of silence passed, before a sound with the intensity of a car-crash boomed from the street below.

Terry didn't move. Nothing made sense. Marta was dead. Vampires were real. Iago had turned into a monster. And Marta was dead.

Everything after that was hazy. She remembered watching Iago change back into a wolf. She remembered trudging up the steps to the flat to call a taxi, Marta's body slumping in the closet. She remembered getting into the cab and reading an address from a business card—but she didn't know where the card or the key had come from.

The rest was a blank.

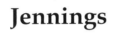

Jennings

London, 1888

David Aarons sat by the water.

There was blood on his hands ... *her* blood.

The Thames was only a few steps away. First, he'd have to stand. Nothing difficult about that. Standing. Simple stuff. Then, he'd have to walk—walk to the water. Also simple stuff. After he'd stood and walked to the water, there wouldn't be anything difficult about placing his hands in the water and washing off the blood. Very easy. Nothing simpler.

And yet, he sat.

Another man approached from behind. David knew who it had to be. He'd introduced himself as 'Arthur.' Not Arthur Jameson or Arthur McCarthy or even Arthur Goldstein. Apparently, these people only had one name.

David Aarons wondered what *his* name would be.

"It's over," Arthur said from behind him.

"But we didn't catch the real killer," he said.

"He's not our concern—not anymore."

"What about us?" David asked without turning.

"Us?" Arthur repeated.

"You and I. We have to drink blood to survive, don't we? Am I understanding that part of this correctly?"

"Yes. But drinking blood and killing don't have to go hand-in-hand."

David placed his hand on his chest. No movement there. His heart would never beat again.

"Can it be undone?" David asked hesitantly.

Arthur said nothing for a moment. "No. We are as we are. We are as we will be for a very long time."

"How long?"

"I don't know. I suppose until the mortals discover and destroy us. I'll be amazed if we make it to the twentieth century."

The blood was dry. David rubbed his thumb and forefinger together, and watched a small part of the stain crumble into tiny pieces he could brush away.

"What now?" David asked.

"We can discuss that another time. You should take a few days to adjust ... "

"I'd like to discuss it now, please," David said. "I need to know if what happens next sounds good enough to keep me from filling my pockets with stones and walking into the Thames."

"That won't be necessary," Arthur said.

"Won't it?"

"No. If you wish to die your final death, you only need to sit here until dawn."

"Good," David said. "I wasn't relishing the idea of searching for stones in the dark."

"The alternative to that—however—would be to join me."

David said nothing for long moments. "What are you about, then?"

"We—our kind—we have no enemies," Arthur said. "We have no enemies because no one knows about us. That's what I'm about. I keep our kind in check. I keep our secret safe. I protect their kind from us, and I protect our kind from them."

"So ... we aren't monsters."

"Oh, we're monsters," Arthur said. "But we're men, as well." Arthur stepped forward and knelt beside him. "Some of us even try to be *good* men."

The blood on David's hands ... it called to him. Even dry and crumbly—even though it had belonged to *her*—it was the most beautiful thing he'd ever seen. David's gums ached.

"Come with me," Arthur said. "If you change your mind, the sunrise will be waiting for you tomorrow. And, the day after that."

David frowned—but Arthur was right. There would always be another sunrise. He stood, and Arthur stood beside him. "I think I'll try it your way, for a while," David said.

Arthur nodded. "Good. We should get going. What should I call you?"

David thought about this for a moment. Not 'Aarons,' it was too ethnic. If he was going to be around a while, he should probably use the name he used when he was trying to blend-in.

"Jennings," David said. "I think I'll go by Jennings."

Arthur smiled very slightly. It was the first time David had seen him smile. It was a kind smile, an honest smile—and yet, somewhat distant. It was a smile that started leagues away before it reached Arthur's face in a diminished form. It looked to David like a smile he could trust.

Arthur pointed his chin towards the water. "You'd better wash off those hands, first," he said. "Tomorrow, we'll start working on that accent of yours."

"What accent?" Jennings asked.

Salamanca, 1986

"Wake up, Jennings."

He opened his eyes in time to see Arthur leaping over the banister, falling to the ground below. There was a moment of disorientation before he remembered where he was: a flat in the Plaza de Mayor. The ambush. Arthur was going into the Plaza, and leaving Jennings with the task of handling the three vampires in the room. Three *confident* vampires, Arthur had called them.

... third story, second from the corner ...

Jennings was on his feet and out of the flat in a blur of motion. He wasn't as fast as Arthur—he didn't have the years—but to mortal eyes his speed was blinding. Unfortunately, he and Arthur weren't fighting seventy mortals. Those vampires in the third-story-second-window-from-the-corner flat would be just as fast or faster than he was.

It took him one preternatural step to reach the landing, another to reach the third floor. The sound of explosions reached his sensitive ears before he was halfway down that long hall. *Bloody-fucking-hell*, he thought to himself. *Whatever's happening, I'm too late.*

He guessed a door—the last door on the right before the bend in the hall. His vampiric strength allowed him to push through it like paper and his vampiric speed threw him into the middle of seven vampires. Jennings took one by surprise, thrusting a thin piece of steel into the centre of his chest, just left of the sternum. The vampire fell to the floor in an inanimate heap. One down, six to go.

He slowed for a fraction of a second to evaluate the situation. One vampire without Gifts against six who could do God-knew-what. It was more than likely most of them were no more than a few days old at best, and they wouldn't know how to use their Gifts. But some Gifts required no learning. *Rapidité*, for example. Speed. One didn't have to learn how to use *Rapidité*, one was simply un-born with it. It was the same with Strength.

His best chance would be to get out of here. Now. Run like the wind and hope none present could catch him. But even that was slim odds. One was standing at the window with a grenade launcher. It was sort of a chancy weapon against a vampire, and rather indiscriminate, but any vampire—no matter how powerful—would be destroyed by being blown to pieces. Even if they only incapacitated Arthur, he would die with the coming of dawn. Alone, against this ever enlarging crowd, he wouldn't stand a chance. After Lyle had the Book (which he would inevitably obtain if Arthur died tonight), he could lead a decades long battle and eventually set things right—but if he took these six vampires now, this could all be over by sunrise. There was no alternative. He had to hope his age and experience would allow him to take these six.

"Sleep," one of them attempted, but the fledgling's Influence was very weak. One of their own number succumbed, but Jennings was unaffected.

"Not tonight, Boss," Jennings said in reply as he thrust a steel wire into a third vampire's chest—a lucky shot. The young girl had been rushing him, and he'd simply held the wire before him and allowed her momentum do the work. Their number was down to four.

Jennings saw the handgun being levelled at him, and felt the twinge of pain in his chest ...

... and then he was someplace else.

It had happened that quickly. His heart had been damaged, and his thoughts had ceased until his heart could heal. The time elapsed could have been the fraction of a second it had seemed, or it could have been decades, centuries. It would all feel the same.

"Good evening, Mr. Jennings," a good-looking man said to him. "At last we finally meet. I can't tell you what a pleasure this is."

Jennings did a complete, instant appraisal of his situation. Sight: an attractive man, confident, gloating, most probably Lyle. He held a thin shaft of steel in his hand, a shaft that had probably just been removed from Jennings' heart. Two women behind him, most probably part of Lyle's cabal. Stone floors, walls, and ceiling, rather nondescript for Salamanca, but at least he knew he was indoors. A wooden table in the centre of the room. Several candles on the table providing the room's light.

Sound: precious little. The stone walls would have absorbed most street noises, but not this much. They might have been in a cellar, or outside of the city altogether. The absence of either windows or a fireplace in the room made a cellar the more likely possibility.

Smell: nothing his other senses couldn't perceive. The candles, the stone, the vampires.

Touch: a strap around his neck held him to some vertical surface, something wood most likely—it wasn't as cold or hard as stone. A second strap across his forehead kept him from moving his head, and a third strap around his waist supported his weight. The odd thing about the weight on the straps was that it wasn't enough—he was heavier than this, or at least, he *had* been. He felt no restraints on his wrists or ankles, in fact, he felt nothing at all in his arms or legs except for a dull pain. Phantom pain, he realised with nauseous rage. His arms and legs had been either cut or torn from his body.

"I don't suppose you would tell me where the Book was if I asked, would you?" the-man-who-might-be-Lyle asked.

"Of course I would," Jennings replied, reining in his useless fury. "In fact, I'm pointing to it right now."

"Ah, yes," he said. "I'm sorry about the amputations; it's purely a security measure. I'm sure you understand."

"Completely," Jennings replied coldly. "In your shoes, I would have done the same thing. Then again, if I were in your shoes, Lyle, I wouldn't be so foolish as to openly oppose Arthur."

Jennings had called him Lyle, and he hadn't blinked or flinched. He could have assumed the vampire was Lyle before that—and it would have been a safe assumption. But like Arthur, Jennings lived by certain codes, and one of them was Take Nothing for Granted.

"Do you even know what the Book contains?" Jennings asked.

"The secrets of power, power like Arthur's," Lyle replied. "With the Book, I would answer to no one."

Jennings laughed, watching while Lyle looked to his girls for reassurance. "What's funny?" Lyle demanded.

"I didn't think you knew," Jennings affirmed. "You are a vampire. You already have that power, but it is locked behind a door. Arthur is many centuries old. Experience has allowed him to wedge that door open a crack—to access a very small fraction of what lay behind. But the Book is a key. Within the Book lie the secrets that will enable you to throw that door open, and bathe yourself in the light of powers you haven't even imagined."

"What kinds of powers?" Lyle asked.

"Weather Control, for one."

"Bah," Lyle dismissed. "There is one among my number who can call a fog whenever she wishes."

"In London? That doesn't take much doing. I'm talking about absolute control of the climate of the world. Do you want it to rain in the Sahara? Do you want to melt the polar caps? Do you want the earth to shake until California falls into the Pacific? Certainly, anyone who could devise that ambush at the plaza could see the use in such a power."

"Yes."

That was all Lyle said. 'Yes.' But in that word, Jennings read volumes.

Not a confident 'Yes.' *Yes, I can see the possibilities because I devised that ambush and I'm that clever.* Not a questioning 'Yes.' *Yes, my ambush was clever but I still have no idea what you're talking about.*

Complete confidence, badly faked. *Yes, and I have to say that because I want my girls—and you—to think I came up with the ambush, but I was really only following orders, I'm only a pretty pawn in a game far more thought out than my feeble mind is even capable of understanding.*

In that single word reply, Jennings could see Lyle wasn't the brains behind this operation. He suspected Drew, but, 'Yes,' wasn't enough to identify Lyle's master for certain. Take Nothing for Granted.

"After this morning, I can only assume Arthur is dead. Yes?" Jennings asked.

"A mortal helped him escape, but he was badly injured. His delirious mind is crying out for assistance, and we shouldn't have a difficult time finding him."

So, he'd learned two more items: this was the night after the ambush, and Arthur still lived. Lyle sucked at this game.

"I can help you," Jennings offered. "I know Arthur better than anyone."

"Thank you," Lyle snorted with arrogant sarcasm, "but in his condition, he shouldn't offer us any more trouble."

"I hope for your sake, you're right," Jennings lied.

They'd blown out the candles before they'd left, and Jennings hung on a wall in the dark.

Arthur was alive for now. Injured, but alive. If he was deliriously sending out some kind of mental distress signal, most likely his brain had been damaged; and if his brain had been damaged, most likely there would be some memory loss. What would he forget? The Book? His codes? His loyalties? It could well be that the Arthur he knew *had* been killed in the ambush, and Lyle was going out to destroy a clean slate. It could be Jennings was on his own—on his own and without arms or legs. It could be he was quite fucked.

A door opened and closed as someone entered, behind him where he could not see. Jennings listened as someone crossed the room to the table. The flare of a match blinded his eyes and filled the room with sulphur. When his eyes adjusted, Stephanie stood in the flickering light of a single candle.

"Arthur's instructions didn't cover this, did they?" she asked.

Jennings could tell by her tone that the Influence had already worn off. "Would now be an appropriate time to remind you that I saved your life?" he asked.

"It might be, if I'd forgotten," Stephanie said. "I'm here to help."

Jennings considered this. Stephanie had led them into the

ambush—unknowingly, yes; but she'd led them into it all the same. It was possible that she genuinely wanted to help. But it was also possible she was being manipulated, just as before.

"Were I in Lyle's position, I would have ordered my arms and legs burned," Jennings said. "Is that what he did?"

"He ordered it, yes," she said. "But I hid them. Am I right in thinking they won't decay?"

"I don't know," Jennings admitted. "Has Lyle found the Book yet?"

"I can't answer too many questions. None of the telepaths here can read your mind, so Lyle has someone flying in from London to try," Stephanie said. "If he reads your mind and learns that I offered to help, Lyle will destroy me."

"Don't worry about that—my mind is unreadable," Jennings said. "It isn't a Gift *per se*—more of a peculiarity. You won't be found out."

"I don't know," Stephanie said worriedly. "They say this man's very good—the best."

'The best?' Jennings allowed himself a glimmer of hope. "When is he coming?"

"I don't know," she said. "I only know they're making arrangements. Why?"

"When he arrives, have him brought straight here."

"That will be done anyway," she asked. "That's all you want?"

"Keep my arms and legs safe," he said. "Where are they hidden?"

"I can't tell you."

"I already told you, my mind can't be read ..."

"I know what you said," she interrupted. "And it's not that. You aren't going to just slip out of here. If you leave, you're taking me with you."

"I'll try, but no promises," Jennings said.

"You don't have to promise," she said, leaning close to the

flame of the candle. "I've got your limbs."

With a gentle breath, the flame was extinguished.

The hours passed slowly. Jennings was bored. He found himself thinking about the past—over a hundred years of it.

There were motion pictures, thousands of hours of film that Jennings drank like blood. *Star Wars. Raiders of the Lost Ark. Terms of Endearment.* Everything Charlie Chaplin ever did. Abbot and Costello. *Casablanca.* James Bond. Walt Disney. Clint Eastwood. Jack Nicholson. Audrey Hepburn.

God, *there* was a woman he'd been tempted to convert. Her and tens of others. Kate Hepburn, Brooke Shields, any of Charlie's Angels. Connie Selleca. But Audrey would always have a special place in his heart. Audrey, who reminded him of Pauline ...

... Pauline from the Resistance. Pauline was a hell of a woman. Strong, intelligent, more beautiful than words. Compassionate. Pauline. Yes, she'd been an exceptional mortal.

And then there was Mary Jane Kelley of London. He'd loved her when he'd still been a mortal ...

Jennings shuddered at the memory. Better not to think of her. Better not to think of any of them, actually; better to hang here and not think of anyone, or anything ...

... gorgeous red hair, her innards neatly placed on the bed beside her ...

... than to to think of Mary Jane. She'd been to Paris once, and they both got a special thrill when he'd called her Marie

Jeanette.

Chewbacca the Wookie. He'd always liked Chewie.

Mary Jane's blood on the walls.

Han Solo, flying in with lasers-blasting to save the day.

Mary Jane's blood on his hands, and he can't stand up to wash it off.

'May the Force be with you.'

The door of the room crashed against the wall with the force of vampiric strength. There was no light, but he could hear a man's footsteps as he walked over to where Jennings was bound.

Fingernails ripped across his flesh like claws; once up the left side of his ribs, another across his stomach, another across his face.

Then his ears followed the footsteps out of the room.

It wasn't precisely like pain. He remembered pain, and this wasn't it. Pain was your nerve endings screaming, 'Injury! We're hurt!' This was more like a statement of fact. 'It's a little chilly in here. By the way, your flesh has been torn open.'

But injury had the unfortunate side effect of awakening the Hunger. The wounds themselves didn't matter, but the body needed blood to heal those wounds. If denied for long enough, the Hunger took over, manifesting itself as a fury that took complete control. Jennings had reached that point twice before. Tonight was his third.

When he woke, he was laying on the cold, stone floor. A dead cat lay on the floor in front of him, an orange tabby with a broken back and fang marks showing through its fur. Jennings' mouth was full of hair. The Hunger was still present—it would never go away as long as his arms and legs were missing—but at least he was in control again.

"Feeling better?"

Jennings looked up and saw Lyle, leaning against the table. *Fuck you*, came to mind, but Jennings only answered, "Yes."

"So glad to hear it. I didn't think you'd be able to break those leather straps. Very impressive, I must say."

"I take it you didn't have any luck with Arthur," Jennings said.

"The crazy bastard Made a wolf," Lyle said. "The girl he left mortal, but he converted a wolf. Took us completely by surprise. I would have thought that was against one of his codes, but apparently he's not as honourable as he would have us believe."

"He didn't use the Influence?" Jennings asked.

"He didn't have the strength."

"Good thing. You'd all be dead if he had."

"Why is it 'good' that I'm not dead?" Lyle asked curiously. "What happened to your loyalty to Arthur?"

"Unlike Arthur, *I* wasn't a knight when I was a mortal," Jennings said. "I was a gambler. I played the odds, just as I do now. Oft times, I tipped those odds in my favour. Staying with Arthur was a safe gamble, because at the time he was the most powerful vampire around. Now, I'm beginning to believe Arthur's reign may soon come to an end. Someone cleverer than him has finally come along."

"And who would that be?" Lyle asked demurely.

"Whoever you're taking orders from."

Lyle stood from the table. "What makes you think I'm taking orders?"

"Just a feeling—an instinct," Jennings replied. "Don't insult me and tell me you aren't."

"Perhaps I am, for now," Lyle said. "But that's going to change soon enough."

"When you find the Book," Jennings stated.

"Yes," Lyle said, lifting an ancient tome from the table which Jennings hadn't been able to see from the floor. "When I find the Book."

"My God!" Jennings exclaimed. "Where on earth did you find it?"

"Your mortal friend had it. It was sitting right on her coffee table, stuffed into the cover of a photo album. It was the damnedest thing. We probably wouldn't even have found it if not for the knapsack of album pages hidden underneath the couch."

Terry had the Book? How the hell had *she* got it? But it was all becoming clear. Something about those early conversations with Terry hadn't made any sense. There'd been a component missing. Jennings had chalked it up to Anne Rice's influence. Un-live and learn.

"I told her I would trade you for the Book," Lyle continued. "Do you know what she told me? 'Fuck right off.'" Lyle laughed a little. "I do love a girl with spirit—they make excellent feeding. Do you read Latin?"

The question had come from nowhere, but Jennings knew why he was asking it: the Book was written in Latin, and Lyle couldn't read it. He wanted to rule the world, and he hadn't the foresight to think that a seven hundred year old text might not have been written in English. Jennings stifled the urge to laugh out loud.

"No, I don't," Jennings said. "Do any in your cabal read Latin?"

"'Cabal,'" Lyle mused. "I've never liked that word. I refer to my vampires as my family."

"Are you a Charles Manson fan?" Jennings asked.

"I used the term long before Manson became famous," Lyle snorted, but Jennings could tell he was lying.

"You didn't answer my question," he said. "Do any of your people here read Latin?"

"Unfortunately, no," Lyle replied. "I don't choose my progeny for their learning, if you know what I mean."

Neither did your master, Jennings thought to himself. "I can help you," he said.

"How, if you can't read Latin?"

"I can tell you what I would do, if I were in your position," he answered.

"I don't need your help, thank you," Lyle said.

"Then what do you plan on doing?" Jennings dared.

"I'd rather not say."

"Why? What am I going to do? I have no arms or legs, and I have no Gifts. I'm a lump of flesh with a mouth—and a hell of a lot more experience than you."

"I don't trust you," Lyle confessed. "Why should I? Why would you want to help me?"

"I told you, I can sense the coming shift of power," Jennings said. "An important part of being a gambler is choosing winners. Your master plans on being the next winner, and you plan on taking that from him. On your own, I don't know what sort of chance you'd have against someone clever enough to set up that ambush in the plaza. With my help, you may just be able to pull this off."

Lyle paced the room thoughtfully. *Pace all you like, pretty boy,* Jennings thought to himself. *There's only one conclusion your slow brain can come to.*

"All right," Lyle said flippantly, "tell me what you would do."

"First, I'd get your chief adviser off the floor and into a chair," Jennings said. "It's hardly comfortable down here."

Lyle breathed an irritated sigh through his nose, walked over to where Jennings lay, and lifted him with one hand by what remained of his jacket. Within moments, Jennings was propped up in a chair.

"Now," Lyle demanded. "What would you do?"

Jennings sighed thoughtfully. "The way I see it," he began, "you're faced with two problems. The Book, and Arthur. The next time you see Arthur, he *will* be at full strength, he *will* have the power of Influence, and he *will* destroy you, unless certain precautions are taken. But I'll come back to that in a moment.

"The other problem: the Book. You either need someone in your family—someone completely trustworthy—to translate it for you, or someone completely impartial with no idea what they have. For the coming fight with Arthur, consider the Book worthless: you aren't going to be able to decipher any of its secrets within the next few days—and it won't take Arthur that long to find you."

"Why do you say that?" Lyle interrupted. "We've stayed hidden in this city for over a week—how would he be able to find us?"

"Because he hasn't seen you as a threat up to now," Jennings answered. "Last night, when he put your family to sleep, he could have just as easily killed every one of them with a single word. But he's been dealing with you with kid gloves. He's intended to slap your wrists and send you back to London. Those aren't his intentions any more, I can assure you."

Jennings could see the effect his words were having on his captor. Lyle had made a slow change from confident, to concerned, to downright frightened. "Maybe now that we have the Book, we should get out of the city," Lyle said, trying to sound thoughtful and assured.

"You could certainly do that," Jennings said. "You could sequester yourself someplace, learn Latin, and study the secrets of the Book for a few decades until you were strong enough to face him. But you have to bear in mind that he's already studied that Book. He already knows its secrets, and in all likelihood, he'll use those secrets to ferret you out no matter how well you hide yourself. You will never have a better chance against him than you do right now—in Salamanca. If you destroy him now, you will eliminate your most dangerous threat."

"We need another ambush," Lyle said.

"That's right, but you need an ambush a little better thought out than that last one. What did you use, a grenade launcher?"

"We had a grenade launcher, and many of the vampires in the plaza were carrying grenades with their pins pulled." Lyle grinned with pleasure at this statement.

You're a sick bastard, Lyle, Jennings thought to himself. *A dangerous, sick bastard.* "Vampires don't use hand grenades against each other in public places," Jennings said sternly. "Do you know why?"

Lyle put his hands on his hips—back to arrogant. "Why?" he demanded.

"Because you risk our discovery by the mortals," Jennings said.

"Once I've read the Book, the mortals will be our slaves—our cattle. We'll breed them for food, and the world will belong to *us*."

"Yes," Jennings said, hiding his disgust, "but for right now, discretion is the better part of valour. Have you heard of tanning beds? Have you heard of lasers? They're using low-powered lasers in security systems that will burn right through a vampire. Just imagine what they could come up with if they knew about our existence—if they were specifically trying to exterminate us. You want to see what they could create? Give them real proof that we exist, and you'll see. The threat of Arthur is nothing compared to four-point-three billion mortals. They would wipe us out like they wiped out polio."

Lyle seemed to be attempting to absorb this. He wasn't convinced, not quite, but he was considering some of the uglier possibilities.

"That's right," Jennings said. "You'd *better* think about it. You were lucky last night. You were lucky Arthur's Influence put every mortal within hearing distance of those grenades to sleep, or else you would have given them their proof and determined the fate for every vampire on the planet. I'll admit, most of the codes of the old Society of Vampires are outdated and completely inappropriate. Staying hidden from the mortals, however, is not.

"That's why you have to be smarter than that when you take out Arthur. You can't think like a human, with hand grenades and bullets. Arthur is fast enough to catch a bullet. You have to think like a vampire."

Lyle took particular insult at this statement. "I *am* thinking like a vampire," Lyle said. "I'm thinking like a vampire of the eighties—that's my advantage over Arthur."

"That's not your advantage over Arthur," Jennings corrected. "Your advantage over Arthur is his code. There are certain things—certain necessary things—he will not do. Your army of vampires is an example of that. And there's a little thing your army can do, that will enable them to take Arthur if you set up another ambush."

"And what is that?" Lyle asked anxiously.

Jennings laughed. "I don't think so," he said. "Not for free. Despite all I've said, I still know you can destroy him. I still know that with time and the Book, vampires can take the world from mortals. But I still have to look out for myself, and I know my advice to you is valuable. Compensation is, therefore, not an unreasonable request."

"What do you want?"

"One arm. Give me one arm, and enough blood so the tissue will regenerate, and I'll tell you how to destroy Arthur."

"Tell me how to destroy Arthur," Lyle countered, "and I'll give you one arm."

"Sorry, no," Jennings said. "Arthur represents the only serious threat between you and your dream world. After Arthur, you'll most likely be able to deal with any problems that should arise without my help. After Arthur, you won't have a need for me. There's nothing threatening about returning one arm. With only one arm, I'll still be at your mercy. And I'm confident you'll find my advice valuable even after Arthur is gone. It's your call."

"I could say, if you don't tell me how to destroy Arthur, I'll decapitate you, and get my advice from your head," Lyle threatened.

"Yes, you could," Jennings said, "if you thought I didn't know that beheading—the separation of the brain and the heart—would kill a vampire."

"I wouldn't even have to go through that much work," Lyle

continued. "I could just leave you out in the open for the sun to claim at dawn."

"You could do that as well, and believe me, I wouldn't like it," Jennings said. "But I still wouldn't tell you how to destroy Arthur, and you and your family would be dead by the following dawn. It's only one arm. In your shoes, I would have ordered my limbs left out in the open for dawn to claim. How much time do we have?"

Lyle checked his watch to learn what Jennings already knew—sun-rise was only a few minutes away. "Let me think on it," Lyle said, heading out of the room.

"Don't think on it too long," Jennings warned. "As of dawn, you won't have anything to bargain with." Lyle was at the door when Jennings stopped him. "You'd better hold on to the other arm and my legs as well—I plan to earn them all back, and I'm going to want you to show them to me before I give any favours."

Jennings could tell by the look on his face that Lyle didn't like that. He'd wanted to leave here indifferently, so his prisoner could sweat it out. But Jennings knew where Lyle was going. He was going to find Stephanie.

The door closed behind the displeased vampire, and Jennings smiled.

Jennings estimated it was less than three-quarters of an hour past sundown when Lyle returned. Two of his girls were with him, carrying bundles wrapped up in cloth. Stephanie was not among them.

"I don't see any blood," Jennings said. "I need blood if the arm is going to reattach."

"Jennifer gorged earlier this evening," Lyle responded. "You can take blood from her. How do we kill Arthur?"

"The arm—and the blood—first, if you please," Jennings said.

Lyle sighed through his nose, and nodded to one of the girls. She unwrapped his left arm from the cloth. It was stiff, and the way she handled it reminded him of the arm of a mannequin. She carefully shoved it up inside what was left of his sleeve until it looked natural. Jennings could feel the tissue of his shoulder reaching out to it, trying to reclaim it.

Lyle nodded to Jennifer, and she approached Jennings, offering him her throat. She was a gorgeous creature, a brunette—mouth a bit too narrow, perhaps—but flawless otherwise. His gums throbbed with painful excitement as his fangs extended, and his breathing became ragged. The thing that lived inside him knew it was about to be fed, and if Jennings had his arms, he would have grabbed her and held her fast with inhuman passion.

His teeth sunk into her neck, and he suckled like a baby. His body cried out in ecstasy as the blood flowed into him. The muscles of his arm reattached with speed even he hadn't anticipated, and the deep scratches Lyle inflicted the night before vanished as though they had never been. The tendons and nerves would require more blood, but the muscle was completely restored within moments. Jennings sucked and drank, sucked and drank ...

... until his jaws clamped on empty air. Lyle had Jennifer by the shoulders, supporting her body. He would have drank the life right out of her if Lyle hadn't intervened.

"Take her," Lyle instructed the other girl. "See that she gets more blood." Within a few moments, Jennings and Lyle were alone. "Now," Lyle said, "how do I kill Arthur?"

Without tendons to support it, the weight of the arm pulled sickeningly on the muscles of his shoulder. There was no feeling in the arm, nothing but the weight, but he had the arm back. The Hunger for more blood, and the pain of the rapid healing, made it difficult to speak. "The Influence," Jennings stammered, "the old Society of Vampires called it *Double Voix*. Two Voices. He speaks with his mouth and he speaks with his mind, and the combination of the Two Voices is too powerful for you to disobey. Take away one of his voices, and he can't control you—some of the fledglings perhaps, but not you."

"And how do I do that?" Lyle urged.

"Deafen yourself to his spoken voice," Jennings said. "Puncture your eardrums. They'll heal the ... the first time you drink blood, but for the fight against him, you need to be deaf."

"And how do I ambush him?" Lyle asked. "He'll be expecting it this time."

"Let him expect it. Some of your cabal ... your *family* ... are going to be naturally resistant to the Influence. If their eardrums are punctured, he won't be able to take them. Even if he Influences only eight out of ten, the ones who are left should be enough to bring him down."

"And where do I strike?" Lyle persisted.

Jennings thought about this for a moment. It was more difficult than he'd anticipated—through the pain and the hunger. If he hadn't spent so many hours last night thinking about it, he wouldn't have been able to puzzle it out on the spot. But he *had* an answer.

"That depends on Terry," Jennings managed. "Neither Arthur nor I knew she had the Book—so she was keeping it secret from us for a reason. Why? Because she doesn't ... she doesn't trust us. Any of us. Or, at least, she didn't. By now, she's beginning to side with Arthur, which means that soon, she'll tell him about the Book and where it's hidden. The other thing about Terry you have to ..." ... Good God this hurt ... "... have to consider is this: is she the kind of person who would check the Book's hiding place? Does she realise ... the Book is missing? You told me she had it sitting on her coffee table. Climb inside Terry's head. She walks ... into her apartment, and she's thinking about Arthur and me and you and trying to decide who to trust. She sees the photo album on the coffee table and if she thinks you don't know who she is, it doesn't occur to her to check the album and see that the Book is still inside."

"You're rambling," Lyle said. "I don't need reasons, I need answers. Do you think Arthur will end up at the mortal's flat?"

"I don't know," Jennings confessed, panting. "But I think it's ... your best shot."

"Very well," Lyle said, gathering up Jennings' other limbs. "We'll try it your way."

Lyle left, and Jennings was alone with his muddled thoughts and his pain. *There you are, Arthur*, he thought. *Served up on a silver platter, as pretty as you please.*

Night came.

Jennings tried the arm—still nothing. He'd never reattached an amputated limb before. He didn't know how much blood it would take to get the thing working. It didn't feel heavy on his shoulder any more, so at least he knew the tendons were coming around. But having it wouldn't do him any good until it no longer hung limp at his side.

He was Hungry. Not irrationally Hungry—not yet—but it wouldn't be long before he was. Jennings knew full well he wouldn't stay in control the entire night if he didn't score some blood. Considering his wits were all he had right now, he absolutely could not afford to lose control.

Jennings stared at his hand, willing it open, close, open, close. His fingers didn't so much as twitch. Maybe it *wouldn't* take that much blood to get the arm back. Maybe a few ounces would do the trick. He looked about the room, his eyes finding the orange cat he'd killed the night before. Its yellow eyes stared into space, its lips were pulled back from its teeth, its spine bent at a sickening angle. He could tell by the position of the front leg that its muscles were stiff with death.

He hadn't drunk it dry—he couldn't have with a bite on the back. Any blood left in its body would have settled at the animal's lowest point, along its side. Of course, if he threw himself out of the chair and the blood in the cat wasn't enough to give the arm back, he wouldn't be able to get back up here. But did that matter?

Jennings thrust his head back, tipping the heavy chair and spilling him roughly to the floor. He rolled off the chair-back, and pulled himself across the floor with his forehead, a few inches at a time. The arm was nothing but dead weight. Even with the unnatural strength in his neck, it took him nearly five minutes to get to the cat.

He took its paw in his mouth, and flipped it over. "Thank God for *rigor mortis*," he mumbled as he positioned himself over the tabby. He nosed matted fur aside, his fangs extending when he saw the dark blue colour of the skin beneath the hair. There was blood there—maybe enough.

He sunk his teeth through the stiff muscles of the cat's side, and sucked hungrily. The blood was cold, and he was getting hair in his mouth, but it was still good. He took what little blood he could from that spot, and bit it someplace else, and then again someplace else, until he suddenly realised that his arm was coming up to grab the animal, to force it deeper into his mouth.

He bit it repeatedly, sucking the dead cat for all it was worth. When he was satisfied he would get nothing more from it, he replaced it where it had been lying, and propped himself up on his good arm.

It wasn't particularly strong or coordinated, but it was an arm. At least he was somewhat mobile again. Of course, getting back into that chair would still be a trick.

It only took him a few seconds to cross the room. He righted the chair, manoeuvred himself around in front of it, and gingerly tried to pull himself into it. But the chair tipped sideways, and he fell painfully on the stump of a leg.

"Dammit," Jennings swore as he turned himself about and righted the chair once more. He wasn't sure how much time he would have, but it certainly wouldn't be that long before Lyle returned. He pulled himself up the side, managing to get his chest onto the seat. If his arm was just a bit stronger, he'd be able to grip the seat and slowly right himself. He tried, but only succeeded in throwing himself from the chair again.

The door opened with Jennings on his stomach on the floor. *Don't use the arm*, he ordered himself. He lifted his head and turned to see Lyle in the doorway, a few of his girls behind him.

"If you're more comfortable on the floor, I could have left you there," Lyle said snidely.

"*I need more blood!*" Jennings shouted angrily, acting out the effects of the Hunger he'd felt when he'd awakened.

"Yes," Lyle said. "I spoke to someone in London about you."

"Who?" Jennings said. "Drew? Your master?"

"I have explicit instructions not to reveal him," Lyle said, pacing over to the table. Four woman entered silently behind him. "He liked your idea with the ambush—said it was lethal enough that he has actually questioned your loyalty. I told him I wanted to keep you here in Salamanca, but he's insisted I ship you to London right away. Don't worry, I'll ship your missing body parts along with you—that was part of my instructions. But you'll have to prove to *him* you're trustworthy enough to get them back."

"I need more blood," Jennings repeated. Each moment made it less difficult to play the role of Hunger-maddened vampire. The act itself was awakening the part of him he was desperately suppressing.

"You'll get blood in London," Lyle said. "There was only one part of our little transaction my master didn't care for." His girls were approaching him, slowly, cautiously. "I'm afraid I'm going to need that arm back."

Jennings jerked his head to flip himself over, but a foot on his back pinned him down. That was when the Hunger took over, reducing Jennings to a bystander. He reached around behind him and grabbed that ankle, jerking the girl off her feet with such force and speed that she cracked her head against the stone floor beside him.

The smart thing to do would have been to face the others—to try and defend himself. But the Hunger wasn't smart. The Hunger saw the opportunity for blood in the vampire on the floor, and the Hunger threw Jennings at her, driving his fangs into her tender throat, drinking greedily.

One of the girls sat on top of him, while the two others grabbed that arm. They twisted it until the still-healing tendons snapped and the muscles tore, and they wrenched it from his body while he fed.

The three of them managed to pry him from the prone vampire, to pin him on his back like a beetle. His head was clearer, but he had no use for a clear head. *You got yourself into this*, he told the Hunger. *Let's see if you can get yourself out.*

Lyle walked over while Jennings struggled, holding a wooden stake in his right hand. "I have a message for you, from my master," Lyle said. "He says he isn't doing this to be cruel, so please, don't take it personally. I suspect the next thing you see will be his face." Lyle raised the arm with the stake. "Good night, sweet prince."

Then the stake was in Jennings' heart, and there was nothing.

He woke to a fire in his throat. It was blood—sweet, warm, nourishing blood. He hardly noticed that his lips were wrapped around the mouth of a bottle, all he felt was the blood rushing through him, the hole in his chest closing, the flesh of his limbs bonding. It wasn't until the blood stopped that he had sense enough to take notice of his surroundings.

He was laying in a large bathtub, the bathtub of the master bath of one of Arthur's houses in Salamanca. Raymond was standing over him—shirt-sleeves rolled up; top button unbuttoned; tie loosened; thick, dark hair brushed back immaculately—holding a two litre Fanta bottle that still showed a film of blood on the inside of the plastic. Jennings almost couldn't believe his eyes.

"I nearly put you on the couch in the living room, but I knew you were going to be messy about this," Raymond said in his feminine way as he wiped the corners of Jennings' mouth with a cloth napkin. "Arthur would kill me if I got blood on his furniture."

"He might not be happy about blood on his porcelain, either," Jennings said.

"I'll scrub it out," Raymond dismissed. "You look just a mess. How do you feel?"

"Better than I've felt in a couple of days," he replied. "The Hunger is still very bad."

"Well, you'll get no more of these," Raymond said, shaking the empty bottle. The blood residue had pooled at the bottom, and Raymond threw the bottle back to drink the last few drops. "The rest of your blood will come more slowly, or you'll get sick."

"Yes, Mother," Jennings said, smiling dryly. Raymond was so maternal, and so very mortal for a vampire his age. He would have made a good mother had his body been born the same sex as his mind. Jennings had actually been quite unsettled by Raymond's homosexuality when he'd first met him. But vampires had little use for sexuality, one way or the other. All vampires were essentially the same sex. All could create progeny. The only aspect of vampirism where sexual orientation manifested itself was in the feeding preference—man or woman.

Arthur had initially taken to Raymond all those years ago because he was trustworthy and because of his Gift. Telepathy was extremely rare, and Telepathy to Raymond's degree even rarer. Jennings had eventually got over his prejudices, and had come to like Raymond because he was a good man. A bit of a sissy, but a good man.

"If I moved you to the couch now, do you think you could keep the mess to a minimum?" Raymond asked.

"Better just to leave me here, for now," Jennings answered, laying his head back and closing his eyes as the healing took effect. "The bonds of muscle are still very weak. I wouldn't want anything falling off."

"I already thought of that," Raymond said, opening Jennings' terry-cloth robe to reveal the white medical tape that criss-crossed his chest and twined around his arms. "Don't worry, nothing's going anywhere. Your legs are taped up, too."

"You think of everything," Jennings said as he was being lifted from the tub.

"Always."

Raymond carried him through the house, into the living

room, and gently laid him on the couch. He adjusted the injured vampire's arms into a position that looked comfortable and stepped back, which was when Jennings noticed the wolf for the first time.

"Oh shit," Jennings said as he stared into its yellow eyes. "Lyle told me Arthur'd Made a wolf, but I didn't believe him."

"Don't start believing him now," Raymond said. "This is just a regular old wolf." He reached down and scratched the animal's head affectionately. "Arthur tells me his name is Iago. He also told me not to mess with him, and I'm not going to. Would you like some more blood?"

"Yes, please," Jennings replied, sending Raymond into the kitchen. "When you were saving me, do you know if you killed a girl named Stephanie?"

"I only kicked-ass, honey," Raymond shouted from the kitchen. "I didn't take any names."

Damn, Jennings thought. He'd intended to keep that promise.

"You'd better not be talking to me telepathically in there," Raymond said. "You know I can't read your mind."

"Where's Arthur now?" Jennings whispered.

"What?" Raymond shouted.

"We both know full well you can hear me," Jennings continued in the same whisper. "I said, where's Arthur?"

"You and your vampire shit," Raymond said disparagingly. Jennings could hear the 'beeping' of the buttons on the microwave—Raymond was heating his blood. Such a mother.

"Why are you avoiding my question?" Jennings asked, speaking in a normal voice.

Raymond stepped out of the kitchen, into the hall. "Arthur took the mortal girl to the hospital."

"What happened to her?"

Raymond's lips went tight. "Acute mental trauma," he said. "I couldn't tell what happened to her—her mind was all over the place—but whatever it was really pushed her over the edge. I've touched minds that far gone before ... it doesn't look good."

Jennings looked away from him, taking this in. His eyes found Iago, who sat staring at him from four feet away—not understanding a word, and perhaps not caring. The microwave gave a final beep—his blood was warm. "That's too bad," Jennings finally said. "She was a sharp girl."

Raymond reentered the room, a steaming mug in one hand and a glass with a straw in the other. "If Arthur would let me, I'd kill that little prick Lyle myself," Raymond said angrily. He set the glass where Jennings could reach it without moving, and bent the flexible straw towards his mouth.

"A bendie-straw?" Jennings asked. "My God, you *do* think of everything."

"'God is in the details,'" Raymond quoted.

Iago perked his ears, got to his feet, and went to the front door. He didn't bark like a dog would have, and he didn't go to the door like he was about to greet someone. He moved like he was moving in for the kill. It was unsettling to watch.

What was more unsettling was that Iago had heard Arthur's footsteps on the walk before Jennings had. Arthur may not have Made this wolf, but he'd done something to it.

Iago had just begun to growl when the door opened, and Arthur stepped in. The growling stopped immediately, and Iago stepped towards him, smelling him cautiously. Arthur patted his massive head as he passed, mumbling, "Good boy."

Jennings was about to say something, but Raymond was already on his feet. "What did they say?" he asked worriedly.

"The doctors don't know," Arthur replied. "They want to run tests and keep her under observation. Maybe they'll know something by tomorrow night."

Arthur stepped into the room, where Jennings got a look at him for the first time. His clothes were shredded, he was covered with blood, and he was walking with a slight limp. "Jesus,

Arthur," Jennings said. "What does the other guy look like?"

"The other *seventy* of them look dead," Arthur replied. "Are *you* all right?"

Jennings lifted his hand from his chest. It was still shaky, but it was moving. "Looks like I'll be fine."

"Well," Raymond said, setting his cup down on the coffee table. "It looks like you had a rough day at the office, dear. How about some nice, warm blood?"

"You're drinking out of mugs now?" Arthur asked dryly. "What happened to the wine glasses?"

"That's for a totally different mood," Raymond said flamboyantly as he moved towards the kitchen. "Fang-less vampires get to be creative too, you know."

"None of that oregano or basil or whatever you put in yours," Arthur ordered. "Just blood."

"Purist," Raymond accused, as though it was an insult. "Now you go upstairs and change and your blood will be ready when you come down." Raymond gave Jennings a quick wink before he turned the corner, an Isn't-Arthur-cute-for-an-asshole wink.

Jennings and Arthur exchanged He's-*your*-friend-not-mine glances.

"I *heard* that!" Raymond sang from the kitchen.

Raymond was already seated in the living room when Arthur came trotting down the steps, Iago right behind him.

"All right," Jennings said as Arthur reached the bottom of the stairs and headed for a chair. "What should we talk about first? How about the wolf?"

"How about the Book?" Arthur answered, turning to Raymond. "Is it here?"

"It's downtown, in an office building," Raymond said. "It'll be fine until tomorrow night."

Jennings could tell by the blank look on Arthur's face that he couldn't believe his ears. "You know where the Book is, and you left it?" Arthur asked calmly.

"That's right," Raymond said defensively. "Saving Jennings was more important."

Jennings and Arthur shared another look. It wasn't what either of them would have done.

"Come on," Arthur said as he stood. "We're going to get it before the sun comes up."

"It's fifteen minutes away, and we have a half-hour before sunrise," Raymond said, his anger really building now. "We might have time to get there and get back with it, but if we run into trouble, we're fucked."

Arthur sighed angrily as he sat back down, desperately trying to keep his anger in. "Too bad you didn't think of that an hour ago," he mumbled.

Raymond leapt to his feet, fuming. "An hour ago, you were in the middle of an ambush I didn't know if you were going to survive, and Jennings was lying in pieces on your bathroom floor! So what would happen if Lyle killed you, and I died trying to get the Book back? Bang, we're dead, they just come and collect Jennings at their leisure because *he* wasn't going anyplace! I know the two of you think I'm incapable of seeing the big picture, that I do things based on friendship, but I was doing the logical thing! I was trying to ensure that *your* cabal wasn't wiped out tonight, because believe me, for a few hours it wasn't looking very good!"

Raymond stood in the centre of the room, so furious there were blood tears welling in his eyes. Arthur looked to Jennings, silently asking his opinion.

"He poses a good argument, Arthur," Jennings admitted. "In his situation, I might have done the same thing."

"No, you wouldn't have," Raymond spat. "You would have left me scattered across the bathroom, or you would have let Lyle put me in a box and ship me to London, just to prove a point about how ruthless you can be—just to prove feelings don't affect your decisions. And do you know what? You would have been wrong."

Raymond vaulted to the hall entrance, springing one-handed from the sturdy coffee table over the furniture in an angry display of his preternatural agility.

"Where are you going?" Arthur asked.

"Your dog is hungry," Raymond said. "You neglect your animals just like you neglect your cabal. Come here, Iago."

The wolf recognised his name, and lifted his head from the floor, perking his ears towards the kitchen. He looked to Arthur, as if waiting for permission.

"Go into the kitchen," Arthur uttered in the Voice. Iago got to his feet, and headed for Raymond, his claws clicking against the floor.

Jennings watched the wolf, fascinated. "I thought you couldn't Influence animals," he whispered with awe.

"I can't," Arthur said. "I tried on a normal dog on my way back from the hospital and got no response. But Iago listens."

"That's bizarre," Jennings said.

"That's nothing," Arthur responded. "You should have seen what he did tonight. Raymond," he called into the kitchen. "Read my mind now, get a good look at what you're feeding."

Arthur closed his eyes and concentrated, and for a moment there was silence from the kitchen. Then Raymond screamed, "Jesus Christ!"

"What?" Jennings demanded. "What did you show him?"

"A scene from earlier tonight," Arthur explained. "You see, Iago is no normal wolf."

"He's a bloody werewolf!" Raymond said, returning from the kitchen. "I don't believe it! I didn't know those things were real!"

"Neither did I, until tonight," Arthur said.

"What?" Jennings said, growing annoyed. "What did he do tonight?"

"He transformed ... changed himself into this ... this monster. He was better than nine feet tall, standing on his hind legs and tossing vampires everywhere."

"And you saw this transformation with your own eyes?" Jennings asked.

"No, but I saw him change back," Arthur said. "In seven hundred years, I've never seen anything like it."

"Can he turn into a human?" Jennings asked.

"I have no idea *what* he can do," Arthur admitted.

"Well, I'll tell you one thing," Raymond said, shocked out of his anger. "The Influence doesn't work on him."

"How do you know that?" Arthur asked.

"Because I'm a telepath, Twit."

"What are you talking about?" Jennings asked derisively. "You can't read dogs."

"I can so, you bastard!" Raymond responded, insulted as though Jennings had forgotten his birthday. "It's *cats* I can't understand. I can read horses too, but they're so stupid, who would want to?"

"One moment," Arthur interrupted. "If the Influence doesn't work, why does he do what I tell him?"

"He wants to please you," Raymond said. "He wants to do what you ask. But he sits there in a blur of non-understanding, listening to the meaningless sounds coming out of our mouths, until you use the Influence. Then, he understands perfectly. When you told him to go into the kitchen, he knew what you were talking about because *you* knew what you were talking about."

"Two voices," Jennings uttered thoughtfully. "One spoken into the ears, one spoken into the mind."

"And it's the voice in his mind that he understands," Raymond continued.

Iago came clicking back into the room, licking his chops.

"*And* he eats like a pig," Raymond said. "He just polished off four entire steaks in less than a minute."

"Time for a little test," Jennings said. "Arthur, call him to you, and have him give you his paw."

"Come here, Iago." The wolf loped over to Arthur, who held out his hand. "Shake," he instructed.

Iago sat, and placed his large paw in Arthur's hand.

"Good," Jennings said, sitting up unsteadily. "Now, say nothing Arthur. Iago, come here."

Iago looked at Jennings, and then back at Arthur, who said nothing with either voice. After a moment, he stood and crossed the room to Jennings.

"Good boy," Jennings said. He held out an unsteady hand. "Shake."

Iago repeated the trick for Jennings.

"All right," Arthur said. "What does that mean?"

"It means he's learning," Jennings said. "He's not only listening to the voice in his mind, he's listening to the one in his ears, and remembering what it means. He's learning English. This is quite a prize you have for yourself, Arthur. I want to see this transformation."

"Better hold that thought for tonight," Raymond said, checking his watch. "It's bedtime."

The western sky was still glowing red when the black limousine pulled up in front of an office building in downtown Salamanca.

"How many do you feel inside?" Arthur asked.

Raymond closed his eyes, concentrating. "Hard to say—less than ten, I think."

"How about you?" Arthur asked Jennings. "Are you all healed up?"

"I'm healed up enough for this," Jennings replied. "Are you sure you want to bring Iago along on this one?"

Arthur sort of chuckled. "You didn't see him last night," he said. "Yes, I'm sure I want him along."

The door to the limo opened, and three men and a wolf stepped out. Little communication was necessary beyond that point. Arthur and Iago took their place by the door, Raymond and Jennings went inside. Jennings took the elevator, Raymond the stairs.

Jennings pushed the button for the fifth floor. He loved modern technology. He was more vulnerable inside this little box, but he didn't mind. There weren't any cameras, and no telepath would be able to see him coming for the same reason Raymond couldn't read his mind. This was going to be a piece of cake.

Jennings reached into his inside-jacket pocket, removing five steel rods. He placed one in his fingertips, and was placing the other four in the palm of his hand when the elevator bell rang, and the car stopped on the third floor. He quickly hid his hand behind his back as the door opened.

A clean-cut, young Spaniard moved to step onto the elevator. "Sorry," Jennings said in Spanish, stopping him at the door. "Going up."

"That's fine, so am I," he said, about to step through the door.

Jennings' finger was on the young man's chest. "In that case, I'm going down," Jennings said, pushing him back out of the elevator.

"The light says you are going up!" the young man argued.

"Take my word for it, you want the next car," Jennings said.

"I want *this* car!" he persisted. "I'm going up!"

He could kill this man. He could kill him and leave him with the dead vampires on the fifth floor—but of course, his body wouldn't disintegrate at sunrise like theirs would. Better to keep this clean.

He leaned his head out of the elevator, finding no one in the hall. Faster than the man could see, he dropped the rods and grabbed the man by the lapels, lifting him easily from the floor.

"Have you ever had one of those moments," Jennings said calmly, "where you know if you'd done something just a little differently, things might have turned out a lot better for you? This is one of those moments. In the name of the Host, take the next car."

Jennings held him there until the doors were closing, dropping him at the last possible moment to get his arm back inside. Sometimes, he wished he had Arthur's Gift of Influence. The rods were all over the floor of the elevator now, and he scrambled to gather and rearrange them in his hand as the car reached five.

The doors opened. Jennings waited. Any vampire near the

elevator door would have heard the exchange two floors below. Any *intelligent* vampire would have seen an attack coming.

The doors stood opened. Jennings continued to wait. Only when a curious, stupid vampire peeked his head around the corner did he make his move.

Jennings gripped him by his skull, his thumb popping one of his eyes, and pulled him into the elevator. Before he could react or even think to react, a rod in his heart paralysed him, and he slumped to the elevator floor.

The door was beginning to close, and Jennings darted through, throwing himself to the far wall. Just as he suspected, another guard stood on the other side of the door. He rushed Jennings, but he didn't have the age. A second rod pierced this one's heart, and down he went.

The door was still closing, when Jennings realised—the body in the elevator. The car would go to three, and the young man would find a body in the car, and the police would be called. "Shit," Jennings whispered as he stuck his hand in the door and forced it back open. He pulled the first felled vampire out of the car and pressed three, mumbling, "There you go, Amigo," before stepping out and allowing the door to close. A third vampire was suddenly at his shoulder, and he drove a rod into her heart before he realised it was Stephanie.

Dammit, Jennings thought, pulling the rod back out and catching her before she fell. The rods were thin, and the damage to her heart minimal. It was only a few seconds before she came around.

"Where's the Book?" Jennings hissed in a vampire-whisper.

"Third door down," she hissed back, indicating a direction with her chin.

"How many others?"

"Six," she said.

"Is Lyle with them?" he asked.

"Yes." Then, hesitantly, "Are you going to kill me now?"

Jennings thought about this for a moment, before grabbing a doorknob and twisting until the lock snapped. "Stay in here for ten minutes," he said. "Don't make a sound, don't move. Once Lyle and his family are dead, you'll be free. Do anything you like but don't stay in Salamanca and don't return to London. Do you understand?"

Stephanie was fast. Had her intent been to kill him, she most likely would have succeeded—but her intent had been to kiss him. She kissed him as long and as hard as circumstances permitted. When she pulled back, there were blood-tears in her eyes.

"I wish I could have got to know you better," she said, before ducking into the office and closing the door behind her.

Six vampires to kill behind door number three. And one behind door number one if Stephanie turned out to be lying.

He rapped on the door to the stairwell with his fingernail. It opened, and Raymond slipped out, a body thrown over his shoulder.

"Any problems?" Jennings asked near-silently.

"None," he replied just as quietly as he lowered the body to the floor. "How do you want to do this?"

Jennings looked up and down the hall, noticing the drop-ceiling. "Take a look up above," Jennings said. "If there's no fire wall up there, you take the highroad."

Raymond stepped onto Jennings' hand and stood up, the other supporting his weight without effort. He popped a tile and looked around. Jennings didn't have to ask how it looked—suddenly the weight was off his hand, Raymond had disappeared into the ceiling, and the tile was replaced.

Jennings walked to the door, removing three more rods from his inside pocket, positioning them in his hand. By now, they had to know something was going on out here. It had all been very quiet, and any humans still in the offices would be unaware. But the vampires behind this door would know something was happening. They were probably waiting on the other side, ready for him to burst through. He decided to surprise them.

Jennings knocked on the door. For a moment, there was no response. Then a girl opened the door—one of Lyle's fledglings. It didn't take her long to recognise Arthur's right-hand man.

She tried to sound tough. "What do you want?"

"A Christmas pony. But, failing that, I want the book and I want some answers."

The door opened wider, to reveal another woman standing beside the first. "Sorry, can't do that," this new girl said. "But if you like, you're perfectly welcome to walk to the end of the hall and leap out of the ..."

A spike in her throat stopped the command before it was finished. Good thing, too—her Influence was strong, and resisting it would have been a struggle. Another vampire burst through the wall to the left of the door, while the first bared her fangs and charged, her arms up to defend herself from the steel rods in his right hand.

One of the funny things about vampires, Jennings had once told Arthur, *is they're so accustomed to their own invincibility, they sometimes ignore the obvious.* Jennings proved his point to the absent Arthur by bringing up his empty left hand, and shattering her nose. Unlike a mortal, the splinters of bone lodged into her brain by the move would only serve to stun her—but that was all he really required. The vampire who'd come through the wall was coming at him.

His next manoeuvre was a single, smooth movement: left arm grabbing the left forearm of the charger, pulling him by; right hand, plunging a rod into his chest; left leg, coming up to back kick into the door in case any more were coming at him—and one was. The wall smasher's now-inanimate body was thrown twenty feet down the hall, and glass shattered as the force of his kick drove the other through the office window.

Shit, Jennings thought. It was too early in the evening to be throwing vampires out of windows—the streets would still be thick with mortals. Arthur would have to handle that one.

Lyle crouched into a defensive posture within the room, a switchblade in one hand. "Stay back," Lyle ordered the other two in the room. "He's mine."

"Oooo," Jennings said, snapping a spike into his left hand so that both hands were ready. "*Mano y mano*, eh? Seems there's a Santa Claus after all."

Jennings almost didn't see Lyle move—he was that fast. The knife lashed out, its objective to remove his right hand at the wrist. But Jennings was able to pull back quickly enough that he was only cut. The rods fell from his hand as the severed tendons made gripping them impossible.

Rapidité; in Jennings' opinion, the most powerful Gift. Even the Influence and Telepathy were of limited use against an opponent who could cover forty feet before you even saw him. *This* wasn't going to be easy.

He lunged again, this time, aiming for the heart. But Jennings was pretty fast himself—fast enough that the blade only punctured a lung.

"A little tougher when your opponent has arms and legs, isn't it?" Jennings said, backing into the hall. A mortal instinct wanted to cough the blood flowing into the lung; Jennings suppressed it. He held back, waiting as Lyle came towards him in tiny, cautious steps without leaving his stance. Jennings waited until he was inside the door frame, hoping the smaller space would restrict his movement just a little. He feinted with his left hand and threw his entire body right, the other vampire reacting just as Jennings had hoped. Lyle blocked the ineffectual blow and lunged forward, tripping over the leg Jennings had left out there. He didn't actually fall—just stumbled a bit—enough for Jennings to get a grip on his ankle and pull him off his feet.

Then Jennings was on him, his good hand gripping the hand

with the knife. They struggled on the floor of the hall in a battle of strength where Jennings should have had the advantage. But Jennings was injured and Lyle was not, and inside of a few seconds, the other was pushing the knife towards Jennings' throat with both hands. Having his throat cut would not take him out of the fight, but he would lose a lot of blood he could ill-afford to lose. Where in bloody hell was Raymond?

With a sudden, unexpected yank, he pulled the knife up into his mouth. It punctured the back of his throat as it was driven in, and Jennings bit down on the weapon, gripping it in his teeth. The knife was trapped.

Lyle gripped the knife-handle with both hands in a vain attempt to free the weapon. Jennings took advantage of his preoccupation with the blade and pushed his thumb into the other's chest; through muscle, between the ribs, into his heart. Lyle's struggle for the knife ceased as his body went limp.

Jennings looked into the room, expecting intervention from the other two, in time to see Raymond drop through the ceiling, plunging a rod into either's chest while hanging upside-down like a bat. It was almost poetic to see—only Raymond.

"Are you all right?" he asked, still dangling from the ceiling.

Enough of the grip had returned to Jennings' right hand to pull the knife from the flesh at the back of his throat. He coughed, blood spattering the wall, before he drove the knife into the chest of the other vampire, allowing him to remove his thumb from Lyle's heart.

I'm fine, was what Jennings had intended to say, but the blood made the sound an unintelligible croak.

Raymond flipped his legs over the rung of drop-ceiling, landing on his feet with a gymnast's grace. "That's all of them," Raymond said. He gestured to the one with the shattered nose. "She's going to come to in a couple of minutes, and I'm sure Arthur's got some questions for her. He's on his way up with the one you kicked through the window. I must say, he's not happy about that one bit."

Couldn't help it, he tried to say, but there was no sense to be made of the bubbling noise that came from his throat.

"I don't speak that language, whatever it is," Raymond said, pulling Jennings to his feet. "Get in there and watch that girl, and let me get the bodies out of the hall."

Jennings walked into the room and looked around. It was a reception area for an office that lay behind another closed door. He walked over to that door and threw it opened, half expecting to find more vampires.

What he found instead was worse. Arthur was *really* not going to like this.

"What are these devices?" Arthur asked, standing inside the office.

The fight was over, the bodies piled in the reception area. Raymond stood in the corner of the office, too angry at himself to speak.

"This is a photocopier," Jennings began. "You lay an object here, on the glass, and press this button." The copier burst to life, filling the room with noise and a brief flash of panning light. "And what comes out is a duplicate of whatever you laid on the glass."

"Uh-huh," was all Arthur said. Jennings could tell he already didn't like where this was going.

"And *this* is a fax machine. You place a sheet of paper here, dial a telephone number, and transmit the contents to another fax machine."

"Another fax machine, where?" Arthur asked.

"Another fax machine anywhere in the civilised world," Jennings replied. "I can hit the redial button here, and see the last number dialled. This," he said, pointing to the LCD display, "is a telephone number in London."

"And *that*?" Arthur asked.

"That is a paper shredder," Jennings continued. "That turns pages of paper into packing material."

Arthur paced the floor of the office. "So you're telling me ...

you're telling me someone could sit in this office in Salamanca and send the contents of the most dangerous book on Earth to London."

"That's what I'm telling you," Jennings answered.

Raymond still said nothing. He'd already made it perfectly clear that he didn't apologise for his decision to rescue Jennings instead of going after the Book, and to say anything now would merely draw unwanted attention to himself.

"So even though I hold the Book in my hand," Arthur said, trying to sound calm, "someone in London, England also holds the Book in their hand."

"At least some of it, yes," Jennings said.

"Can you tell how much?"

"There was no marker in the Book, no way to tell how far they'd got through it," Jennings explained. "Judging by the amount of shredded paper, I'd say they had a lot of it. There might still be some information I can get out of the ..."

Arthur's fist came down—one of the only times Jennings had ever seen him display his anger physically. The fax machine exploded in a burst of plastic and circuit-boards.

"... fax machine," Jennings finished pointlessly.

"We can't stay here," Raymond said quietly. "Our fight wasn't as discreet as we might have hoped. The authorities will be here soon."

"Wake him," Arthur said, pointing to Lyle.

"Arthur, we can't ..." Raymond began.

"*Wake him!*" Arthur shouted furiously.

Raymond and Jennings moved in silence, like cowed children before an angry parent. Raymond removed the knife from his heart. Jennings held the arm of one of the paralysed vampires over his chest, cracking the elbow backwards like a cook preparing an egg. Blood poured into the wound in his chest, then dribbled up his chest as he moved the flow over his mouth. Lyle's throat began to bob as he swallowed. Jennings threw the arm aside as soon as he was awake.

"Who were you answering to in London?" Arthur demanded.

Lyle laid on his back, struggling to speak.

"Wait ... !" Raymond cried, but it was too late.

Lyle's hand moved to his chest with amazing speed. His fingers pinched something under his skin and pulled, and he screamed as light consumed his body.

Jennings, Arthur, and Raymond stared down at the empty clothes in amazement.

"I ... I tried to tell you ... " Raymond said. "I'm sorry ... I couldn't see it in his mind until it was too late ... "

"Tell me what?" Arthur demanded as Jennings searched the clothes. "What the hell happened?"

"Jesus, I've never seen anything like this," Jennings whispered, holding up a tightly packed cardboard tube about six inches long. "*This* just happened."

"And what is *that*?" Arthur asked angrily.

"It's a modified flare," Jennings explained. "It probably burned for less than a second, but that's all it took. He had it shoved into his chest cavity, with a cord attached to the cap under the skin. Pull the cord, the cap comes off, and that's all she wrote."

"I could see the command in his mind," Raymond said. "He was to pull that cord and destroy himself before revealing whom he was working with."

"But he was definitely working with someone?" Arthur asked.

Raymond nodded that Yes, he was.

"Fine," Arthur said. "We'll wake the others, and see if they know anything."

It took less than half-a-minute to discover that none of them did.

"Bring the bodies to the roof," Arthur instructed. "Raymond will guard them. If the authorities come to the roof, use your Telepathy to fool them into thinking there's nothing there. Let the lot of them burn at sunrise."

Arthur stormed out of the room, Iago right behind. Jennings stood thinking for a moment, before chasing him into the hall.

"Arthur," Jennings said. "That fax machine would be able to do more than just send faxes, it could receive them as well. There could be some shredded correspondence from the source in the trash in there. It will take time to piece it together, and I might not find anything, but there'd be no harm trying."

Arthur nodded, distracted by Iago, who was sniffing the floor intently. The two of them watched while he followed an invisible trail to another door—Stephanie's door.

Jennings could feel Arthur pushing his Presence, searching behind that door with vampire-senses. He hoped Stephanie had climbed out the window, or slipped out while they were in the other room, or ...

"Come out of there," Arthur said.

The door slowly swung open. Iago backed away from the door, his ears flattened against his head. Stephanie stepped out. If Arthur recognised her from Tito's, he made no indication.

"To whom were you sending the Book?" Arthur asked.

"We weren't given a name," she said unsteadily. "Only a number."

"Was Lyle answering to Drew?"

"I don't know."

"No, I didn't think so." She fell to the floor of the hall, a steel rod in her heart. "Raymond," Arthur said loud enough for the other vampire to hear, "you have another body out here in the hall." To Jennings, he said, "Get your shredded paper, and let's get back to the house."

"Uh ... perhaps I should stay behind and help Raymond with the cleanup," Jennings suggested.

"Raymond earned himself this cleanup—and perhaps worse," Arthur said coldly. "I need you to search for that correspondence."

Jennings returned to the office. Raymond was dejectedly stacking bodies in the reception area, and didn't even look up.

There was nothing to say and nothing to do. Jennings had seen Arthur like this before. The elder vampire would listen to nothing that suggested any of Lyle's family should live. Stephanie would die when the sun rose, and that was all.

Jennings carried his bag of paper into the hall, and followed Arthur and Iago down the stairs.

Pasting together shreds of paper was every bit the pain-in-the-ass Jennings knew it would be. A night and a half of labour found him in his room at Arthur's house, surrounded by little piles of paper. But at least he didn't have to think about Stephanie.

There was a light knock on the door, and Raymond entered. "Arthur wants to talk with us downstairs," he said.

"Tell him I'm a little busy right now," Jennings said, irritated. "I'd really like to have something accomplished here before the end of the millennium."

"It's important, Jennings," Arthur's quiet voice came floating up the stairs.

"So is this, unless I'm mistaken!" Jennings retorted. Then, more calmly, "I'll be down in a minute."

Raymond stalled a moment. "Would you like some blood when you come down?" he asked.

"Yes, please," Jennings answered distractedly.

He didn't notice Raymond leaving, and he didn't notice when one minute became five, and then fifteen. "Jennings!" Arthur called from downstairs.

"Shit," he mumbled to himself, leaving his work to join the others.

Raymond and Arthur were sitting in the living room when Jennings came down the stairs. "Thank you very much for joining us," Arthur said dryly.

Fuck you very much for asking me to come, Jennings thought to himself as he silently took a seat on the sofa.

"Now, Raymond," Arthur began. "Am I to understand we have no established connection between Lyle and Drew during this entire incident?"

"Drew is a telepath," Raymond said. "He's not as powerful as me, but were I to read his mind, he would know it. Most of my information I read from the people around him—and to the best of their knowledge, Lyle was acting on his own."

"He was allied to *someone* in London," Arthur said.

"But that could have been anyone," Jennings said. "I can name ten vampires in London who are more powerful and more ambitious than Drew. There's Jonathan, Lawrence, Elizabeth ..."

"Lawrence is gone," Raymond interrupted. "Remember Eric?"

"The Russian?" Arthur asked.

"The German, living in Russia, until he moved to London," Raymond corrected. "He and Lawrence had a bit of a feud over territory, and Eric won."

"I had no idea Eric had returned from behind the Iron Curtain," Jennings said with contempt. "He always had too much ambition for his own good. Did Lyle have any contact with him?"

"I can't say for certain—but it's possible."

"Jennings," Arthur said, "I know you and Eric have something of a past, but we have a city full of candidates—and Drew is still pretty high on my list."

"He still has a prominent place on my list as well," Jennings agreed. "But just listen to what I have to say. Drew is a theatre-fag—no offence, Raymond."

"None taken," Raymond said, without meaning it.

"Drew likes pretty things and pretty boys and pretty dance numbers. Drew isn't the type to try and steal the Book to rule the world—which is what Lyle had in mind. Drew keeps his little status quo and he's happy with that. Eric, on the other hand, perfectly fits the profile of someone who would inspire this sort of madness. That flare-trick smacks of Eric. And the bastard is clever enough to have set up that ambush at the plaza. Despite the gross use of explosives, it was well thought-out and well executed. If not for the intervention of Terry, you'd be dead and I'd be flying third class mail to London."

"So, what can we prove?" Arthur asked.

"Nothing," Jennings said. "Not a damn thing. Maybe I'll be able to paste something together in the next few weeks, but I wouldn't count on that. Whoever planned out this attack wouldn't be stupid enough to sign his name to something, even if he knew it was going to be shredded."

"What is your recommendation?"

"Send Raymond back to London," Jennings said. "Have him keep an eye on things, see if he can spot any developments. We take some time, get ourselves situated. Then we go to London, and you start pushing. You are the czar, they are the peasants. Perhaps it's time you reminded them of that."

Arthur nodded thoughtfully. "I've been thinking of taking the Book to America," he said.

Raymond and Jennings both protested in surprise.

"America?" Raymond asked. "What the hell is in America?"

"We don't know anything about the States," Jennings said. "Considering what the mortals there are like, the vampires must be completely uncivilised."

"I've been thinking about this for some time," Arthur said. "War is a great concern of mine. Americans send their armies into battle all over the world, but never in their own country—not for over a century. If I'm going to stash the Book somewhere, it seems to me America would be the perfect place."

"What about nuclear war?" Raymond asked. "If they start World War III, the two places you don't want to be are the Soviet

Union and the United States. Are you forgetting the Cuban Missile Crisis? It was only two decades ago."

"And it turned out to be nothing," Arthur said. "The Americans never fight at home."

"The American *military* never fights at home," Jennings countered. "The American *citizens* never stop fighting. They all carry guns, and it's perfectly legal."

"That's an exaggeration," Arthur defended.

"Not much of one," Jennings said. "They can't even go three years without a major incident. They have race riots, earthquakes, AIDS—who knows what AIDS does to a vampire?"

"Americans didn't invent AIDS," Arthur said. "In case you haven't heard, we have that here, too."

"No, they didn't invent AIDS," Jennings conceded. "But they did for AIDS what the Japanese did for the transistor radio. It hasn't changed since I was a mortal—it's like the Wild West out there. Cowboys and Indians—that's all Americans know."

"I get your point," Arthur said. "And I know it's going to be a whole new world out there. But America is where I want the Book. America is where I've wanted the Book for fifty years, I've just never had the inclination to move it. Now, I *have* to move it. All of the stronger vampires are in Europe."

"Leiberman is producing movies in Los Angeles, but he's the only one I know of," Raymond said unobtrusively.

"That's fine," Arthur said. "I was thinking of staying on the East Coast anyway."

"Where?" Jennings asked. "New York City? When the bombs start dropping, that'll be the second place to go."

"Not New York City," Arthur said.

"How about New Orleans?" Raymond asked. "I hear Anne Rice lives there."

"*Not* New Orleans," Arthur said steadfastly. "There are plenty of cities within driving distance of New York. Boston, Hartford, Albany, Newark ..."

"Newark?" Jennings demanded. "There's an idea. Or, we could hide the Book in Hell—no one would ever find it there."

"There's more to this than the Book," Arthur said. He took a moment to gather his thoughts, while Raymond and Jennings waited respectfully. "Terry isn't doing well," he began. "The doctors say she may not ever wake up. She didn't just grab me up out of the plaza—she stood by me when we were stranded out in the middle of nowhere and Lyle was coming for us. I owe her. I'm making arrangements to have her flown back to the States, and I plan to accompany her."

"When?" Jennings asked.

"They wanted to fly her out tomorrow, but I persuaded them to wait until tomorrow night. It wasn't that difficult, considering I'm footing the bill. Bringing Iago is causing all kinds of problems, but they aren't anything I can't handle."

"And what are we to do?" Raymond asked.

"I need time to acquire some property, set up housekeeping. I have a lawyer working on a place right now, but considering his lack of awareness of our ... special needs ... whatever he arranges will probably be temporary. I'm selling my holdings here in Spain, all except for this place and one other flat Jennings doesn't know about. I suggest, Jennings, that you do the same.

"What I need you two to do is clean up this mess in Salamanca. Lyle still has some progeny left in this city—they must all be destroyed. Once that's done, Raymond will return to London to keep an eye on things there, and Jennings will join me in the States. I should be all settled in by then."

"A move like this isn't going to be cheap," Jennings said. "Do you know what real estate costs out there?"

"Which brings us to our second order of business," Arthur said, grabbing a speakerphone from the table beside him, and placing it on the coffee table in the centre of the room. His fingers began dialling numbers. "Whether Drew had a part in this or not, his progeny is still his responsibility. Restitution must still be made."

The telephone in London was ringing, and all were silent while they waited for an answer.

"Hello?" a young man's voice answered.

"Hello, this is Arthur. I need to speak to Drew."

"One moment, please," the voice said. There was no sign of recognition whatsoever. *Must be a brand-new fledgling*, Jennings thought.

It didn't take long for Drew to reach the phone. "Arthur, this is Drew, what's happened?" he said hurriedly, not even trying to sound calm.

Jennings found himself feeling sympathy for the bastard, reminded of his own disappointment with Stephanie.

"It's over, Drew," Arthur said.

Nothing but silence came from the speakerphone for several long moments. "You mean it's ... you mean it's *over*?" Drew asked in a quivering voice.

"He died by his own hand, if that makes you feel any better," Jennings said.

"Oh, I'm sure Arthur didn't give him a little Push towards *that*!" Drew said angrily. Jennings didn't have to see him to know he had tears in his eyes. "You are the most powerful vampire alive ..."

"Whoa!" Jennings said, in response to the use of the word.

"Drew!" Arthur commanded sternly. "You know better than to use that word over the phone, where anyone can hear you! If you can't use this form of communication responsibly, I'm going to have to terminate this call."

"I'm sorry, I'm sorry," Drew said. "I'm ... I'm just upset."

"I'll be honest with you, Drew," Arthur said. "If he *hadn't* destroyed himself, *I* would have. We aren't talking about some minor breach of etiquette, here. He tried to kill me on three occasions. You know me, Drew. You know I don't come to such decisions lightly."

That was one thing they had to fall back on. If Jennings had had his way, they would have killed Lyle as soon as he got to Salamanca. But Arthur had a reputation for being fair—a hard-earned, well-deserved reputation.

"I know ... I know you don't," Drew admitted quietly. "I just ... it's just that I loved him, okay?"

"We've all lived long lives," Arthur said. "I think we can all say that at one time or another, we've loved someone who was unworthy."

Jennings had heard that story before—Arthur was thinking of Anne, the vampire who'd Made him. Personally, Jennings had *never* loved anyone who was unworthy.

"But believe me," Arthur continued, "Lyle was *particularly* unworthy. *Three times*, Drew—wouldn't you say that justified extreme measures?"

Drew's end of the line was silent for a few moments. "Yes," he finally admitted.

"Besides, when you get right down to it, this entire incident wasn't *my* fault," Arthur said, the sympathy leaving his voice.

It took a moment for Drew to catch the implication. "*My* fault?" he demanded. "How on earth could this be *my* fault?"

"I spoke with Dr. Del Rio, Drew," Arthur said.

Silence on the other end of the phone. *Dr. Del Rio?* Jennings thought. *Who the hell is Dr. Del Rio, and why the hell wasn't I told about him before this conversation began?* This whole interrogation was sloppy and getting sloppier.

"Oh?" Drew asked, with a weak attempt at nonchalance. "And what did he say?"

Now, Arthur was angry—so angry Jennings could see his fangs had extended. "Drew: I want you to listen and I want you to listen very closely. We know Lyle was reporting to someone in London. Jennings and I have not ruled out the possibility that someone was you. Do you know what the consequences could be, if we found out it *was* you?"

"Yes," Drew answered timidly.

"Then why don't you tell us what *you* think Dr. Del Rio might have told me? Why don't you tell us what's really going on in London?"

Drew took a deep breath, an all-right-it's-time-to-come-clean-breath. Jennings knew this was the portion of the conversation he'd have to pay attention to. Of course, it would have been better if he'd known about Dr. Del Rio, or if he'd taped it ...

"He called me about two weeks ago," Drew said.

"Dr. Del Rio?" Arthur asked.

"Yes," Drew said. "Eduardo. I know him as Eduardo."

"Go on," Arthur urged coldly.

"He called me and told me some girl had come around asking about ... about our kind ... and that she'd shown him a book—*the* Book. Eduardo knew about the Book because I'd been looking for it fifty years ago when I met him."

"And why were you looking for the Book fifty years ago?" Arthur demanded.

"The same reason Lyle was looking for it. I wanted to be more powerful than I was, plain and simple."

"I see," Arthur said, coming to his own conclusions. "Please continue."

"I told Lyle about the call," Drew admitted. "I didn't tell him because I wanted him to go to Salamanca. It was just a casual conversation—pillow talk. He'd heard that I'd got a call from Spain and he wanted to know what it was about. So I told him, and I told him about the Book. That's when he disappeared."

"Did he have contact with any other elders in London—anyone ambitious enough to try something like this?" Arthur asked.

"Lyle had contact with *all* the elders here," Drew said. "Lyle had a way of making himself known. But if he had anything close with anyone in particular, I would have gone to them and asked to have Lyle brought back myself. I never wanted any of this to happen."

"Excuse us for a moment, Drew," Arthur said, pushing the mute button on the speakerphone. He addressed the room: "Any thoughts?"

"I think he's telling the truth. He admitted more than he needed to with his confession that he was looking for the Book fifty years ago. And he passed up a perfect opportunity to finger another elder. Then again, I wasn't privy to the conversation between you and this Dr. Del Rio," Jennings added with some annoyance. "Does his story match what you learned from the doctor?"

"Yes," Arthur said. "Raymond, do you have any observations that contradict Jennings'?"

"No," Raymond said uncertainly.

"Raymond," Jennings said steadily, "if you heard something I didn't, say so. I'm not flawless, my mind is still open. Maybe Drew is *that* good a liar. You're a telepath—you know what it sounds like when a man's words don't match his thoughts. I know you hear things the two of us can't. So share your insights before I come over there and slap you around."

Raymond smiled slightly at the mock-threat. "I was just noticing he was awfully coy when Dr. Del Rio's name came up—that's all."

"That's understandable," Arthur said. "He didn't want that connection to be made, because it lays the blame for Lyle's death on him, and he's trying to get out of reparations by blaming me alone for the unwarranted death of his progeny."

"You're right," Raymond said. "That's why I didn't want to ..."

"*No!*" Jennings shouted, cutting him off. "You noticed something else, didn't you?"

Raymond visibly squirmed in his chair. "In regular speech, Drew's a clumsy talker. He stammers. He hesitates. That speech he just gave sounded a bit too rehearsed to me."

"Jennings?" Arthur asked.

"I don't know Lyle that well—but I trust Raymond's judgement."

Arthur seemed confused. "So you're going back on what you said before?" he asked.

Jennings gave a little smile. "Looks that way."

Arthur rubbed his chin thoughtfully. "All right," he said, thinking. "All right. The Society of Vampires is dead. I am perfectly aware of that, although many would accuse me otherwise. All the same, I am respected within the vampire-community because I hold to the old society's standards. Drew is holding himself accountable to me right now because it is known I hold to those standards—because he knows if I declared him my enemy, most of the elder vampires would follow. The fact that I am honourable gives me far more power than the Gift of Influence.

"Given that, I have to make all of my decisions based on what the Society would have done. I must do this to keep my respect, because if I lose my respect, I'm just another bloodsucker. And based on what I know right now, I cannot find Drew guilty of conspiracy in this instance. It may well be that he's an excellent liar, and he was behind Lyle the entire time. But if I cannot prove that to the vampires of the world, I cannot take action against him. Can either of you give me any reason whatsoever to condemn Drew, given these standards?"

"I might be able to turn something up with that number on the fax machine," Jennings said. "But for now, I have nothing on Drew aside from the fact that he Made Lyle."

"Raymond?" Arthur asked.

"Do you plan to send me back to London?" Raymond asked.

"Yes," Arthur replied.

"Then I'll look into things once I get there," Raymond replied. "But for now, I have to agree with Jennings. I have nothing on Drew."

"Very well," Arthur said, pushing the mute button again. "Drew, are you there?"

"I'm here," Drew answered unsteadily.

"I've discussed this with Jennings," Arthur said. "We've decided we currently have no reason to believe you were allied with Lyle during this incident."

"But?" Drew asked. Even *he* could see the other shoe about to drop.

"But, you are to be held responsible for Lyle's Making," Arthur said. "Wouldn't you say that perhaps you bear some responsibility for Making someone who tried to kill me three times? That perhaps, if you'd taught him respect, none of this would ever have happened?"

"I didn't know he was going to do this!" Drew retorted. "Lyle was spirited. He had an independent streak."

"He was a psychopath, and he never should have been Made," Arthur said evenly. "*You* never should have Made him. If you had any doubts about being able to control him, you should have left him as he was."

"I thought time would mellow him," Drew defended.

"You were wrong," Arthur said. "In the old days, the Society would have forbidden you from Making any more progeny—if for some reason they let you live."

"You can't stop me from Making progeny," Drew said.

"Care to test that?" Arthur asked.

Again, silence. Drew knew full well how powerful Arthur was. Drew's own upbringing had been proper in at least that respect.

"Are you forbidding me from Making progeny?" Drew asked pathetically.

"No," Arthur replied. "Not yet. I think this incident with Lyle has taught you a lesson. Reparations, however, must be made."

"What kind of reparations?" Drew asked.

"Monetary," Arthur said. "I'm going to have to relocate because of this incident. You are going to have to pay for this relocation."

"How much?"

"I don't know yet," Arthur said. "Think in the neighbourhood of a million pounds."

Drew gasped, but Jennings had to interrupt. "A million pounds?" Jennings asked. "Do you know how expensive America is? I know your tastes, Arthur. Five million would be a conservative amount. You'd better count on closer to ten."

"Ten million pounds?" Drew exclaimed. "I don't have that kind of money!"

"Don't worry, I'll front the expense," Arthur said. "I certainly don't expect you to come up with that kind of money by tomorrow. Once I'm all settled in, I'll let you know how much you owe."

"I lost here too, you know!" Drew snapped. "There should be some reciprocal restitution. I'll cover half the expense of your move."

Jennings flinched—Drew never should have said that.

"You're right," Arthur said. "You're absolutely correct ... I'm handling this inappropriately. It was foolish of me to offer you the opportunity to make restitution for your mistakes. There should only be punishment. You should die. Of course, I'll have to exterminate your entire family, just to make sure no pretty young fledgling comes back to cause trouble, but I think the punishment fits the crime of irresponsibility you've committed. It's what the Society would have done."

"Arthur, listen," Drew said, now trying to be rational.

"No, *you* listen," Arthur said. "I don't want to kill you. More so, I don't want to go to the trouble and expense of tracking down your entire family. But you have to pay for your mistake, be it by punishment or restitution. I'm not asking for revenge money. I'm not asking for money on the basis that your mistake nearly cost me my life. I'm asking for you to pay the damage caused by your mistake. If you're unwilling to do that, then you leave me no choice but to come to London and destroy you all. Choose. If you believe you're powerful enough to take me, by all means, choose the punishment. The resulting demonstration of power will be enough to keep our kind in line for a hundred more years."

Drew said nothing for a long time. Arthur looked to Jennings, who shrugged his shoulders. "Well?" Arthur asked.

"I'll pay the ten million," Drew finally said. "But it's going to take time."

"Don't worry about time," Arthur said. "I'll tack on a reasonable interest rate, and you'll be straight with me before you know it. I'll even cut you a little deal ... if you can find out who Lyle was allied with in London, I'll only charge you half of the money. Does that sound fair?"

"Is that all?" Drew asked.

"I asked you a question, Drew," Arthur said evenly. "Does that sound fair?"

"*Yes*, it sounds fair," Drew said without meaning it. "Is that all?"

"Yes, that's all for now. You'll be hearing from me, Drew."

The line clicked as Drew hung up. Arthur hit a button on the speakerphone, and returned it to the table beside him.

Raymond was nodding his head. "He didn't mean it when he said he'd pay you," he said. "He's planning something."

"I got that too," Jennings agreed.

"For now, perhaps," Arthur conceded. "But he's just upset. Over time, he'll realise it's easier just to pay the money. No, I'm not worried about Drew. On to our third order of business."

"Which is?" Jennings asked.

"Iago," Arthur said. The wolf lifted his head from the floor at the mention of his name. "We have to find out what he can and cannot do, and since Raymond seems to be able to read him, I want to do that before I leave tonight."

"Well then," Jennings said as he stood. "If you won't be needing me, I'll be returning to my room to push a very large rock up a very steep hill."

There was a downside to having the acute hearing of a vampire—it made it damned difficult to concentrate.

Raymond's voice floated up the stairs. *See if you can get him to change.*

Iago, transform.

Slight pause. *I don't think he wants to.*

Why not?

I'm not sure. I don't think it's a very pleasant experience for him; is it, Iago?

Be that as it may, I need him to change. Iago, transform.

Jennings suddenly realised that he was no longer working, but listening intently to what was going on downstairs.

Jesus, Mary, and Joseph, he heard Raymond say with awe.

Jennings leapt to his feet and ran out the door—this he had to see. He'd nearly reached the bottom of the stairs when he saw something hunched in the living room. The size of it made his senses tell him, *Bear. Big bear.*

It turned towards him, growling with an intensity that would have made Jennings shit his pants if his bowels still worked.

Big, pissed-off bear with yellow eyes. Run.

Arthur shouted, "Iago, no!"

"Jennings, don't be afraid," Raymond ordered. "He can smell your fear, and he translates fear as aggression."

"How can he smell my fear?" Jennings shouted in reply. "I'm a vampire, for Crissake!"

Iago was ready to pounce.

"Don't argue, he just can!" Raymond cried.

"Iago, stay! Heel!" Arthur continued.

What Jennings did next, he would later count as one of the bravest things he'd ever done.

"Iago?" he said in playful baby-talk. "Is that my big, pretty, Iago? Ooo, look at the great, big puppy. Yes!" Jennings walked right up to him while he was talking. "Look how pretty! Yes!" he continued, as he reached up and petted the coarse ruff on Iago's neck. "Aren't you just a great big puppy? Yes you are! Yes you are!"

Jennings stole a glance at the other two. Raymond was close to laughing, Arthur's mouth had fallen open.

"Don't laugh," Jennings said, as though he was still talking to Iago. "'Cause Jennings is still alive, isn't he? Yes he is! Look at the size of the jaws on you! I'll bet you can crush a fucking lamppost, can't you? Yes you can! Yes you can!"

"Laying it on a little thick, aren't you?" Arthur asked.

"Not at all, 'cause Jennings is going to live another hundred years!" He was petting him with both hands now. "Isn't Jennings going to live another hundred years? Yes he is!"

Iago began licking his face.

"Oh my ... God!" Jennings said, flinchingly trying to keep his tone, and periodically closing his mouth to keep Iago from licking his teeth. "You've just got the ... biggest, wettest tongue, don't you? And I think that's the ... worst case of ... dog-breath ... I've ever smelled! We're going to have to train you not to do this, aren't we?"

"You want me to fetch you a rolled-up newspaper to smack his nose?" Raymond asked, no longer trying to contain himself.

"Not even if your life depended on it," Jennings replied.

"I'd better grab some more steaks," Raymond said, getting

up and heading for the kitchen. "The change made him hungry."

Iago sat hunched on the floor, happily eating steak after steak.

"Those are all we have left," Raymond said as he returned to his place on the couch.

"We can't even stand him up in here, get a good look at him," Jennings said.

"The house in America will have cathedral ceilings," Arthur answered distractedly.

"Is this as far as you've taken him?" Jennings asked.

Both looked puzzled. "What do you mean?" Arthur asked in reply.

"I mean that according to legend, werewolves are men who change into wolves. Maybe Iago can turn into a man."

"How would I get him to do that?" Arthur asked. "If I ask him to change into a man, he's not going to know what I'm talking about."

"*He'll* know if *you* know," Raymond said. "The second voice speaks directly to his mind."

Iago had finished eating, and was looking up at them expectantly.

"Iago," Arthur commanded, "become a man."

The three of them sat and watched with bated breath. "Nothing's happening," Jennings finally said. "Maybe he can't ..."

Something popped in Iago's back.

"... or maybe he can," Jennings finished in a whisper.

Other sounds followed. Jennings was reminded of what he'd heard when Lyle had torn off his arm, and he shuddered. Iago's coat thinned, until they could see white skin beneath. His shoulders narrowed, his hock joints broadened into heels, his muzzle drew back into his face, his ears changed shape, his sloped forehead became more pronounced.

The entire change took three full minutes, although none of them were paying attention to their watches. When it was over, a pale, muscular man—hairless except for the dark blonde on his head—squatted on the floor of Arthur's living room. He looked up at them with yellow eyes.

Arthur sighed with disappointment. "He'll never pass for human with those ... eyes."

In the middle of his statement, Iago's eyes faded to grey.

The three of them were soon standing, and Raymond was at his side, helping him up. He shakily stood on the balls of his feet, his knees slightly bent, like he had when he'd been half-wolf half-man—and gave the appearance of a dog being taught to walk on his hind legs.

"No," Raymond said, bending to force Iago's knees straight and his feet to the floor. "Like that. Isn't that better?" He stood from the task of correcting the new human's stance. Raymond was just over six feet tall, and he only came up to Iago's chin. "He's a big one."

"Not quite inconspicuous, is he?" Jennings asked rhetorically.

"With that accent, you're one to talk," Arthur retorted.

"Come on," Raymond said, taking him by the arm. "I'll show you the kitchen ... uh-oh."

"What?" Arthur asked.

"He has to go to the loo," Raymond said. "I guess it's something he's going to have to learn eventually, isn't it? Any volunteers?"

The silence was deafening.

"Very well, I'll teach him myself," Raymond said, guiding him into the hall. "As long as the two of you trust me with this big, gorgeous hunk of man, alone in the powder room."

"You behave yourself!" Arthur shouted into the hall.

"It was just a joke," Raymond said, helping him through the door. "That would be like molesting a child, and I'm not a boy-lover. My God, do you know how long it's been since I've *gone* to the loo? I don't know if I'm qualified to teach this."

"I'm sure you'll both do just fine," Jennings said, returning to his chair. The bathroom door closed behind them. "Arthur, do you know what you've found here?"

"A six-and-a-half foot tall toddler?" Arthur replied, rubbing his temples.

"Well, yes—for now," Jennings admitted. "But think of the possibilities. No other sane vampire believes these things even exist. He can sit and listen to entire conversations, and no one will suspect anything because he's just a dog. He can get into places even we couldn't get near. And best of all ..."

"Best of all?" Arthur urged.

"Best of all, he can walk around during the day, and kick ass when we can't. Iago may turn out to be the best friend you've ever had."

"I thought when someone saved your life, you became their responsibility—not the other way around," Arthur said.

"Maybe that's precisely how he sees it," Jennings said seriously.

The toilet flushed, and the two of them emerged from the bathroom. "I can't believe what they've done with modern plumbing," Raymond said, shaking his head.

"Any problems?" Jennings asked.

"He pulled it off just like a pro!" Raymond said like a proud mother, pinching Iago's cheek.

Jennings rolled his eyes—Raymond's maternal instincts were about to get ugly. A quick glance at Arthur told him the other was thinking the same thing.

"I *heard* that," Raymond said.

Back to the room. Back to turning shreds of paper into sheets of paper.

It was the following night. Arthur and Iago had left for Madrid the night before, and would leave for the States tonight. Crossing the Atlantic from east to west was an easy trip for a vampire to make, because one travelled with the darkness. Returning to Europe was another matter entirely. Unless the flight was timed perfectly—and you couldn't count on these things running smoothly—you had to box yourself up and fly as cargo.

Iago presented a whole new set of problems. They'd discussed it last night, and it was decided it would be easier to ship him as a wolf than to try and come up with a Spanish passport in a matter of hours. But that presented problems of its own. Wolves were, after all, an endangered species. Arthur'd had to Push a veterinary doctor to get papers proving Iago was a domestic dog, and he'd have to continue to Push anyone who questioned those yellow eyes every step of the way—something he wouldn't be able to do from a box in cargo. If Iago ever made a return trip, it would have to be as a man.

But Jennings didn't have to worry about these things. True, he would probably be saddled with the task of arranging identification for Iago. But Jennings had a million strips of paper to sort before that became a problem.

Raymond rapped lightly on the door before he entered. "I'm going to need your help," he said.

"What for?" Jennings asked.

"I've found a group of stragglers—ten of them. I don't want to go up against them alone. I'm sorry, I know you're doing important work here ..."

"Don't worry about it," Jennings said. "There's nothing to find here, anyway."

Raymond looked about the room at the thin strips, and couldn't argue. "You know," he began, getting off the subject, "I ordinarily don't have to ask this question. I ordinarily know what's bothering someone. But you being a Blank Spot and all ... do you want to talk about it?"

Jennings sighed angrily, throwing down a handful of paper. Enough was enough, already. He stood from the floor, stuffing shreds of paper into a plastic bag as he answered. "There was a girl in Lyle's cabal—his family. I owed her. She hid my arms and legs after Lyle told her to burn them. I promised I would help her escape the family, and instead I let Arthur kill her."

"The girl in the hall," Raymond stated.

"Yes—how did you know?"

"I couldn't hear what you were saying, and I couldn't read your thoughts, but I could read *her* thoughts as you were saying it. I caught pretty much the entire exchange," Raymond said. "That was why I let her live."

Jennings stopped stuffing paper. "You *what*?"

"I figured you wouldn't be hiding her if you didn't have a good reason for wanting her to live," Raymond explained. "I took her to the roof with the others, but removed that thing from her heart after the two of you left. It wasn't long before she was up and gone. I don't know where she is now."

"Why didn't you tell me?" Jennings demanded.

"What, with Arthur around? And chance he might overhear me?" Raymond was shaking his head. "I don't think so."

"Then Stephanie is alive?"

"I can't say for certain she's alive right now, but she didn't die on that rooftop that night," Raymond said.

"Did she say anything to you?"

"There wasn't much for her to say. I told her if she stayed in Salamanca, she put both you and me at risk. She nodded, and then she was gone."

Jennings was nodding his head slightly, a faraway look in his eyes. Stephanie was alive and gone. She could be anywhere in the world by now, and he would most probably never see her again. But at least she was alive. "Well ... I'm glad she got away," he told Raymond.

"So am I, if it will make you less bitchy," Raymond said, backing out of the room. "I'll be downstairs when you're ready."

"Ready?" he asked.

"Ten stragglers?" Raymond repeated. "You and I have to deal with them? Don't worry, the girl from the hall isn't with them."

"I'll be down in a moment," Jennings said as Raymond closed the door behind him.

Stephanie was alive. He'd kept his promise.

"Thank you, Raymond," Jennings said under his breath.

"You're welcome!" Raymond sang from the stairs.

Iago

Place unknown, time unknown

Alpha Male led his pack in the hunt.

It had been four days since they'd finished devouring their last kill. If they didn't find something soon, pups would starve. Alpha Male was determined not to let that happen, as was the rest of the pack.

Epsilon Male was the first to catch the scent of meat. He gave a few short yips, and the others stopped, smelling the air. Within moments, they all knew it was there. All could tell by the slight scent of decay this would not be a Hunt. This meat was already dead—carrion. But it would feed the pups as well as any meat, and conserve their own fat supplies by avoiding the exertion of a Hunt.

The pack trotted towards it for a hundred yards before finding it—a dead, partially eaten reindeer. A single, rogue wolf stared at them from the carcass, taken by surprise by their downwind approach.

Alpha Male ran towards this wolf with a menacing snarl, his teeth bared. He pounced on the rogue, bowling it over. He was a large wolf, but older—perhaps a displaced Alpha from a neighboring pack. He didn't fight back, but instead rolled over and showed his belly while Alpha Male stood over him, growling, demonstrating his dominance.

The rogue whined and cowed, his ears flat against his head,

his tail tucked under his belly. Alpha sniffed his sex and didn't recognize the scent—this rogue had not violated the territory before. The other members watched and waited anxiously as Alpha Male continued his demonstration for several long minutes. Eventually, he was satisfied his message was clear and that the rogue understood his place. With a final snarl and lunge for the throat, he walked away to sniff the ground around the perimeter.

Other wolves had been here—he recognized scents from another pack—but none had been here recently. Alpha Male found a tree and marked his territory.

When he returned to the carrion, most of the females had already fallen on the meat, gorging. Gamma Male was establishing his own dominance over the rogue. Scrawny Omega Male was feeling a bit uppity, knowing he would have dominance over this rogue (albeit briefly)—and was currently being put back in his place by Epsilon Male.

They weren't far from the den. Alpha and Gamma Females headed for the pups and the yearlings, to bring them to the carrion, while Alpha Male sniffed the meat. It hadn't been dead more than a week, and the cold had kept it reasonably well-preserved. He also detected a slight smell of Man, but that had never stopped him before. He began to eat.

Only a few hours had passed, but already it was established that this would be the new den. The former Omega Male (now Zeta—second to last—with the tentative induction of the rogue into the pack) continued to show his dominance over the new Omega Male, who showed amazing restraint considering the difference in size.

Beta Male was the first to show signs of the tainted meat. He whined at the pain, flattening his ears in deference to the unknown force that caused his stomach to convulse. Gamma Male took advantage of the situation, seeing this as his chance to take Beta Male's slot—but it didn't go on for more than a few minutes before he, too, felt the poison wracking his body. Despite the fact that the new Omega Male had earned a brief respite from harassment, he still hadn't gotten off his back. Alpha Male sniffed him cautiously—he wasn't dead yet, but he was close.

Next, it was the pups; and soon after, the yearlings. They'd eaten the meat last, but the poison affected their smaller bodies much more quickly. Alpha Female lay on the ground, each breath an effort, while the pups climbed on her. They yelped pathetically at the pain in their tiny bodies, but nothing could be done. Some of the pack ate grass, but most of them now lay on the cold ground, panting.

Alpha Male felt it too, but looking around him, he knew he wasn't feeling it like the rest of his pack. His back legs stopped working, and he dragged them around behind him for half-a-minute before succumbing. By the time he went down, none of the pack remained standing and better than half of them were dead. The yelping of the pups had ceased, as those few who still survived now lacked the strength to voice their pain. Their mother—Alpha Female—whined with every pained breath. She whined at the pain in her body, and she whined at the pain in her heart. Six dead or dying pups surrounded her—two of them actually on top of her.

The sun was setting as Alpha Female died. The whines of his once-noble pack diminished with the light, until Alpha Male was alone.

The sun was coming up by the time the pack-less Alpha could stand again. He had survived. He had no way of knowing how or why, but he had survived. Cautiously, he sniffed every member of his pack, his nose confirming what his heart already knew. He was an Alpha no longer—an Alpha needed a pack. He was a rogue.

He threw back his head and howled his pain. Others heard him in the distance, and they joined him. They couldn't tell from the nonspecific language of the howl what had happened, but they heard great sorrow in that sound, and they answered with sorrow of their own.

The rogue began to wander. He didn't know where he was going, except that he was going away. He wandered for many seasons, sometimes through areas where no wolf-mark could be found and the scent of Man was thick and oppressive. He wandered to a place where smaller wolves hunted smaller prey, where there was no need to form packs and hunt in an organized fashion. He was a rogue in a land of rogues. He was home.

He hardly remembered the severe winters of his former life. He hardly remembered prey so large, the pack ate for days. But he never forgot his pups, his yearlings, his Alpha Female, his pack. Every night at dusk, and every morning at dawn, he commemorated them with a song as sad and as lonely as any wolf had ever sung.

New Jersey, 1986

"Zymotic. Adjective. Relating to or produced by or from fermentation, as certain epidemic or contagious diseases. Zymurgy. Noun. A branch of chemistry treating of processes in which fermentation is the principal feature, as brewing, making of yeast, and winemaking."

Iago lifted his head from the couch and pointed to his stomach. "Hungwy," he said.

"We're almost finished," Arthur replied. "Zyrian Autonomous Region. A former name for the Komi Autonomous S. S. R. Zyryanovsk. A city of northeast Kazahk S. S. R. near the Russian S. F. S. R. border. There—we're finished."

"Hungwy," Iago repeated.

"In a moment," Arthur said, flipping back through the dictionary and finding a word at random. "Space ebullism."

"Pafowogicaw. Da vapowizing or bubbwing out of body fwuids undew de abowmew condisuns of tempwatew and pwessew expewienced at owtitudes in esess of abou sisty-fwee fousand feet."

"Posset."

"A dwink of hot miwk cuwdewd wif wiquor, sweetened, and spiced."

"Very good," Arthur said. "Your diction needs work, but otherwise, very good. Congratulations, you have mastery over every word in the English language. Once you get used to talking, maybe I'll teach you French. Steak?"

"A swice of meat, as of beef ..."

"No, I was asking if you wanted a steak."

Iago leapt from the couch. "Bowito!" he answered excitedly.

"You'd rather have a burrito than a steak?" Arthur asked.

"Bowito-bowito-bowito!"

"All right," the vampire said, checking his watch. "It's early yet—Chi Chi's should still be open. I'm getting a little hungry myself."

"Hi, guys," their waitress said as she walked up to their table. "Let me guess: burritos?"

"Bowitos!" Iago replied with unbounded enthusiasm.

"How many?" she asked.

Iago held up all the fingers on both hands. "Jack," Arthur said sternly—despite Terry's choice of the name 'Iago,' Arthur insisted on calling him 'Jack.'"In English," Arthur requested.

"Ten," Iago replied.

"Ten burritos," she said as she scribbled onto her pad. "Hungry tonight?"

"Hungwy," Iago repeated.

"The usual to drink?" she asked.

"Yes, please," Arthur answered.

"One Gin and Tonic, one water," she said aloud as she wrote.

Iago's mouth was already watering at the thought of food. He poured some water into his mouth and swallowed, knowing it would take some time for the food to get here.

Arthur leaned over the table to Iago. "Your eyes have turned yellow," he said quietly. "If you keep letting that happen, you'll never pass for one of them."

Iago was perfectly aware his eyes had changed—he was seeing the world as he was accustomed to seeing it: grayer, less definition, less acuity. It happened when he became too caught up in his more basic thoughts: hunger, anger, lust—anything that dimmed the inquisitive side that had made him Change to a Man in the first place. With an instant's concentration, his vision sharpened, and he was a Man again.

"Better," Arthur sighed. "You know all the words now," he began, changing the subject. "Describe Claudette."

"Cwawdette?"

"Our waitress. Describe her."

Iago concentrated. "Pwetty."

"That's right," Arthur said. "Claudette is very pretty. What else?"

Iago thought for a long time. "Pwetty?" he finally said.

"What color hair does she have?" Arthur asked.

Iago shrugged.

"What color eyes does she have?" Same response. "Is she tall? Is she thin? Is there anything else you can tell me about her?"

"Pwegnant." Iago said.

"Pregnant? How can you tell?"

Iago pointed to his nose and sniffed. "Pwegnant," he repeated.

"How can a woman smell pregnant?" Arthur demanded.

Iago shrugged again. "Pwegnant."

She was passing at that moment, and Arthur stopped her. "Excuse me," he said. "Claudette, this may seem like a personal question, but are you pregnant?"

A look of shock came over her face. "I'm ... I'm two weeks late," she managed to answer. "Why?"

"Forget I asked the question," Arthur instructed quietly, and she walked away as though nothing had happened. "I'll be damned."

"Bwonde haew. Bwue eyes," Iago said.

"What?" Arthur asked. "What is it?"

Iago was sitting in the passenger seat of Arthur's Porsche, struggling to find the words to express himself. Apparently, that struggle had shown on his face.

"Tewwy," he finally said.

"Yes?" the vampire asked. "What about Terry?"

"Where?"

"She's in a hospital," Arthur answered. "She's very sick."

"Smeoo."

"Sorry, I haven't the slightest idea what you're saying. You *really* are going to have to work on your diction."

"Heoo."

"No, she's not 'here.' She's in a hospital."

"See. See!"

"'See?' You want to see her?"

"See!"

"If you want something, you're going to have to ask for it like a Man. Say, 'I want to see her.'"

"I want to see hew."

"That's better. You can't."

"I want to see hew!"

Arthur pulled the car to the side of the road and stopped. "Listen to me, Jack, and understand what I'm saying. Terry is sick because of *us*. Because of you and me."

"No."

"Yes, she is. She isn't like us. She doesn't drink blood to survive, she isn't going to live forever, and she can't smell when someone is pregnant. She is a normal, mortal, human. Most mortals don't know we exist—they don't even accept it as a possibility. And when some humans are confronted with the fact that we do exist, they get sick. Their minds can't handle it. It's our fault she's sick, and she isn't going to get better if we see her. She has to forget she ever knew us."

Iago's mouth twisted and contorted as he tried to express clear thoughts in a foreign language. "No," finally escaped his lips. "Sse no ... sse is no ... sse is not ... sick ... a'cause ... of ... me. I ... I pwotect hew. I want to see Tewwy."

Tears were welling up in Iago's eyes, and Arthur had to look away.

"Pwease."

"*Sacre Merde*," Arthur swore under his breath. "Very well, Jack. You can see her."

"Excuse me," the woman at the reception desk said as Arthur and Iago walked past. She leapt from her seat, and moved in front of them. "Ex*cuse* me! You can't go in there. Visiting hours are over."

"Really?" Arthur asked. "Check your list—I'm sure you'll find that we have unlimited access."

"Of course," the woman said distantly. "Unlimited access."

"Call Theresa Butler's doctor ... get him here right away."

She walked away from them, reaching over the desk to pick up her phone.

Iago was sitting in a chair beside Terry's bed when her doctor entered, some time later.

"What are you doing here?" the doctor demanded. "You aren't allowed in here!"

Arthur stood from the wall where he'd been leaning. "Of course he is," the vampire said. "He's allowed to go anywhere he wants. He's a specialist from Europe—his English isn't very good, but he can make himself understood. Tell everyone who works in this area Jack is allowed to go anywhere he likes, any time he likes."

The doctor straightened, a queer look in his face. "I'll speak to the staff right away," he said, before leaving the room.

"There," Arthur said. "It's done. You may watch over her until she wakes—but after that, we're going to leave Terry's life forever. If we don't, she won't ever get better. If you really care for her, you'll do as I ask."

"I do as you aks," Iago said. "When Tewwy betto."

"Good."

Iago stroked Terry's hair while she slept. A nurse had recommended he read to her, but he didn't know how. Spoken language was getting easier, but written symbols on paper were still a mystery.

She stirred in her sleep, moaning a little. Iago studied her closely, and noticed her expression had changed. He didn't know Man's Faces well enough to know what the change was, but the fact that there was a change seemed very important.

"Tewwy?" he said uncertainly.

She opened her eyes, turning her head towards him. Terry was awake.

"How you feewe?" he asked.

Terry swallowed and licked her lips. "Thirsty," she croaked.

Thirsty. Affected with thirst.

Thirst. A distressful feeling of dryness in the throat and mouth, accompanied by an increasingly urgent desire for liquids.

Iago leaned forward and took a cup of water from the wheeled-table, handing it to her. Her eyes darted about the room nervously as she drank. When she was finished, she asked, "Who are you?"

"A fwiend," he answered. Arthur had been very clear on this point—she was not to know that he was the wolf she'd adopted in Spain, or to be reminded of anything that had happened there. "I not 'upposed to say moa," he said.

He was suddenly caught up in how beautiful she was. It was a new experience for Iago: desire for a human. He'd never mated in this shape before. Vaguely, he wondered how it was accomplished.

A strange look came to her face. "What's the matter with your eyes?" she asked as the scent of her fear washed over him.

It only took him a moment to realize—his eyes had gone yellow. Lust had stolen his Man-thoughts from him. "I sowwy," he said, embarrassingly jumping from the bed and turning away from her. "It happens if I don' concentwate," he explained. "Pwease don' be afwaid." He thought about words from the dictionary, and about driving. Arthur had promised to teach him how to drive someday, but for now, the entire process was a complete enigma. Puzzlement cleared his vision, and he knew his eyes had changed back. "See?" he said, facing her again. "'Dey all betto."

Terry continued to look at him strangely "Do it again," she asked.

"Why?" he asked warily.

"Because I want you to do it again," she answered. "And sit back down."

He walked over to the bed, cautiously sitting at her feet.

"No," she said, patting the bed beside her like she'd patted her legs that first time he'd seen her; trying to get him to come closer. "Up here," she added.

Reluctantly, he moved closer to her.

"There we go," she said. "Now, do it."

It wasn't difficult. He thought about Terry's hairless skin against his own, and his vision blurred once more.

Terry stared at him closely. She reached up and touched his face, and his excitement grew. His skin began to prickle with the urge to grow hair, but denying that urge was much simpler than denying the eyes.

"Ee ... Iago?"

He didn't say anything for a second. Arthur would not be pleased. "Yes," he admitted. "Ahfo wantsa caw me 'Dack,' but I don' wike 'Dack.' I wike 'Iago.'"

"I remember now," she said. "Jesus, I remember all of it. You changed into a big bear-thing and went over the balcony with Lyle."

No point in keeping secrets anymore. "He dead now," Iago said. "Awe of dem dead."

"What about Jennings?" she asked. "And the Book?"

"Dennings fine, dey have de Book. I not 'upposeda talk about dis stuff. Ahfo s'gon be mad, I talk 'bout dis."

"Why?"

"'Cause he say you went to sweep 'cause you no wike us," Iago tried to explain in his child's voice.

"That's silly," Terry said. "Of course I like you, Iago. You saved my life."

Her hand went back up to his face. The touching felt good. Iago never wanted it to stop.

"Do you like that?" she asked.

"Yes," he replied.

Suddenly, her hand was on the back of his neck. His instincts would have told him he was being attacked, but they weren't given time to react. She pulled him towards her until their lips touched, and she moved hers against his. It was an altogether pleasant feeling.

"How about that?" Terry asked after she'd released him.

"What *was* dat?" Iago asked, opening his eyes. They were gray again.

"It's called a kiss," she said. "Do you like it?"

"I don' know," he lied.

"Here, try it again."

She was rougher this time, and the Wolf in him sang out. Were he the Alpha of Arthur's pack, he would have taken her right then.

"Now, what do you think?" she asked after it ended.

"I fink I wike it."

"So what's your deal?" she asked. "Are you a human or what?"

"I human wight now," Iago answered.

"But you aren't really a man," Terry said. "You're just a wolf who can turn into a man."

"I don' know," he admitted. "When I a Woof, I more dan a Woof. When I a Man, I more dan a Man. I can't expwain, maybe when I wearn to talk betto."

"Are you tired?" she asked.

"Yes," he replied, amazed she'd been able to tell that somehow. He doubted he *smelled* tired.

"I'm tired, too," she said. "Why don't you lay down with me and go to sleep for a while?"

Iago nodded, and Terry slid over as much as she could to make room. He lay down with his back to her. "You gonna wake up, wight?" he asked, suddenly worried. "You not gonna sweep for a weewy wong time, wike befoa?"

"No, I promise I'll wake up."

She wrapped her arm around him. It was funny ... in all his years of observing Man, it had never occurred to him that they were much better designed for intimacy than Wolves.

It wasn't long before they were both asleep.

"What are you doing, Jack?"

Iago sat up straight at the sound of Arthur's voice. "Nofing," he blurted.

"Did you tell Terry who you were?" Arthur demanded. She was waking now as well.

"No," Iago answered. "She guessed."

"She guessed you were a werewolf?" he asked with impatient anger. "She just pulled that out of the blue?"

"His eyes turned yellow," Terry interjected. "Besides, I saw the transformation too, if you remember."

"I've told you about your eyes," Arthur reprimanded. "You'll never pass for human with your eyes changing color every five minutes, will you?"

"No," Iago replied humbly.

"It was a mistake," Terry shot back. "You can't expect him to learn everything in a few days."

Arthur blinked. "Jack, will you wait outside?"

"He prefers 'Iago,'" Terry corrected.

Iago stood. He had to do as he was told—Arthur was the Alpha. He had to walk out of this room, even though he knew Arthur would never let him see Terry again. Dutifully, he shuffled into the hall, closing the door behind him.

Jesus, he heard Terry say from inside the room. *If he had a fucking tail, it would be between his legs. What have you been doing to him?*

Iago leaned against the wall, sliding to the floor and wrapping his arms around his knees. He wanted to be the Wolf. He wanted the sounds they were making to be just sounds, instead of words that carried meaning. But even if he Changed, he would still know what Arthur was saying. Besides, the vampire would not be pleased if he came out and found Iago was the Wolf.

Are you going to make me a vampire now? Terry was saying. *Is that the plan?*

No, that's not the plan.

Then what's the plan?

Iago knew what fear smelled like. Terry's question had just shown him that fear also had a sound.

The plan is for you to put this behind you. You're going to forget about me, forget about vampires and werewolves and all of this mess. You're going to finish school and get on with your life and be a happy mortal.

And just how do you propose I ... the Influence.

Iago could stop this right now. He could get up off the floor, walk into the room, and take control of Arthur's Pack by beating Arthur. Physically, Arthur was no match for him. But he was in the world of Men now. Although Iago didn't fully understand it, he knew that among Men there was more to power than strength.

I don't want to forget everything. I don't want to forget Iago.

Iago wanted to hear his own howling voice, echoing through the halls of this awful place and its awful smells. He wanted to be one with the pain and sadness that surrounded him here. But Arthur wouldn't like it.

No, she shouted. *Iago!*

Iago leapt to his feet. Alpha or not, if Arthur hurt Terry ...

Don't cry out. Don't fight it. Arthur was using the Voice, speaking into his head. No, not his head. Terry's head. Iago was only eavesdropping.

Just ... let me say good-bye ... to Iago.

He put his hand on the door, expecting to be called in. It was a reasonable request. There was no reason he would deny ...

You don't remember Jennings or Lyle or myself or any other vampire. Vampires do not exist. Neither do werewolves. You have no memory of Iago.

No ... Iago ...

You have no memory of Iago. *You have no memory of Iago.*

Iago took his hand off the door. He wasn't going to be asked inside. Terry wasn't going to get to say good-bye.

Presently, Arthur emerged from the room. "We can never see her again," he said flatly. "I told you from the start that was the way it had to be." He paused for a moment, as though waiting for some protest, before starting down the hall. "For God's Sake, Jack—if you can't keep your eyes from changing, at least put on your sunglasses."

Iago hit the wall with a sound that reverberated through every hall of the hospital. Arthur stopped walking and turned towards the werewolf—uncertain what to expect.

Iago's trembling lips were pulled back in a snarl that showed his lupine teeth. His ears prickled with hair, and the cartilage there was shaping into points. His fingernails had pushed into claws, and there was pain at the base of his spine where a tail was slowly growing. When he spoke, it was slow and careful—even around his canines—so that every word would be clear.

"My name ... is ... Iago."

Arthur didn't say anything for a moment, as though waiting for more. "Very well," he finally conceded. "Put on your sunglasses, Iago."

the end